SEASON OF WRATH

AN AGE GAP, RUSSIAN BRATVA BILLIONAIRE ROMANCE

LISA CULLEN

© Copyright 2023, by Author Lisa Cullen .

All Rights Reserved.

No part of this publication may be reproduced, distributed or transmitted in any form or by any means including photocopying, recording, or other electronic or mechanical methods except in the case of brief quotations embodied in critical reviews and certain other non commercial uses permitted by copyright law. Unauthorised reproduction or distribution of this work is illegal.

This book is a work of fiction. Names, characters, businesses, places, events, and incidents are either the products of author's imagination or used in a fictitious manner. Any resemblance to actual persons, living or dead, is purely coincidental.

This book is intended for adult readers only. Any sexual activity portrayed in these pages occurs between consenting adults over the age of 18 who are not related by blood.

DESCRIPTION

My attraction to the older mafia boss is undeniable...
He says he's stealing my youth, but I want him to have it.
Until a *baby* bump ruins all my plans...

I never wanted to strip for money... but a job is a job, and one check later, I've spent the night with a gorgeous, loaded mafia boss and paid off my mom's hospital bills.

Four years later, the handsome stranger comes back into my life...
Except Maksim Federov has no idea I had our baby girl years ago after the night we spent together.

I'll keep the secret until I can make sure Maksim has a place in my daughter's life...

Until then, our relationship will be governed by my boundaries.

Even if it does mean I end up in his bed every night, begging for more of his sensual touch. Now I just have to keep my mouth shut about the baby he gave me.

But life has other plans.

1

HEIDI

Taking several steadying breaths, I try to stitch together the splitting seams of my emotions as I wait for Zoe to answer her door. She flings it open a second later, her tornado of energy bursting through the air as she greets me with a brilliant smile, her pixie cut a wild halo of wispy edges around her head.

"Heidi! You ready to get wild for our girls' night?"

Short, with dark hair, angular features, and beautiful olive-toned skin, Zoe's the polar opposite of me in both looks and energy, but we've been inseparable ever since my mom and I moved to California before my first year of high school. And she can read me better than anyone.

Her excitement dies now as she sees the expression on my face. "What's wrong?"

Gripping my wrist, Zoe hauls me through the door and into the five-bedroom San Francisco apartment she shares with four of the girls she works with. I follow her mutely, terrified to say the words out loud because then they might feel true.

"Are the other girls asleep?" I ask, not wanting to fall apart in the middle of Zoe's kitchen if they might come waltzing in.

My best friend plunks me down at the dining table and sits across from me. Dark eye makeup completing her rebellious punk-rock look, the smokey cat-eye accentuates her light hazel eyes. Currently, they assess me with an intense level of concern. "Amber is. The other three went in to work early. I guess things are picking up at the club, so Howie's offering overtime."

I nod numbly, scarcely able to comprehend her answer when all I can think about is my mom.

"Seriously, Heidi, you're freaking me out. What's wrong?"

Swallowing hard, I take a moment to steel myself. "Mom got her lab results back."

Zoe's perfectly shaped brows press into a deep frown. "And?" she asks softly.

I shake my head, my eyes dropping to my hands, which lie folded in my lap. "It's a Glioblastoma M-something-or-other—a brain tumor—which I guess is very aggressive and hard to beat." A single tear trickles down my cheek, and I sniffle as the emotions start to leak out despite my best efforts to contain them.

"Oh, honey. I'm so sorry. But . . . they can treat it, right?"

I shrug, wiping my cheeks before covering my eyes with my hands. "She starts chemo Monday. Not that the doctor sounds confident at all that it will help."

Zoe falls silent, and that makes it so much worse because my outspoken friend is never short on words—or opinions. Dropping my hands, I meet her eyes through my tear-blurred vision. And I can see my deep sense of fear and loss reflected on her face.

"What can I do?" she asks, reaching across the table to grasp my hand.

I shake my head. "I don't know that there's anything *to* do."

A sob rips from me, and in an instant, I'm falling apart completely, unable to hold it together any longer. At least I made it out of the house so my mom didn't have to see this. She has enough to worry about without watching my meltdown.

Zoe comes around the table and pulls me up into a tight hug, letting me cry it out. And despite my best efforts to get it back together, I can't seem to stop the tears from falling. I don't want to lose my mom. She's all the family I have in the world, and I don't know what I would do without her.

It feels like all the stress and anxiety I've been shouldering since her appointment this afternoon has finally hit me full force, and I can barely breathe. But as Zoe keeps her arms circled snugly around my waist, the emotion slowly drains from me.

After several agonizing minutes, I find the strength to collect the jagged pieces of my heart and put them back together. Breathing raggedly, I straighten and dry my tears as I release Zoe from my death grip.

She gives me a sad smile, dropping her arms. "How's your mom taking it?"

"Better than I am, I think. She just says she's tired when I ask her. Though I know she's in pain. But the only thing she's complained about so far is that I'm quitting school." I give a disbelieving chuckle, thinking about how obstinately Mom objected when I told her my decision.

Leave it to my mom to be worried about my education when her health is on the line.

"You are?" Zoe asks, her eyebrows arching.

"Well, yeah. I could barely afford it, even though I'm working at the store full-time. And of course Mom can't afford health insurance, so how else are we going to pay for her treatment? She can barely maintain the hours she's got, her headaches are so debilitating. I need to get a second job."

"But you're so close to graduating," Zoe objects as she heads toward the white-painted kitchen cabinets.

"Yeah, well, I can finish my last two semesters once Mom's cancer is in remission. I'm not about to tell my mom she can wait to get treatment until after I finish my degree."

Zoe snorts and rises onto her toes as she feels around for something on the shelf above her line of sight.

"What are you doing?"

"Getting us glasses. We're opening a bottle of wine because you need a drink, so unless you want to pull straight from the bottle, we need something to drink it out of."

My shoulders sag in relief. A glass of wine sounds incredible right now. Something to dull the debilitating anxiety that's tightened my chest ever since we got my mom's prognosis. I join Zoe at the counter and use my extra five inches to reach the glasses she's working so hard to get. Not that I'm exceptionally tall. My friend is just short at five feet, one inch tall.

"Thanks," she says, dropping back onto the flats of her feet and heading toward the pantry for a bottle of wine. "I just hate that you're having to postpone school when it's already taken you five years to get this far."

"I couldn't care less about interior design right about now."

Zoe nods, cranking the corkscrew into the bottle and removing the seal with a pop. Then she pours me a generous glass and gestures for me to head to the living room couch. I take a swig of the rich, thick liquid, appreciating the bitter tang that promises a quick numbing dose of emotional relief. Then I follow her directions and lead the way to the overstuffed gray loveseat.

"I know you have your pride, but Heidi, maybe now's the time to think about joining me at Lady Venus. We make good money, and if finances are that tight, stripping could help—even if it's just temporary. To get your mom through chemo." Her expression is almost apologetic. She knows how I feel about dancing half-naked in front of drunk, horny men.

Of course, I would never judge her or the girls who are willing to do it. Hats off to anyone with enough confidence to expose themselves like that. But it makes me squeamish. I can't stop blushing just thinking about it. I haven't even been to see Zoe at work.

But I need the money. *Mom* needs the money. *And it's just dancing, isn't it?*

I take another swig of wine, searching deep inside myself for courage. I picture being up on stage wearing lingerie and heels, swinging seductively around a pole. It's so far from who I am. Sure, I enjoy dancing when Zoe and I go to the clubs. But that's entirely different from taking off my clothes and subjecting myself to the sexual fantasies of countless strange men.

Draining the last of my glass, I hold it out for a top off. Zoe obliges, pouring me another generous amount of wine without a word.

"Alright," I say as the alcohol finally starts to hit my bloodstream, giving me the courage I'm so desperately seeking. "Will you introduce me to Howie?"

The strip club manager has been good to his girls, from what I've gathered of Zoe's stories. I suppose, in the end, it's better to set aside my pride and see it as an opportunity if it will help my mom's fight with cancer.

Zoe gives a crooked smile, seeming to read the thoughts in my eyes. "We can go in before my shift tomorrow."

I nod. "Thanks, Zoe."

2

HEIDI

Six Months Later

"I'm sorry, Mrs. Turner, but the cancer is still growing. See this light-gray mass here on the frontal lobe?"

Dr. Humphreys uses his pen to circle a baseball-sized milky-gray blob on the right side of my mom's PET scan, and my stomach plummets. Before, it was about the size of a quarter. Even after all that chemo, she's definitely getting worse.

"I'm afraid chemotherapy isn't a viable solution."

"What is?" I ask, my desperation apparent in my voice.

Mom gives my hand a gentle squeeze, assuring me that everything is going to be okay. But it's not. None of this should be happening. My mom is barely fifty-five. She shouldn't be dying. It hurts to see her so frail. Even her lips have turned a pale grayish-brown. And her beautiful honey-blonde hair I inherited has all fallen out. Now she wears colorful bandanas to cover up the sad, sparse bristles that are able to grow on her scalp.

She tried the wigs but felt they weren't her. But without her thick signature locks, she looks so tired and beaten down, it breaks my heart. *And now the chemo hasn't even helped?* I hate it. I feel so absolutely useless. All I can do is sit by and watch as the cancer eats away at my mom's sharp and wonderful mind.

"We can look at alternative options. There's a trial drug currently available at UCSF. You could apply for that. I think you have a moderately good chance of being accepted into the study, given your specific tumor and its lack of response to treatment." Dr. Humphreys's expression is grave as he looks over his glasses at us.

"And how much will that cost?" Mom asks, her voice sounding tired.

"It depends. Insurance wouldn't likely cover it, but potentially, the program would cover some of the costs."

"We'll figure out how to pay for it," I assure her. Working full-time at Lady Venus has managed to cover her treatment over the last six months. And though finances are tight now that mom has gotten too weak to maintain her job at the flower shop, I can work overtime if I need to.

Finishing up the appointment, we head outside to the little beater of a Honda Civic I have sitting in the parking lot. I hold my mom's hand the entire way because her tumor has made her balance unpredictable, and I don't want to see her take a spill on the asphalt. We get into the little navy car without a word. Mom waits patiently, her purse clutched on her lap as I stare out the windshield.

And now that we're alone, I can feel the tears starting to sting the back of my eyes. Try as I might to keep it together, I can't help but sniffle. I'd really been hoping for good news—despite mom's persistent headaches. I'd almost convinced myself they were due to the chemo and not the fact that her tumor was still present.

"It'll be okay, Heidi," Mom says gently, and I nod, gripping the steering wheel firmly in both hands.

"I'll look into the program as soon as we get home. I have about a half-hour before I need to go to work."

"Heidi, you're wearing yourself ragged. You need to slow down."

"I'll slow down once we kick this cancer," I tell Mom, meeting her eyes with conviction.

She gives a sad smile, the exhaustion apparent in the sagging lines of her face. Just a year ago, we'd talked about going on a road trip to celebrate my graduation. Now, it feels like I'll never get out from under the mountain of financial stress bundled with the fear that I'm losing my mom.

I know she's made her peace with it. But I can't. I'm not ready to let her go. I don't know that I'll ever be ready for that. But I'm not even thirty. It's not fair. My mom is one of the best people in the world, and she shouldn't be dying of cancer. Not after we already lost Dad to it when I was just a child.

Aren't there enough people in the world that we could spread the misfortune around a little?

But it seems to follow me, my family, picking us off one by one.

The house is silent as Mom shuffles into her room to rest, exhausted from even the briefest of outings anymore. I get on the computer to look into the program Dr. Humphreys mentioned. It's not going to come cheap, even if we can get her into the program. But it looks like a promising new way of specifically targeting brain tumors, so it might do what chemo couldn't. We have to try.

I work quickly, filling out her initial application in the few spare moments I have before I need to head in to work. Then I grab my makeup bag and race across town to Lady Venus. I can't be late, not if I'm going to try to convince Howie to give me overtime. I'll need it to cover the extra expenses if Mom gets accepted into the experimental treatment program.

Plopping into the makeup chair next to Zoe, I give a breathy greeting as I get to work on my face.

"How'd it go?" she asks tentatively, and I know she's asking about Mom's doctor's appointment.

I press my lips into a tight line, unwilling to cry when I need to be on stage in ten minutes. Rather than go into detail, I just shake my head. I don't have time to fall apart now.

"I'm sorry, honey," she breathes, her shoulders slumping.

Rising from her chair, she comes to stand behind me, getting to work on my hair rather than pressing for more information. She knows better than to let me get emotional at the start of a shift. The last thing I need right now is to get sent home. No man likes to watch a stripper crying when she's supposed to be helping him forget about the problems in the world.

We're here to inspire pleasure, beauty, fun fantasies.

So there's no room for tears.

Plucking my pink sequin thong and matching top from the rack, I strip quickly out of my street clothes and don my outfit for the first '90s-themed song-and-dance routine. Zoe's already in her bright lime-green one, standing at the front of the room as she glances nervously toward the DJ.

"Come on, Heidi. He's giving me the go sign."

"I know, I know," I breathe, stumbling into my strappy pink heels before my top's even tied.

Zoe pulls it closed around my ribs, cinching it deftly. Then she dashes back to her place just in time to take her cue and head out on stage. Her signature strut raises a wave of hooting cheers, and I shake my head as I straighten myself out, making sure everything's in place.

Behind me, Tiff is standing in her blue sequin outfit, ready to take the pole on the near side of the catwalk. Amber and Kat are already backstage once more, having entered through the far opening, where we typically exit to keep a smooth flow between numbers. They'll have a dance or two to change and recuperate before they go back on stage.

Luke, our DJ tonight, gives me a signal, and I know it's my turn to flaunt my body as I make my entrance. But I don't strut like Zoe. She's got the fiery personality and rebellious glare to pull it off, and while I've gotten perfectly comfortable on stage over the past six months, I'm still not overtly sexual in my walk like some of the girls can be. But I do know how to walk a catwalk now.

Scooping my blonde waves over one shoulder, I take long, confident strides, placing one foot directly in front of the other as I make my entrance. I don't rush as I head toward the center pole, keeping my eyes up, aloof to the sea of men on either side of the stage. It's easier not to look at them until I reach my place. Though Zoe never seems to have a problem with eye contact, it unnerves me to think about so many eyes on me.

But once I get to dancing, it's easy to slip into the rhythm of the song, to find my comfort in my own skin. And I can appreciate the good workout I get from pole dancing. It keeps me focused.

Reaching my pole, I grip it, finding confidence in its firm stability as I allow my eyes to scan the sea of faces for the first time. My heart skips a beat as I spot a man sitting right beside the stage.

He's gorgeous.

Dressed in a black suit, he looks like he might have just come from some formal event—a wedding, maybe. He's loosened his tie and opened the top buttons of his shirt to reveal a hint of the muscular chest beneath. The perfectly trimmed scruff that colors his jaw is the same dark color as his thick head of wavy locks that shine from the product that keeps them perfectly styled.

From here, I can see the black ink of tattoos that just barely start to climb up his neck. I imagine every inch of his broad shoulders and back are covered in the artwork. He looks large, in both height and build, even from this vantage point above him. Large in the intimidatingly muscular way. He's in magnificent shape.

But it's not his impressive figure or the chiseled line of his square jaw that stops my heart. It's his steely gray eyes that hold as much haunting sadness as I feel. And he's sitting right in front, staring up at me as if daring me to chase his unfathomable troubles away.

I shiver as our gazes lock.

Something about this man screams danger. Death. And I wonder if he might not be the grim reaper himself, come to escort one more Turner family member to the afterlife. If so, I'm not so sure I would mind.

His server appears to deliver the finest bottle of Russian vodka we keep in stock, and when she leaves the bottle, I know he's here for one thing and one thing alone. To numb the deep and terrible pain that darkens his soul.

I take one lap around my pole, leaning away from it as I make a slow circle, starting my dance. But I find it almost impossible to focus with him watching me. I can feel his eyes tracking my movement, and it makes my skin prickle.

And when I make it around to his side of the stage once again, I know he's the one I'll be dancing for. Dipping low, I spread my thighs as I move to the song's seductive rhythm, offering him a fantasy world in which his sadness does not exist.

His eyes drop, following the curves of my body to the peak of my thighs, the way my ass rests lightly on the backs of my heels. And as I lean forward onto my palms, his eyes dart back up to find mine.

God, he's striking. The intensity of his gaze. It's smoldering, lighting my body on fire just by focusing on me. He leans forward in his chair, resting his elbows on his knees as he clasps his rocks glass casually in his large hands. And I wonder what they might feel like wrapped around my body.

Excitement blossoms in my belly, catching me off guard. I never have sexual thoughts about the men who watch me. If anything, my feelings toward them hover somewhere between pity and disgust.

But this tall, dark stranger has my heart thrumming an unsteady beat. To distract myself, I return to my pole, reaching high above my head and taking a running start so I can spin my way down it.

I hook one knee around the cool, smooth surface, using it as leverage so I can arch back. And when I find my anchor point with my eyes, once again, it's the sad-eyed man watching me. Muscles tight with anticipation, my pulse ringing in my ears, I almost don't notice as the song delivers its last resonating notes.

A hint of disappointment trickles into my gut as I catch Zoe's subtle message to get the hell off stage. Releasing my pole, I don't dare look back at the eye-grabbing, distinguished gentleman. Instead, I walk deliberately back down the catwalk toward the quick-change dressing room backstage.

3

HEIDI

I'm already stripped completely naked and changing into my next outfit when Howie walks in, his bearing all business as he approaches me.

"Heidi, you've been purchased for a private dance. A Mr. Federov. He's paying top dollar, so make sure you give him his money's worth. Put on your white outfit and go to room fifteen." Then he turns his attention to Amber without another word to me.

My stomach sinks as I change tracks, collecting the lingerie Howie ordered me into. I would usually brush off my disappointment as my typical response to lap dances. They're too personal for my taste, and though Lady Venus has strict rules about the lines customers are not allowed to cross—and the bouncers to reinforce those lines—it still makes me uncomfortable.

But tonight, I find my physical response stems more from the fact that I won't likely see the sad-eyed man again. My pole will be taken by a different girl, so even if he sticks around long enough for me to return, I'll be dancing in a different spot.

Though I haven't said a single word to him, I find I want to understand better what loss he's suffered to show such pain in his eyes. And to see if I can't relieve his pain in some small way because it might just help me forget my own.

Working my white fishnet stockings up to my thighs, I hook them deftly, then finish my look with a pair of feathery high heels. An angel costume to match my stage name. Though without the wings, I think it tends to make me look more like a slutty bride. Not that Howie gives a crap what I think in that regard. Not to mention, no client wants to have angel wings smacking him in the face. So, really, I'm an angel only in name.

Finding my off switch for my pride, I take a fortifying breath and head back to the black-velvet-curtained alcoves Howie calls rooms. Small numbers hang from the curtain rods above my head, marking which room is the one I've been designated.

I give a smile of acknowledgment to Peter, the bouncer who stands with his hands clasped in front of him at the far end of the hall. He'll be the one who comes running if this Mr. Federov gets handsy and I need help. His bulging arm muscles, broad chest covered by a skin-tight black T-shirt, and thick neck are visually intimidating enough that, typically, just his presence in the hall deters any misbehavior. He gives me a curt, silent nod.

Then I turn to slip inside alcove fifteen, parting the curtain just enough so I can enter before I pull it closed behind me. Mr. Federov will already be here, waiting, an intentional choice we adhere to for each of our clients. The anticipation of a dancer's arrival makes the reward that much sweeter.

I can feel his eyes on my back even before I turn to face him, and my instincts raise the hair on the back of my neck, warning me that I'm in the presence of danger. But Peter is just down the hall, I remind myself. Then I turn to face the man who purchased my private attention.

My breath catches as my eyes meet the steel-gray eyes from before. It's the same sad-eyed man who was watching me on stage. His gaze follows me with an undiminished level of haunting intensity, the emotion behind them making my heart hammer. I dread experiencing the loss I see so clearly in the depths of his soul.

He's older than I had realized from my place on stage—his dark hair flecked with silver that's more prominent at his temples, though not quite enough for me to call it gray. I would place him in his mid-forties. And though I don't normally go for older men, I have to admit he's even more attractive than I first thought.

The brooding intensity of his demeanor makes my stomach tremble. He makes me nervous, but in an oddly good way. I don't quite know what to make of my physical reaction to his presence. I've had boyfriends before. I'm not completely naive when it comes to men. But this heat that consumes my body now is something else entirely.

In the dim, red-tinged lighting, he looks somehow more treacherous than he did when I was on stage, though his posture is relaxed, his arm slung casually across the back of the red vinyl bench where he sits. The small enclosure of the alcove suddenly feels far smaller than usual. And yet, his penetrating gaze compels me to come closer.

The curving booth-like seat surrounds a circular platform in the center of the room, where I typically prefer to dance. But tonight, a sense of daring rises inside me as I fall prey to my curiosity. I want to touch him.

"Evening, Mr. Federov," I say softly, my voice almost breathy with the quick pace of my heartbeat.

Soft, sexual music surrounds us, guiding my movements as I mask my inexplicable nerves with the familiar movements that appeal to men. And for the first time, I find myself wondering if I entice this tall, handsome stranger as much as he does me.

I bite my lip at the thought, approaching him slowly as I get closer than I typically might.

"You know my name?" he asks, his voice deep and almost rasping in the sexiest way. But what I note most is the distinct Russian accent that matches his name. He's a transplant just like I am. Only he traveled much farther to get here.

The similarity puts me slightly more at ease, though I can't say why. Perhaps it's a relief to know we have one small thing in common besides the heaviness of grief. But he's not here to get to know me or see how similar we are. He's here to address a far more basic desire.

I smile alluringly, releasing my lower lip as I climb up onto the red vinyl bench, placing one knee on either side of his thighs. Heart thudding in my chest, I feel electric arousal as I straddle him, though our legs only lightly touch.

"We make a point of knowing all our high-paying customers' names," I assure him, though I'm sure his will vanish from my mind within a week or so, just like the rest of them do.

Heat radiates at the peak of my thighs as his eyes burn intensely into my soul. And though the sadness remains predominant, I can see a new light in his gaze, a hunger that raises goosebumps along my arms and tightens my nipples inside their low-cut white-lace cups.

His arms tense, but he doesn't move them, and my breath catches as I feel the desire to touch me radiating from him. His lips part, releasing a soft caress of warm air across my chest, and I find myself desperately wishing he might break the club's rule.

Just this once, I want him to shatter the invisible barrier separating us.

Daring to push things farther than I ought to, I settle onto his lap, rolling my hips in time to the music as I lightly grind against him. I let my arms fall gently over his impressive shoulders to grip the back of the seat.

I can feel the iron proof of his excitement pressing adamantly against the seam of his black slacks, and I gasp as a wave of arousal washes through me. I should stop, shift my position, do something to alleviate the mounting pleasure building deep in my core.

But I can't seem to control my body anymore. Instead, I lean into his chest, shivering slightly as my breasts graze across his shirt's fine silk. He smells intensely masculine—the combined scents of leather, sandalwood, and a hint of motor oil that makes me think he does something physical with his hands—for work or pleasure, I can't even guess.

"Where are you from?" he rasps, his voice hoarse, and I sense that he's as lost in my dance as I am, using conversation as an attempt to maintain control of the situation.

Somehow, I find his discipline—his ability to resist touching me when I'm so far past the acceptable limit—that much sexier. *Who is this man, and why am I so insanely attracted to him?*

"Not here," I breathe.

Though I'm dying to know more about him, I know better than to give out personal details of my life. We have stage names for a reason. Stalkers can be both dangerous and insanely difficult to get rid of. Howie made it clear when I took the job that we aren't supposed to give out any information, innocuous as it might seem, that would help someone find us. And for all I know, the fact that I'm from Austin, Texas, could be all this dangerously enticing Mr. Federov needs to hunt me down.

"Have you been in the city long?" he presses, his tone growing more conversational, and a spike of anxiety lances through me as I wonder if I misread his tactic and he's actually lost interest in the dance.

"Mm-hmm," I respond, doing my best to control the emotions wreaking havoc inside me.

"Then how come I've never seen you here before?"

I release a soft laugh, though I know his inquisition is anything but funny. I've just never met a man who seems more interested in me than the service I'm here to provide. His probing conversational technique is challenging my ability to follow Howie's strict rules that keep us safe. "You are full of questions, aren't you Mr. Federov?" I ask, trying to keep my tone light, teasing.

"I want to get to know you," he murmurs, and the confession sends a tingle racing up my spine. The statement sounds genuine enough that it makes my heart flutter.

"You didn't pay to get to know me," I reason, changing my position to face away from him so I can clear my head. His appealing cologne is making it too hard to think, and I need to keep my head on straight. This is a job, a paid lap dance, and if I'm not careful, I might do something I regret.

Because having my face so close to his was making it almost impossible to resist kissing him.

Reclaiming control of the dance, I gently grind back against his lap. But the feel of his cock twitching inside his slacks only intensifies my excitement. I'm playing with fire, and I know it.

And though I shouldn't, I take his impressively large hands and guide them slowly up my body. Starting at my hips, I let him feel the curve of my waist, the sides of my ribcage, then I dare to slide them higher until his callused palms cup my lace-clad breasts.

"What if I did?" he asks, the ragged sound of my voice making me throb with desire. "What if I paid you to spend the night with me?"

His offer freezes me in place, and my fingers tighten instinctually around his hands as horror grips me. This is what I get for taking things too far, for letting my own attraction drive the dance. I crossed the line, the one Howie put in place for this very reason, and now I'm furious with myself—and this gorgeous stranger—for having taken that last step into a world where I promised myself I would never go.

I'm aware that some of the girls take side offers from their clients. They'll give a blowjob in a guy's car for an extra hundred, spend the night for an extra five. But it's strictly against the rules, and I would never stoop so low as to sell my body. And yet here he is, offering me money for a night of sex.

I shove his hands away, jerking to a stand as I spin to face him, my disgust overcoming my guilt at having blurred the line and brought us to this point. "I'm not a whore," I say adamantly, the hurt dripping from my tone. Though I can hardly see how he's supposed to think otherwise when I was putting his hands all over me just moments ago.

His face registers mild surprise, though he doesn't argue or defend himself. Instead, he observes me with a casual calm that completely contrasts with my emotional response.

"Fifty thousand dollars," he offers boldly, throwing out a number that makes my head spin.

And though I promised myself that I would never cross that line —that I would never sleep with someone for money, even if that's what so many of the other girls do to cushion their bank accounts— fifty thousand is a massive amount. It would make all the difference in the world when it comes to the medical bills Mom and I are facing.

But as significant as it is, that would still put me out of a job, and I need the income. "I can't," I say, though the words feel painful as they leave my lips. "I need this job." But I could really use that money. *And would it really count as prostitution if I only did it once?*

Even I know that reasoning is too flimsy to hold up. I would definitely feel guilt and shame after the deed was done. But fifty thousand dollars is a staggering amount to pass up.

"A hundred thousand," he offers, his gray eyes sharp as they watch me closely.

I breathe heavily at the astonishing new amount. *He can't be serious, can he? A hundred thousand dollars to sleep with me one time? Is this some kind of test? A challenge to see how long I'll hold out? What price I'm willing to sell my dignity for?*

I shiver violently as my will to resist crumbles. Deep, agonizing shame grips my chest in an iron fist. Mom would never want this. But a hundred thousand dollars could save her life—and change mine. With that much money, I could even finish college and get my life back on track—after paying off Mom's medical bills.

Closing my eyes, I fight off a wave of self-disgust.

Apparently, everyone has a price, and Mr. Money Bags has just found mine.

But somehow, even more shameful is the excitement that pools deep in my core at the thought of spending a night with him. I find him dangerously attractive. I can't deny that. And though he's probably closer to my mom's age than my own, I might have set that aside to consider dating him.

But that's not what he's asking for. He wants to give me money for sex. Which means he doesn't see me as anything more than an object. He doesn't want to get to know me, like he suggested. He wants to use me, to discover only my body. That's it. End of story.

And for a hundred thousand dollars, I'll let him.

"Okay," I breathe, fighting a wave of self-disgust. Then my eyes snap open, and I glance over my shoulder, feeling like a naughty child who could get caught breaking the rules at any second.

And when I turn my head to face him once again, Mr. Federov's striking features have transformed into a dark, dangerous smile of satisfaction. "Good. Tell your boss you're feeling sick and need to go home. I'll meet you out front in fifteen."

He stands, and for the first time, I get a good look at just how large he is. Well over six feet tall, he towers over me by nearly a foot, and he must weigh twice as much as I do in sheer muscle.

I quiver as a surge of intimidation washes through me. This man is large enough that he could do whatever he wants to me. I would have no chance of fending him off. And I've just agreed to spend an entire night with him. Alone.

4

MAKSIM

The limo idles by the curb, waiting for the long-legged beauty the club introduced as Angel when she walked on stage. She's taking long enough to make her excuses and leave the club that I'm starting to wonder if she changed her mind. Not that it would destroy me if she did. I don't intend to take this past one night.

But after my brother Alexei's wedding today and seeing both of my younger brothers so happy, all the pain of knowing what I've lost has come back in full force. So rather than stay for the reception, I left early to get drunk. To drown my sorrows and suffer in solitude so as not to ruin my youngest brother's happy day.

But sex is far more effective than alcohol, and something in Angel's eyes makes me think she understands the kind of loss and suffering I've endured. So I sincerely hope she hasn't bailed on me because just a few minutes with her have left me feeling less alone.

And then the doors open.

Our eyes meet for a moment, the flicker of relief in her hazel depths—as if she thought I might have given up and left without her. Then she casts them down to descend the club's steps, her body language almost shy now that we're in a less structured setting and she's fully clothed.

She's dressed in a casual sweater dress and white tennies that somehow make her look just as sexy as the skimpy lingerie she wore for my lap dance. This girl is striking in a very understated way, natural in her look—entirely different from my fiancée.

My dead fiancée.

Pain lances through me as Symphony's face appears in my mind's eyes. My last moments with her. The shock and fear in her expression as she died in my arms.

It's been less than a year, and while I've slept with several women purely to try and numb the agonizing hollowness of her loss, for the first time since Symphony died, I feel like I can actually *see* a woman.

Angel intrigues me—something about her subtle Southern charm combined with the devastating sorrow in her eyes. It speaks to me, the way her sadness doesn't waver even as she smiles tentatively at me now.

"Ready?" I open the limo door, gesturing for her to slide in first.

She hesitates for the briefest moment before nodding and slipping into the dark interior. I follow her inside, and the driver pulls away from the curb a moment later, heading toward the sex club I've frequented with my casual encounters lately. A conscious choice because I can't bring myself to let them into the bed I shared with the woman I thought I would spend my life with.

Angel's gaze roams the limo's interior, and her innocent, wide-eyed expression makes me wonder if she's far younger than her sad expression had me believe.

"Have you ever been in a limo before?" I ask, studying her closely.

The beautiful dancer turns her head sharply to look at me, her cheeks warming to a soft rose color. "No."

"Have you ever slept with a stranger before?"

Her blush intensifies, making her appear even younger and more naive, and a doubt settles into my stomach about whether I should have made the offer to her in the first place. While she works in a strip club, she's unlike the other women I've slept with until now. I'm quickly coming to realize how far off I was in my estimation of her.

"No," she whispers shyly.

Before I can press her further, the limo pulls up outside Temptation. Opening the door, I slip outside and offer Angel my hand. Hers is petite against my palm, and I can feel the slight tremor in her fingers that reveals her anxiety. She might seem calm on the surface, but she's nervous.

Still, she lets me guide her through the front doors, my hand on the small of her back. She stands silently as I speak with the young, leather-clad receptionist who books our room and hands me a key.

"Have you ever been to a sex club before?" I ask, watching her from the corner of my eye as I guide her toward the thrumming music of the bar area.

This time, Angel only shakes her head. Several men eye her appreciatively as we enter the room, their gazes combing down her long legs. But as soon as they glance in my direction, their attention shifts as they purposefully avoid eye contact with me. They know better than to touch what's mine.

At the bar, I order two vodka sodas and hand one to Angel as soon as they're delivered.

"Thanks," she murmurs and takes a large swig.

"Nervous?" I press, a hint of amusement curling my lips because it's growing more apparent by the second.

Angel releases a breathy laugh, her cheeks coloring once again. "Is it that obvious?"

I give a one-shoulder shrug and force a smile that feels somewhat stiff after so many months without smiling at all.

Angel bites her full lip, her embarrassment intensifying. "Honestly, I've never done anything like this." Her eyes dart around the room to encompass all the scantily clad clubgoers, the secluded communal alcoves where people are in various states of undress and busy getting it on. "I'm pretty ... inexperienced, I guess."

"How old are you?" I ask, curious whether she might actually give me a straight answer now that we're not at Lady Venus anymore.

"Twenty-three."

She doesn't miss a beat, leaving me confident that it's the truth, and I'm struck by the realization that she's young enough to be my daughter. A flicker of guilt tightens my stomach. I shouldn't have made the offer. It doesn't matter that she's the first woman who's seemed to somehow comprehend the agony of my existence. We're worlds apart in our experience.

"Perhaps this was a mistake," I state, studying Angel's face. "I shouldn't have brought you here. I shouldn't have asked you to spend the night with me."

Her face falls, her anxiety spiking as Angel reaches out to grasp my forearm, and the unexpected contact sends electrical jolts of attraction up my arm and through my core.

"You can't back out now! I mean . . ." She worries her lips as if concerned that she did something wrong. "I went into this with eyes wide open, and twenty-three is certainly old enough that I'm capable of making my own decisions. If you're serious about the money, then I want to go through with this."

My gut clenches as I realize how terribly I've misjudged this girl. She must be desperate for cash to go so far out of her comfort zone. And while I'm ruthless when it comes to business and destroying my enemies—like Aleksandr Volkov, who had my fiancée murdered—I don't like the thought of taking advantage of this young woman.

"I wouldn't make the offer if I weren't serious about the money," I state, setting aside my drink.

"Good. Then it's a deal, so let's seal it with a kiss." Angel follows my lead, setting her drink aside, and before I can muster the self-restraint to stop her, she grasps the collar of my dress shirt and pulls my lips down to hers.

Electric excitement crackles between our lips, igniting my attraction for her with a white-hot intensity. I could feel it at Lady Venus as well. Every subtle brush of her flesh against my own sent my instincts into overdrive, wiping away my better judgment as she turned me on.

A low snarl rumbles up from my chest as my hands find the curve of her hips, and without thinking, I pull her firmly against my body, relishing in the feel of her athletic yet yielding frame.

Angel gasps, her lips parting as her arms snake around my neck, and I take advantage of her surprise, delving my tongue into her mouth to taste her deeply. She tastes fresh and citrusy, like the drink she just set down, and the cool softness of her lips mold to mine in perfect submission.

I know I shouldn't want her like I do, not when she's so clearly in a compromised position, but I can't help myself. When she releases the softest of sighs, I wrap one arm around her waist and let my free hand travel up her side, her shoulder, her neck, until my fingers tangle in her luscious honey-blonde locks.

I can't stop kissing her until my lungs are screaming for air, and even then, I only break away to gaze down at her soft, feminine features. Her hazel eyes—almost green and gold with a dark-brown rim containing the burst of color—stare up at me with a combination of determination and trust.

"W–Where do you want me?" she breathes.

Releasing my breath, I ease my hold on her, allowing her to settle back onto her feet. Then I press her drink into her palms and finish off my drink with one large gulp. She follows suit, drinking it down quickly and coughing slightly from the burn of carbonation on the back of her throat.

Taking her delicate hand lightly in my own, I guide her toward the private rooms at the back of the club. She follows without a word, and when I open the room and gesture her inside, she leads the way.

Normally, when I bring women here, I might ask what kind of play they enjoy then go from there. But with Angel, I sense that we'll be exploring from the start. She stops in the middle of the room, her eyes traveling over the complex and unique furniture built to maximize pleasure and punishment alike.

Stepping up behind Angel, I rest my hands lightly on her hips and lean close to murmur in her ear. "You're sure you want to do this?"

She shivers delicately beneath my palms, then nods.

"I want to hear you say it."

"Yes, Mr. Federov."

"Call me Maks," I insist. Hearing my last name on her lips only reminds me of our age difference.

"Maks," she agrees, then adds, "I want this."

Intrigued by her conviction despite her apparent nerves, I feel compelled to put her at ease. I want to take it slow and explore what she might find pleasurable since she might not know herself. She said inexperienced, not a virgin, and I'm curious just what that might mean.

Scooping her thick waves of hair away from her neck with my fingers, I press my lips to the soft spot behind her ear and am rewarded with a soft gasp.

"Do you like it when I kiss you, Angel?" I murmur, working my way slowly toward her shoulder and the collar of her scoop-neck sweater dress.

"Yes," she whispers, tilting her head to give me better access.

"Good. Because I intend to kiss every inch of your body tonight."

5

HEIDI

The deep rumble of Maks's low voice raises goosebumps along my neck and arms and sends a tingle down my spine. He's a terrifying juxtaposition—dark and brooding, possibly even dangerous, and yet, I get the sense that he wants to protect me, to take care of me in some way. Or at least to put me at ease.

His apparent concern over our age difference contradicts the way he so willingly threw money at me to get his way. Like he's used to getting what he wants and doesn't care what it takes, and yet, he doesn't like to think he's taking advantage of me.

His touch is powerful, commanding, but it feels like he's entirely focused on pleasing me. Yet he's supposed to be paying for *his* pleasure.

I can't make sense of him, and that mystery makes him all the more intimidating. But now that I'm committed to spending the night with him, I don't want to let this opportunity slip through my fingers.

The thought that I could finally afford all the expenses that have come with Mom's cancer and still have plenty of the money he's promised left to turn my life around . . . it's brought me such intense relief that I nearly panicked when he started to back out.

But now, as his lips travel expertly over my skin and his strong hands move slowly down my hips toward the hem of my dress, I'm not just glad I stuck with the deal for the money. Because Maks is a phenomenal kisser, and he's making my body go wild at the slightest touch.

His fingers curl around the bottom of my dress, and inch by inch, he guides the soft, knitted fabric up my thighs, over my hips, past my waist and breasts. His lips leave my skin as I raise my arms, allowing him to undress me. And somehow, though I have danced in little more than a bra and panties at Lady Venus almost every night, having Maks strip me of clothes feels intensely more intimate.

"Turn around," he commands, dropping my dress onto the floor beside me.

I do as he says, turning tentatively to face him. His eyes travel appreciatively down my body, undressing me further with his eyes before they come back to find my face. Then he slowly kneels before me.

My breath catches in my throat at the way his eyes never leave mine. Stooping before me, he looks like some kind of Greek deity lowering himself to worship at my feet.

His fingers deftly go to work on my shoelaces, then one strong hand grasps the back of my knee, bending my leg so he can slip my foot out of my white tennis shoe. He does the same with my other foot, tossing my tennies carelessly over his shoulders as he watches my face. I'm too spellbound to look away.

All the while, my lungs feel as if they're frozen in a block of ice, the oxygen trapped there as my ears start to ring. With a deliciously soft caress, Maks's hands travel up my legs, my hips, following the lines of my body as he comes back to a towering stand.

Then he tips his chin toward the freshly made bed that occupies one corner of the room.

"Go bend over the edge." As he orders me, his hands find the edges of his suit jacket, and he starts to undress with a casual confidence that makes my heart stutter.

When do the whips, gags, and restraints decorating the room come into play? Is he about to spank me? Would I like that? Questions race through my head at a million miles a second, and I find it nearly impossible to think as I turn to follow his command.

I can hear him step out of his own shoes behind me, the soft whisper of silk hitting the floor that makes me think he's discarded his fine dress shirt. But I don't dare sneak a peek and look back. Then my stomach knots at the sharp snap of his belt coming free of its loops.

I keep my eyes pinned to the crimson sheets before me and force my nerve-stiffened body to bend at the hips so I can rest my cheek on the firm mattress. Close behind me, Maks looms with his intense presence.

As my new position puts my body on full display, Maks releases a low, appreciative growl. My heart flutters when his large palms find my waist, and he slowly trails them across my skin, exploring the planes of my back, the dimples at the base of my spine, then the round orbs of my full ass.

"Tell me, Angel, has anyone ever kissed you here?" Maks rumbles, one hand shifting from my ass cheek to stroke between my thighs.

I gasp as the heat of his fingers singes my skin through the silk of my thong, and a deep, throbbing ache starts in my clit after being touched so brazenly. The feel of his hand boldly petting my most intimate parts sends my body into a frenzy that makes it nearly impossible for me to retain the question he asked.

"No," I gasp after I can make sense of his words.

He hums approvingly, then his fingers hook around the waistband of my panties, and he strips me of them in an instant. The whisper of fabric sliding down my thighs makes my core tremble, and my panties pool around my ankles a moment later.

"Spread your legs," Maks commands as his hands find my ass cheeks once again.

And though I'm shivering with a heady combination of fear and excitement, I do as he says. His palms grip and knead my ass, then he spreads my cheeks wide.

A throaty groan escapes me at the intense euphoria of his warm, wet tongue finding my clit and stroking across it. Explosive excitement heats my flesh as Maks expertly licks the length of my slit, his tongue delving between my folds. Warm arousal gushes out to meet him as I find myself instantly on the verge of climax.

I've never felt anything so tantalizingly erotic as a man's face buried in my pussy.

My legs shudder violently, the strength leaving them as they turn to noodles, and somehow, Maks seems to know just what to do. His strong hands brace me against the firm edge of the mattress, holding me up when I lack the ability.

"You taste like heaven," he rasps, his hot breath whispering across my clit and making me whimper with need. He repeats the motion several times, intensifying my arousal with every bold stroke. I cling to the satin sheets, trying to stop myself from falling apart completely.

But I know I'm hovering on the brink of climax, ready to topple into oblivion as soon as he'll let me. From the purring rumble of appreciation, I suspect that Maks is taking his time, enjoying the way I shiver and gasp with every delicious stroke of his tongue.

Just when I think I can't stand it any longer, he tilts my hips higher. The stubble covering his chin and cheeks tickles my thighs as he shifts his angle, and then his lips wrap around my clit, and he sucks softly.

I cry out as the explosion of ecstasy bursts through me like a thousand tiny stars. Colors dance behind my eyes as I orgasm with such force that it makes my toes go numb. Panting, I cling to the soft crimson sheets, shuddering against Maks's face with uncontrollable relief.

Only after the trembling euphoria slowly subsides does Maks release my clit, then he laps between my folds once again, as if slurping up the dripping goodness of an ice cream cone.

"Now, turn around and lie on the bed," he commands.

Still tingling from my release, my limbs heavy with contentment, I do as he says, crawling up onto the bed and making my way to the center of it before reclining on the pillows as I face him.

The fiery arousal in his eyes makes my skin heat. Consumed by lust, he seems to have shed, if only for a moment, his deep sadness that struck me so powerfully at the strip club. As I watch Maks now, I can see him in his full glory.

Wearing nothing but a pair of boxer briefs, his muscular body is on full display, the chiseled lines of his chest and abs flexing beneath an intricate collage of tattoos that covers almost every inch of exposed flesh. His arms bulge with strength, his broad shoulders ensuring me that whatever unbearable burden he might carry could never be too heavy a load.

If ever a man could capture the strength of Atlas, it would be this man, and I scarcely know where to look now that his glorious body is mere feet from me and prowling closer with catlike grace.

Where the silver hair at his temples would place him in his mid-forties, his body is clearly at the peak of its strength, far from that of a middle-aged man. I don't think I've ever seen a sexier sight, and for a moment, I'm struck dumb.

"Spread your legs for me, *krasivaya*," he murmurs. "I want to see how wet you are."

I don't know that I've ever been this excited by the sight of a nearly naked man. And from the impressive bulge in his boxer briefs, I suspect the best is yet to come. But it takes every scrap of my self-confidence to do as he says and open my legs to his hungry gaze.

A hiss of anticipation issues between his teeth as I take a deep breath and slowly let my knees fall open, spreading my thighs.

With impressive speed, Maks is on top of me, his hips coming to rest in the valley of my thighs as his muscle-bound chest grazes lightly across my bra-clad chest. The soft dusting of hair that covers his pecs tickles in the sexiest way.

My breath catches as he leans in to capture my lips once again, and the tangy, almost bitter taste of my excitement on his tongue sends a silent thrill through my body.

"You're positively dripping," he observes, his tone hovering somewhere between playful and predatory.

Then he reaches between us to stroke two thick fingers between my folds. His touch is silken with the lubrication of my juices, gliding through my slit with a sinful kind of friction. A soft cry parts my lips as his fingertips brush across my swollen, sensitive clit, lighting up my nervous system.

"You like that?" Maks purrs, his lips so close they brush across mine as he speaks.

Consumed by my euphoria, I can only bring myself to nod. My next cry vanishes into his mouth as he claims my lips at the same time as he presses two fingers inside my entrance. Then he groans. I writhe beneath him, my heart hammering as my excitement skyrockets once again.

Maybe it's that I haven't been with a man since my mom got so sick, or maybe this god of a man knows just how to provide women pleasure after years of experience. But every brush of his thumb across my clit, every penetrating thrust of his fingers, is driving me wild.

Hips rolling in time with his hand, I grind against his palm, relishing in the calluses that release jolts of blazing pleasure through my core.

"Come for me, Angel," he breathes against my lips, and I have no choice but to obey.

I groan as my second climax rolls through me like a tidal wave, washing away all my troubles and leaving me in a sweet, euphoric oblivion. My walls clamp down around his fingers, begging for more as he curls them to stroke my G-spot.

When I finally come down from my high, my body is so intensely relaxed that my eyes start to flutter closed.

Somewhere in the back of my mind, I'm aware of the fact that he's still calling me by my stage name. I probably should have told him my real name when he told me to call him Maks. But it feels too late now, and since this is a one-time deal, I suppose it doesn't matter if he calls me Angel or Heidi.

"You aren't going to fall asleep on me, are you?" Maks teases softly, calling me back to the moment, his facial hair whispering across my cheek as he leans close to my ear.

"No," I breathe, shaking my head to reinforce it. We had a deal, and I mean to see it through. Though his attention to my pleasure before his own has put me at ease in a way I never could have anticipated.

"Are you up for a little fun, then?"

He leans up onto his powerful forearms to gaze deeply into my eyes, and for a moment, I'm captivated by the molten silver of his own. I hadn't realized how beautiful they were beyond the sadness.

"We haven't been having fun already?" I ask with a hint of exasperation.

And for the first time, I detect the hint of a smile curving his soft lips.

"For what I have in mind, you would have to be willing to trust me."

My heart skips a beat at the dare reflected in his gaze. Once again, my mind sets off warning bells, reminding me that this man could be dangerous. But for some reason, I feel safe with him. And now, I'm dying to know his definition of fun.

"I trust you," I murmur.

6

MAKSIM

What started as an unusual sense of protectiveness for the young, eager dancer has turned into a fascination. Her almost shy hesitation in the beginning gave her a dignity that seems to vanish the instant money gets involved. But now that she's nearly naked beneath me, her body my playground, I seem to have unlocked a daring, adventurous side of her, a willingness to explore and immerse herself in my world of pleasure.

God, she's sexy. Her innocent expression of euphoria that seems completely without expectation is turning me on. I want to explore her, see what kinks she might enjoy, how she'll react to the intense combination of punishment and reward.

"Follow me," I command.

Standing from the bed, I offer Angel my hand as she reaches the edge. Even her smallest gestures are elegant, and when I pull her to a stand, she watches me with intense curiosity.

"Is this when all the . . . toys come out to play?" she asks, her slight Southern drawl giving her question a hint of impertinence.

"Would you like to play with toys?" I counter, curious if the question stems from fear or anticipation. Arching an eyebrow, I reach around her to unclasp her bra while I wait for my answer.

Angel urges the straps down her arms and lets the lacy cups fall to the floor. Her breasts are perfect, pert, round, firm, beautiful in their naturally modest size. As a model, Symphony had paid well for her curves—or I had. She'd insisted that the agencies would only hire women with above-average breasts. But that doesn't seem to concern Angel.

"Well?" I press when the silence stretches between us, and to urge her response, I give one pert nipple a soft pinch.

Angel inhales sharply, her chest flushing with fresh excitement. "I don't know," she finally admits.

How a girl as beautiful as she is could possibly be so inexperienced at the age of twenty-three, I can't quite fathom, but I intend to broaden her horizons tonight. Taking her hand, I lead her to the standing bondage frame. Then I deftly tie a knot around her left wrist and guide her arm up over her head.

"If, at any point, this is too much for you, just tell me to stop. I want us both to have fun with this."

"What does that mean? Too much?" she breathes, her eyes wide as they shift from watching my hands to reading my face.

I pause to meet her eyes directly. "I don't suppose you've ever been spanked before?"

This time, she giggles, and a moment later, she bites her lip to cut the embarrassed laughter short. Because, as much as I find the melodic sound pleasant, I'm far from joking.

"No," she agrees once she has herself under control.

"I want to see how many times I can spank you before you're ready to come."

Angel swallows hard, and I give a dark smile before resuming the knot attaching her right hand to the frame. I check to ensure she's secure but still loose enough that the rope won't be cutting off the circulation to her hands.

She naturally grips the ties, holding onto them for support as they force her to stand tall, her arms stretched to their lengths. Then I capture her chin between my thumb and finger, tipping her face up so I can steal a kiss.

Her lips are soft and yielding, just as she's proven to be, and I linger there, tasting her tongue as mine strokes into her mouth. Then I release her to go to the wall of toys. I pick the fur-tipped riding crop, a toy that can bring both pleasure and pain. A soft introduction when used appropriately.

Still, it makes a nice loud snap when I bring it sharply against my palm. Angel yelps, her back tensing as she looks over her shoulder with nervous anticipation. I smirk when she releases a shaky breath.

"Are you trying to frighten me?" she asks, her chin lifting defiantly.

"Anticipation is half the fun," I tease, prowling forward slowly to stand behind her once more. Then I brush the soft tip of the crop slowly up the inside of her thigh.

Angel shivers, goosebumps rising across her flesh, and I give her ass a playful tap, not hard but enough to make her gasp.

"Spread them," I command, indicating her ankles with the riding crop.

She does, stepping wide for me.

"Good girl," I praise and scoop her hair over one shoulder so I can reward her with a light kiss on the neck. "Do you like being told what to do, *krasivaya*?" I tease, walking slowly around her body so I can take in her beauty from every angle.

She's glorious, soft and yet lean and athletic, with just enough cushion to make her curvy but with the muscles of a dancer.

Angel frowns, as if the question confuses her somehow, and when she doesn't answer, I take it as an opportunity to flick the whip sharply across her nipple, just grazing her breast. She squeals, her muscles tensing from the shock, but the sound tapers into something of a sinful moan.

"Answer me, Angel. Unless you want me to even the score." I tickle her other nipple with the crop's soft fur as I make my threat.

"No," she blurts, and then her cheeks color, telling me without words that she's not being entirely truthful with me—or herself.

"Hmm." I continue my slow circle around her, nearing her backside once more, and after a moment's delay, I give her ass a sharp smack with the crop.

"Ow!" she squeals, drawing her leg up defensively. "What was that for?"

I respond by delivering a quick snap to her other ass cheek, and Angel squirms as a soft groan escapes her. One that tells me the sharp sting of her punishment is also turning her on.

"I ask the questions, not you," I state calmly. "And don't lie to me. I can tell when you're lying."

"I'm not lying," she insists as I circle back around to her front side.

With a flick of my wrist, I catch her nipple that I spared the first time around, and Angel jerks against her restraints, but she doesn't tell me to stop. Drawing close, I trail the soft fur down from her collarbone and between her breasts, tracking closer to the peak of her thighs.

"You said you don't like being told what to do," I murmur. "But I can see it in your body language. You liked it when I told you to bend over the bed. You liked it when I made you spread your legs for me. Admit it."

I give her clit the softest of warning taps, letting her know where I intend to strike her next if she lies again. Her eyes flicker with a fiery defiance, and for a moment, I think she might just stand her ground. Her lips twitch, then part, and she releases a breathy sigh.

"I like it when you tell me what to do," she admits, and the confession turns me on far more than it should.

To reward her honesty, I lean down and capture one hardened nipple in my mouth. I soothe the sting from the crop, gently circling the taut nub with my tongue and sucking gently until Angel moans with pleasure. Then I give her other nipple the same gentle caress.

From my periphery, I can see her knees weaken as her arousal takes control. And with a light pop, I release her breast.

"You understand the game now, *krasivaya*? If you're a good girl, I'll reward you. Do something naughty, and I'll punish you."

"I understand," she says breathlessly.

"Good," I praise. "Now tell me, Angel, does it turn you on when I spank you?" I rasp, stroking the whip's fur down the length of her body once more.

She shudders, seeming both excited and instinctively afraid of the toy's potential sting.

"Yes," she whispers, and her eyes dip momentarily to confess her naughty pleasure.

I can tell it takes courage to be honest about it, and to reward her, I reach between her thighs to stroke her slit and circle her clit. She's positively dripping, and her clit twitches at the lightest touch. Angel whimpers, her knuckles turning white as she grips her restraints convulsively.

"Dirty little minx," I praise, resting my free palm against the small of her back to support her twitching body.

Her breathing quickens, her trembling growing more distinct as I bring her to the edge of a third climax. But this time, I want to draw out her pleasure and build it to see how hard I can make her come.

"Oh, please!" she gasps, her hips jerking forward as I roll her clit between my finger and thumb.

Then I release her, and Angel groans at the sudden loss of contact. Confusion flickers across her face, and her chest heaves as she works through the physical frustration of having reached the precipice but not quite achieved release.

"Did you want me to keep going?" I tease quietly, nipping her ear and extracting a tortured gasp.

"Yes!" she cries desperately.

In a flash, I bring the crop down across her ass with a sharp crack.

"Oh, holy sugar honey iced tea!" she yelps, and the phrase is so unusual, it brings me out of the spicy moment and makes me pause.

Then, to my utter astonishment, she laughs.

"Sorry, that one stung."

"Too much?" I need to make sure I'm not pushing her past her limit, but her reaction was so far outside my level of comprehension, I don't quite know how to interpret it.

Angel bites her lip, a reticent look crossing her face, but she shakes her head no. Scowling, I step closer and tip her chin so she has to meet my eyes.

"Don't lie to me," I repeat, my tone low and commanding.

"I'm not..." Her words die on her lips as she reads the warning in my eyes. "Okay, maybe it was a little much," she admits. "But I don't want you to stop..."

How is her vulnerability so insanely sexy? She drives me wild just by telling me the truth.

"Are you ready to take all of me?" I rasp, my anticipation so acute I don't think I can keep playing our little game.

"Yes," Angel breathes, and though her voice cracks, I sense that she's telling me the truth.

Capturing her lips, I leave her with a scintillating kiss that makes my blood boil. Then I release her to walk back to my slacks and extract a condom from my wallet. Stripping the last shred of fabric separating me from her, I drop my boxer briefs and tear the condom foil with my teeth as I stalk back toward her waiting figure.

Angel watches with hooded anticipation, her lips parted slightly in the sweetest look of surprise as she takes in the size of me and swallows nervously.

"Don't worry, *krasivaya*. I'll take it slow," I purr before slanting my lips over hers once again.

She sighs, leaning into me as she melts into my embrace.

Slowly, I let one hand follow the curve of her breast, the flat plane of her stomach, and out over the flare of her hip before I grasp her supple thigh and hook her leg around my waist. It leaves her perfectly exposed to me, and as my swollen tip slides adamantly into her slick folds, a ravenous hunger consumes me.

This is the release I've been seeking, the sinful oblivion that can wipe my mind clean if only for a brief time, and as I press against the tight ring of her entrance, Angel releases the single sexiest sound I've ever heard.

I ease inside her, feeling her walls stretch, yielding to my iron girth.

"Merry *Christmas*," she gasps, her breaths bordering on hyperventilation.

Once again, I pause, unsure of how to take her unusual expression, though this time, her tone holds the distinct note of an expletive. She's responding to my size, which even for a woman with experience would be considered above average.

But when I begin to withdraw, Angel whimpers in disappointment.

I press forward a second time, entering her just a little deeper, and her leg wrapped around my waist starts to quiver.

"You want more?" I tease, holding her firmly against my body to support her weight as I rock my hips.

"Yes," she breathes.

And this time, I press all the way inside her glorious depths. Angel cries out as her pussy tightens around me, warning me that she's just moments from release, and I want to feel her fall apart around me.

Tightening my arm around her waist, I rock inside her, grinding against her clit at the same time to stimulate her.

"Fudge triple ice cream, I'm coming!" she cries.

And she does, her pussy gripping my hard length with agonizing force as she begs me to join her in ecstasy. God, but I want to. But not yet. I intend to draw this out and deliver a night of pleasure before I take what's mine.

It's surprisingly easy to hold onto my load, despite the sinful way she milks my cock, because her mind-boggling expletives drive me to distraction. She must be replacing curse words with these odd phrases, and a bubble of amusement rises in my chest at their astounding innocence. Compared to the sinful nature of our desire and the depravity of my kinks, I find her inability to say "fuck" nothing short of adorable.

As she grows limp with the aftershocks of her climax, I have to pause as the chuckle rumbles up from my chest, unbidden. I haven't laughed in so long, the feeling is foreign in my throat, and the humor dies as soon as it fractures the sexual tension in the room.

Angel's eyes find mine, widening in shock, and I wonder if she's as surprised to hear me laugh as I am, or maybe she's just realizing her choice of vocabulary for the first time. But her shock is mingled with a heady lust, and as she breathes heavily against my chest, the sensation of her taut nipples pressing into my chest reignites my passion.

The intensity of my attraction for her heats my gaze, and without a word, I scoop her other leg up off the floor and wrap it around my waist. Then, holding her against me with one arm, I reach up to untie her wrists.

She watches my face with open anticipation, her arm falling around my shoulders as soon as her right wrist is free. And when the last of her restraints falls away, her fingers tangle in my hair as she leans in to kiss me.

Still buried in her warm, wet depths, I carry her back to the bed, never breaking the kiss that sets my soul on fire. Something about this woman lights a passion in me that I haven't felt in far too long. I'm intoxicated by her beauty, captivated by her innocence, enraptured by her eager appetite.

I want more of her. I want all of her, and I want to hear my name on her lips when I make her come again. Falling on top of her, I drive deep inside her pussy as her thighs spread to accommodate my hips.

Angel moans, her head tipping back as she takes all of me inside her for the first time. My cock throbs at the seductive sound, and her walls tighten in response, sending a jolt of anticipation up my spine.

Consumed by this raw, passionate moment, all I can think about is how good it feels to be one with the beautiful girl beneath me. I want to make her feel the same level of soul-consuming fire she's ignited in me.

As I thrust inside her, we find a rhythm, moving in a smooth and scintillating dance of bliss.

"Come with me, Angel," I command as the pressure at the base of my spine builds to unbearable levels.

She nods, her honey locks forming a halo around her head. When I rock inside her this time, burying myself deep inside her warm depths, she tightens, gripping my cock like a vise. That's all it takes to send me over the edge, and I snarl as I release my seed inside her to the hilt.

Her walls flutter around me, her clit throbbing against the base of my cock as she moans my name like a prayer. I wait until the last of her pulsing aftershocks subside, then I slowly ease out of her.

Rising from the bed, I leave her there to dispose of the condom. Then I start to dress.

After catching her breath, Angel seems to get the hint, and she slides off the crimson bed sheets to collect her own clothes and don them. As she bends to tie her shoes, I pull my checkbook from the breast pocket of my suit.

She glances my way from the corner of her eye, and when she straightens, her back is stiffer than I've seen it before. Still, when I tear the check from the book and offer it to her, she takes it without a word.

"This is for twice as much as we agreed upon," she observes after reading it.

Rather than gratitude or even amazement like I had anticipated, Angel seems to shut down, close off, almost as if she's ashamed about taking the money or insulted that I want to give her more than the original offer.

Baffled by her reaction, I don't know how to respond. The dynamic between us has shifted too quickly, and I sense that any explanation I might give would further cool the atmosphere between us.

"Come, I'll take you home," I offer instead, gesturing toward the door.

"Thank you, but I can find my own ride," she says and leads the way back through the club.

"It's no problem," I object, that odd sense of wanting to protect her and see her safely inside her front door tightening my chest.

Then again, perhaps that's exactly why she refused my offer. She might not want me to know where she lives. *After all, what does she know about me?* Nothing except that I'm a considerably older man who would offer her an ungodly amount of money to sleep with me.

"Let me at least flag you a cab," I offer, stepping up to the curb and raising my hand.

A yellow taxi pulls up just moments later, and I open the door for Angel.

"Thank you," she murmurs, her gaze shy once more as she slips into the back seat of the cab.

Then she's gone, vanishing into the night like a figment of my imagination. And though I assured her that this would only be a one-time deal, I suddenly find that I don't like watching her drive away.

Something about this innocent, young, Southern Belle stripper has me hooked, and I don't know that I can just let her go. I didn't even get to the bottom of her adorably PG curse words.

I might have sworn off love, surrendered to a life in which my family and my role as *pakhan* are my sole priorities, but I suspect I'll be making another trip to Lady Venus much sooner than I had anticipated.

7

HEIDI

Tapping my pencil against the textbook laid out before me, I try to focus on my coursework, but my mind is anywhere but on my assignment. Thanks to my one night with Maks, his generous payment wiped away my financial troubles and I was able to enroll in classes for the spring semester.

Now, as spring break swiftly approaches, I feel nothing but gratitude for the leg up he gave me. It was enough money to not only see me through school without having to hold a full-time job, but it also covers the best medical treatment money can buy for my mom.

Not that it's made a difference.

We might not have to worry about the cost of care anymore, but at the rate she continues to waste away, I fear I'll lose her anyhow. She's as sick as ever, with no sign of her Glioblastoma diminishing or even slowing. Thankfully, we can afford full hospital care now, which is what she needs after the last round of experimental treatments left her so weak that I can't take care of her on my own.

It's the thought of her bedridden and alone in the hospital that haunts my thoughts now. With midterms in just a week, I need to study, but I don't like wasting the potential last precious moments with my mom.

"If you keep chewing on your lip like that, you're going to put a hole through it," Zoe observes from her spot on my mom's couch.

While I thought she'd been busy watching the drama-filled reality show flickering across the TV screen, when I glance her way, I find her sharp gaze watching me closely.

"Worried about your mom?" she presses.

My shoulders slumping, I nod. "I haven't been over to see her today, and she looked so weak and pale yesterday."

Zoe's expression softens, and I know she's at a loss for what to say. All her reassurances that my mom is a fighter, that she'll kick cancer and be back on her feet in no time, have died off over time. Because Zoe sees it too. There's no escaping the cold, hard truth of my mom's condition. Even the hospital has suggested that we prepare for the inevitable and ensure my mom's affairs are in order.

She's already signed the house over to me, and with little else to her name, it won't take much to reconcile her worldly goods. But that seems so insignificant in my mind compared to the gaping hole that will open in my life when she's gone.

I don't want to think about it.

I'm not ready to face it.

I don't know that I ever will be.

"You want me to go with you before work?" Zoe offers.

I don't know what I would do without my best friend. She's been around almost nonstop lately, here to support me emotionally, to let me cry it out all I need. But some days are worse than others, and today, I feel sick with anxiety over how frail my mom has grown.

My gut twists at the thought, and I'm shocked to find that sick feeling in my heart could spread to my stomach. Frowning, I shove my textbook off my lap and make a mad dash for the bathroom as I realize I'm on the verge of vomiting.

"Heidi?" Zoe calls, bolting out of her seat as she follows close behind me.

I barely make it to the bathroom in time, and I throw myself down on my knees before my lunch comes back up and hits the porcelain bowl with a revolting sound.

"Ugh."

Zoe quickly backpedals, giving me some space as I hold my hair back with one hand and grip the toilet seat with my other.

"You think you got food poisoning?" she asks tentatively after I finish dry heaving and collapse onto the bathroom tiles. "I told you that chicken smelled a bit off last night."

But I get a sinking feeling because I don't think this is food poisoning. My period is several weeks late. I thought I might have missed it due to stress over starting school a week after the semester already began and then having my mom take a turn for the worse. But it was just over six weeks ago when Maks and I had sex. The timing is too coincidental.

Sure, we used a condom, but those aren't a hundred percent effective, and I didn't touch the chicken that Zoe was complaining about.

Looking up at her from my seat on the floor, I press my eyebrows into a reluctant frown. "I think I need a pregnancy test," I confess.

Zoe's face falls. "No," she objects. "Not with the sexy Russian billionaire you said was old enough to be your father. You said you used protection."

"We did. But I'm also two weeks late, and I'm never late."

"Fuck." Zoe combs her fingers into her wispy pixie, and when she releases the short strands, they stand even more wildly around her face. "Stay put. I'll be back in five." Then she vanishes from the doorway.

Slumping against the cabinets, I tip my head back and close my eyes. *What have I done?* I'm not ready to be a mom. I've barely gotten my feet on the ground to start my career. I don't know the first thing about being a mother, and with my mom so sick, I can't even imagine trying to take on the responsibility of caring for a baby of my own.

A surge of denial washes through me. I'm getting way ahead of myself. Maks and I used protection, and we only had sex the one time. I can't be pregnant. Zoe's probably right. After all, that chicken dish came from the same Chinese restaurant as the Mongolian beef I ate. It's probably food poisoning.

Talking myself down, I manage to rein in my panic. When Zoe

finally returns, I've nearly convinced myself that this is not as bad as it seems. I just have a stomach bug. I'll be fine by tomorrow with no more life-altering surprises on my horizon beyond the terrifying fact that my mom is likely terminal and not going to be with me much longer.

"I got you a latte too," Zoe says, handing me the box of tests and the coffee all at once.

"Thanks, Zoe." She knows me so well. Coffee's my comfort drink, and right now, I could use a splash of caffeine to help my flitting thoughts focus.

Taking a deep breath, I push myself up off the bathroom floor and set my coffee on the counter so I can open the box of pregnancy tests.

"I'll, uh, give you a sec," she says and steps back out of the bathroom, pulling the door closed behind her.

I read the instructions carefully, though the principle seems basic enough. Then I take the test and cap it before setting it on the edge of the tub to wait the three minutes it's supposed to take.

"Can I come in?" Zoe asks, her voice muffled by the wood of the door.

"Yeah." My knee bounces, jiggling my elbow as I watch the test from my perch on top of the toilet lid. Stomach in knots, I can hardly breathe. *What if I am pregnant?*

I don't have an answer for that yet.

Zoe leans against the counter, her hip within a foot of my shoulder, and wordlessly, she passes me my latte. I take a gulp and relish the burn as it scalds my throat on the way down.

When the timer on my phone goes off, I nearly jump out of my skin. In a flash, I snatch up the test and stare down at the two innocent pink lines looking back at me.

"Well?" Zoe demands, bringing her head next to mine to read over my shoulder. "Oh, shit."

All I can do is nod. My lips are too numb to form a sentence. But for once, my Southern upbringing can't wash away the word ringing in my mind. *Fuck.*

"What are you going to do?" Zoe asks gently, kneeling beside me and giving my wrist a gentle squeeze. "Whatever you decide, you know I'm here for you, right?"

Tears sting my eyes at the immediate support. "Thanks, Zoe."

"Will you . . . keep it?"

"I can't see myself getting an abortion." That's not entirely an answer to her question, but as soon as the words leave my lips, I know they're true. And quickly following that, I nix the idea of putting my child up for adoption.

Mom raised me by herself after Daddy died. Surely, I'm strong enough to do the same. And as soon as I think of my mom, of the deep love and friendship we have, I know that I want this child. Because I want to have that connection with my own baby. *Especially* if I'm going to have to find my way in this world without my mom.

"Yes," I whisper. "I want to keep it."

Zoe gives me a soft smile, her eyes seeming to grasp the tumult of emotions roiling inside me. Then her sharp brows press into a delicate frown.

"What about your baby daddy?"

My heart skips a beat as she brings up a very valid point. I hadn't even considered Maks when I was panicking over what to do about the baby. Of course, I should tell the father of my child that I intend to keep it. He could be a part of the baby's life or not, as is his right.

But I don't have the first clue of how I might get in touch with him.

"Have you seen him at Lady Venus lately?" I ask, chewing my lip.

"Honestly, I didn't get a good look at him that night, but from how you've described him, I don't think so. Definitely no sexy Russians going by the name of Maks. But of course, Howie insists we only call the customers by their last names."

"I can't remember it," I confess. "It was definitely Russian."

"Smirnoff? Romanov?" Zoe suggests.

"I don't think that's going to help," I chide. Maybe I would recognize it. But I only used it once or twice, and all I can hear in my mind is Maks telling me in his low, sexy accent to call him by his first name.

"Well, maybe it's for the best. He wanted a one-night stand, so how reliable would he be as a father, anyway? Right?"

"True," I agree.

Still, it bothers me to think he'll have a child he will never know about. And that child will never know their father. All I can do from here is my best to love this child enough for two parents.

While it terrifies me to think that I'm going to be a single mother, at least Maks left me with a considerable cushion that will ensure our baby gets a good start in life while I establish my career.

8

MAKSIM

Four Years Later

"Gentlemen, thank you for agreeing to meet with me today," Frank Thompson says as he welcomes us into the luxurious conference room of the Bay View Hotel.

He stands to shake each of our hands in turn as I enter the room first followed by my younger brother, Dimitri, and our youngest brother, Alexei. The three of us own the company known as Federov Brothers Investments together, a lucrative business acquisitions venture my father passed down to us when he died.

It also makes the perfect front to the shadier Bratva business I inherited after my old man was murdered in cold blood. That world, too, my brothers share in, each of us handling our own specialties. But it falls to me to be the head of the family, the *pakhan*, and as such, I bear the weight of ensuring our clan thrives. Good, bad, and hard, ugly truths that entails.

"I assume this means you've had enough time to consider our

offer?" I ask, keeping my tone professional as we settle into the seats across from Frank and his lawyers.

The bodyguards Alexei now insists we tote everywhere, due to Aleksandr Volkov's increasingly reckless behavior, take up silent sentinel behind us. And while their constant presence normally drives me crazy, I don't mind them now, as they offer an extra level of intimidation to push this offer through.

Dimitri and I agree, the Bay View Hotel is a jewel we need to acquire, whether Frank considers it on the market or not.

"Ah, yes. That's obviously why I requested this meeting today." His eyes dart between me, Dimitri, and Alexei before flicking to the solid wall of muscle standing behind us. "But I hadn't meant to disrupt your business as usual. I simply wanted to convey a message."

I can tell what direction this message is going to take based on the sweat beading on Frank's brow. But I keep my calm. Strong-arming the hotel owner into a deal is often better done with flattery and incentives than actual brute force.

"Nonsense. We couldn't leave such a momentous occasion to receiving the news by messenger," I schmooze, adding a hint of charm to the intimidation technique. "We look forward to doing business with you and feel it's only right to demonstrate that by respecting your time with our presence."

Frank shares a glance with the lawyer to his right, who shifts nervously in his seat.

"About that," the lawyer says, clearing his throat. "Mr. Thompson has received a better offer from another interested party."

"Did you, now?" Dimitri asks, one eyebrow creeping higher on his forehead. "Let me guess. By one Aleksandr Volkov?"

The bastard's been sniping our intended acquisitions for years now, moving in on our territory like the slick git he is. And after his disgusting show of force four years ago in which he shot up our family yacht, took out multiple members of the ballet troupe on board at the time, and murdered my fiancée, we've been in nothing short of all-out war.

"Ah, the gentleman requested that we keep his identity under wraps until negotiations are final." Frank dabs his forehead nervously, his eyes darting between me and my brothers without ever fully making eye contact.

"I'm sure he did," Dimitri sneers.

I shoot him a warning glance, knowing full-well my brother's temper can get the better of him if he doesn't keep it under tight wraps.

"And how much is this better offer you've received?" I ask, resting my elbows on the conference table and interlacing my fingers.

"I'm sorry, but we can't release that infor—"

"You're not even going to let us make a counteroffer?" I ask in mock surprise.

The lawyer cuts short glances in Frank's direction, and the hotel owner swallows as he considers his options.

"A hundred and twenty million," Frank blurts without consulting his lawyers.

I give a cold smile, silently acknowledging the man's weakness that could afford us the opportunity to fight back. His greed made this acquisition possible in the first place. As long as we can outmaneuver Aleksandr in negotiations, the Bay View will be ours.

"We can offer you a hundred and fifty million," I state, making an executive decision, though I know I will have my brothers' support if it means crushing Aleksandr. "And trust me, you would much rather do business with us."

"Is that a fact?" Frank says as if to play his hand close to his chest while he considers our offer. But he won't refuse a sum that large, no matter what agreement he might have made with Aleksandr.

"If your other offer is from Aleksandr Volkov, then I can assure you he is a crook who wouldn't hesitate to swindle you as soon as the contract is drawn up. But our family has been doing business in the Bay area for generations now, and I guarantee you won't regret selling to us." Rising from my seat, I offer my hand, adding silent pressure for him to make a fast decision before the offer walks out the door.

Coming to a stand, Frank gives my hand a hearty shake. "I never should have doubted it. Thanks for making the trip across town to get this venture back on track."

"We'll start drawing up a contract and be in touch," I state with a curt nod.

He shakes my brothers' hands as well, and we depart in a calm procession, leaving Frank's lawyers to hash out how they are going to handle his rash decisions mid-meeting.

I suspect Aleksandr must be applying his own form of pressure, and the legal system can only help a man so much when he's trapped between two Bratvas in a tug-of-war. I wonder if Frank's lawyers know how deep in their client is just yet.

We're silent until we reach the armored Escalade Alexei has hired to drive us to and from our meetings around town. As soon as the door closes behind the last of our guards, my temper spikes.

"I want him dead. Yesterday. You keep telling me we're getting closer to finding a way through Aleksandr's defenses, and then more time passes. Why is he not dead yet?" I demand, leveling my frustration fully on my youngest brother.

Alexei scowls and runs a hand through his close-cut dark hair that's just starting to show its first strands of silver. "I want him dead just as much as you do. But unless you want to resort to a *Scarface*-type shootout and get all our asses thrown in jail, you'll have to be patient."

"I've been patient for four fucking years. How much longer is this going to take?"

"Lay off, Maksim," Dimitri cuts in, for once, the cool head in the car. "You might have lost more than the rest of us, but we all have our own reasons for wanting Aleksandr Volkov dead."

"I'm sick of picking off his underlings and pretending like we're making a difference. Meanwhile, we're cowering behind living, breathing shields. I can't take a dump without having them within breathing distance."

I know I'm being difficult, but I'm beyond irritated about Aleksandr's tactics. He's a leech, a parasite trying to take over the business my father, my brothers, and I have built from the ground up. And to top it off, he stole my future from me, the one thing I chose for myself—a woman I wanted to marry.

On the other hand, Alexei—who has always excelled at security tactics and getting in the minds of our enemies—has taken this whole bodyguard plan to an obsessive level. I get the need for increasing our protection with the escalating violence between our two Bratvas. But the lack of space is driving me crazy. I just want this war to be over. And to end it, we need Aleksandr Volkov dead.

The car pulls up outside our office building, and as we pile out, I stop to look up at the towering skyscraper.

"You coming up?" Dimitri asks, pausing to look back at me.

Alexei stops as well, both watching me expectantly. Typically, I'm the first one in the office and the last to go home. While my brothers are busy making and enjoying a home with their wives and growing families, work has been my obsession since Symphony died.

But after the day's turn of events, I'm in a bad mood, and I need to unwind.

Glancing down at my watch, I check to make sure it wouldn't make me too much of a degenerate to hit the bar at this time. It's after four. Good enough.

"I'm calling it a day," I state. "I need to blow off some steam. You guys won't want my mood darkening the office anyway."

"What's your plan now that you've cut loose your newest fuck toy?" Alexei ribs me, a smirk curling the corners of his lips.

"Don't start," I warn. "She was getting too clingy. I had to cut her loose before she completely lost perspective. I'll settle for a drink tonight."

"Or maybe, you could try and put the past behind you and start thinking about a real relationship. It's been four years, Maks. Symphony wouldn't want you to be stuck like this. It's time to move on, and I think you'll find that a meaningful relationship is a lot more effective in generating happiness than alcohol and meaningless sex."

There was a time in life when I never thought I'd hear those words leave Dimitri's lips. Of the three of us, I'd always thought he would be the eternal bachelor. That was until he met his wife,

Camille. Now, my brother is a father, a husband, and the happiest I've ever seen him.

Same goes for Alexei. He and his wife have a second child on the way, and their lives are nothing short of perfect—at least when it comes to their loving relationships.

"You say that, but I've come to understand the hard truth—that *pakhans* don't get love. You should be happy you're the younger brothers. You don't have the responsibility of running the family. I'll take the target on my back if it means you two can have good, full lives." I clap them each on a shoulder as I try to keep the bitterness from my smile.

"Maks," Alexei objects. "That's now what our father worked so hard to pass down to you."

"And yet, his untimely death is further proof, isn't it?"

"Or maybe you're just being stubborn because you don't want to risk losing someone again," Dimitri counters, working his way beneath my skin like no one else can.

Though I know they're trying to help, it rubs me the wrong way to have my younger brothers trying to coach me on personal relationships. I don't want their concern. I don't need it. I've made up my mind, and I'm far happier knowing that I won't be the reason another beautiful young woman might lose her life. "Go home. Enjoy your families. Tell Nadia and Camille I say hi. I'm going for a drink."

"Maks!" my brothers chorus as I head toward the parking garage and my red Corvette.

Hopefully, a fast drive back to my penthouse apartment will help diminish my bad mood. And if not, I'm sure a drink or ten at the new bar that opened down the street will work.

9

HEIDI

"We're celebrating," Zoe announces as soon as I walk through the front door of my sweet three-bedroom home on the outskirts of the city. "Aren't we, Sarah?" she adds, scooping my daughter up off the ground and giving her a twirl.

Sarah's peals of laughter fill the house and make me smile.

"Celebrating what?" I ask, setting my purse on the entry table and kicking off my nude heels.

"The fact that you actually have a client moving into one of the *Painted Ladies* and they want *you* to decorate it."

Zoe sets Sarah down, and my little girl skips over to me, offering me the doll she'd been playing with before I walked in.

"Why, thank you. Can Mama get a kiss?" I ask, stooping to say hello.

Sarah obliges, throwing her chubby little arms around my neck to plant a wet kiss on my cheek. It doesn't matter that my job allows me to spend most of my day with my little girl. I still miss her when we're apart for any length of time.

Zoe's a godsend, watching Sarah whenever I have to make house calls to clients and even driving her home on days like today. I don't know how I would survive day to day without Zoe as my assistant-slash-roommate. Since Mom died, she's all I have to rely on, and I know I need her an unhealthy amount.

But she and Sarah are thick as thieves. And like Zoe's said whenever I voice my concerns, my offering her a job has made all the difference in her quitting Lady Venus to have a more comfortable nine-to-five job.

"We're going out for a drink," Zoe continues, undeterred by my half-attention as I greet my daughter. "This is your highest paying client to date, and they'll open doors to even more amazing opportunities."

"Zoe, I'm a full-time, working single mom. I can't just go out for a night on the town. I have responsibilities," I scold, combing Sarah's hair away from her face and kissing the top of her head before I stand.

"Not a night on the town. *One* drink. Besides, I've already hired a babysitter, so you can't back out now." Zoe flashes me a devious grin.

"You did not," I counter.

The doorbell rings in answer, and I plant my fists on my hips.

"Come on, we need a girls' night," Zoe pleads, her dark eyes innocently wide.

Sighing heavily, I concede. "Fine. One drink."

Zoe gives an excited little squeak as I head to the door to see who she's hired.

"Hi, Miss Turner," Annie says brightly as soon as I open the door.

"Hi, Annie. Thanks for coming on such short notice." I step aside to let the smart young high school girl enter our home.

She's babysat Sarah for an hour here or there if Zoe doesn't have time to help, and I adore the enthusiastic teen. She's more than capable of watching Sarah until we get home.

"Happy to help. Zoe said you had an exciting day today?"

"I have a new client," I explain, heading to the kitchen to ensure she's all set up with an afternoon snack. "We should be home before dinner, but I'll set out some lasagna to thaw. Feel free to help yourself as well."

"Thanks, Miss Turner."

"Heidi, the Uber's here. Let's go!" Zoe calls from the front door.

I guess I won't be changing out of my work clothes. The tea-length navy wrap dress I wore to work will be fine, and I slip grudgingly back into my heels as I head toward the door.

"I'll be back in a bit, Sarah. You'll be good for Miss Annie, won't you?"

"Yes, Mama," she agrees, her dark head of curls cascading around her sweet heart-shaped face and into her hazel eyes.

The eyes she gets from me, but the dark curls must be from her father. I get my honey blonde waves from my mom. The stray thought of my mom brings stinging tears to my eyes. She's been gone for over two years now, and I still miss her every day.

"Love you, pumpkin." I press a last kiss to my daughter's forehead, then I follow Zoe through the front door.

As soon as I step down from the front porch, Zoe hooks her arm in mine and drags me toward the Uber. "They'll be fine. And we're going to have a great time," she insists. "I heard about this cute little bar that just opened in Pacific Heights. It's supposed to be chic with fantastic martinis."

"Martinis? You're incorrigible," I state, laughing lightly as I slip into the back seat of the car with her.

"Live a little!"

Zoe chatters lightly as we ride into town, telling me about how her afternoon with Sarah went before diving in with the fact that my little girl is picking up vocabulary like Zoe can't believe.

"Why do I get the feeling you've taught my daughter some terrible word?" I ask, quirking an eyebrow.

"I would never! But . . . she may have inadvertently picked up the phrase 'double damn'." Zoe gives a bashful smile, silently asking forgiveness.

"Are you kidding me? She's three, and she already has a worse mouth than I do. This is what I get for trying to raise my daughter anywhere but the South," I joke.

"Oh, please! You couldn't leave me!"

Giving Zoe a playful nudge with my elbow, I flash her a smile. "I still can't believe you're teaching my toddler curse words."

"At least it wasn't a *real* curse word." Zoe opens the car door right as we pull up to the curb, fleeing before I can scold her further for teaching my daughter bad words.

The street is humming with the excitement of the workday coming to an end, people entering a cute little brick-faced building with the name *Fiasco's* in bold black letters above the door.

Hits from the eighties and nineties trickle from the speakers as we enter the finely decorated establishment. A natural wood counter wraps around the bar with brushed nickel stools holding several patrons still dressed in work attire. The oak tables filling the rest of the small establishment have adorable spindle chairs painted in an array of pastel colors surrounding them.

"Okay, you're right. This place is adorable," I admit as we snag the last two open stools at the bar.

"Right?"

"What can I get you ladies?" the bartender asks, greeting us with a broad smile and straight white teeth.

"I'll take a Cosmo," Zoe says without missing a beat as she leans her elbows onto the bar and flutters her eyelashes flirtatiously. "And my friend would like a dirty martini, three olives."

"Coming right up." The bartender gives Zoe a subtle up-and-down glance before getting to work.

And as he leaves, I release a soft snicker.

"What?" Zoe asks, spinning on her stool to face me.

"Having fun?"

"Hey, a little bit of flirting never hurt anyone." She gives the bartender a nod of gratitude as he sets our drinks before us, then she raises hers in a toast. "To Heidi for catching her first big fish," she says.

Laughing, I raise my martini glass and tap it lightly against hers, then I take a sip. "Mmm. This really is good."

"Try mine."

Zoe swaps our glasses and steals a sip of mine while I try her Cosmo.

"Now, tell me exactly what you have in mind for our new clients' Painted Lady."

I lay out in detail the decor I discussed during the home visit today, and as Zoe and I talk furnishings and upholstery, the alcohol slowly starts to set in, allowing me to relax and let loose like I rarely have time for anymore.

"And they've given you free rein to spend as much as you want?"

"Their exact words were, 'After seeing what you did with the Russels' home, we have full confidence in your abilities. At the end of the day, we want a place that feels like home but looks like it's straight from a magazine'," I quote.

Zoe gives another excited squeal and leans in for a hug. "I think you've really made it," she gushes. "Just like your mom always knew you would. If Evelyn could see you now."

"I miss her so much," I admit, my heart aching with the loss that feels as fresh as ever. "I wish she were here to celebrate with us."

"Me too," Zoe agrees, her smile nostalgic and sympathetic all at once. "Evelyn was the best. But she must be looking out for you from heaven if you're landing deals like the one you did today."

That makes me smile, the thought of my mom putting in a good word, supporting me even after her last breath.

"How are those drinks treating you ladies?" the bartender asks, coming around to check on us.

"They're amazing," I admit, my slight buzz from my martini increasing my enthusiasm.

His gaze shifts to Zoe, waiting for her vote of confidence, and she props her chin in her palm as she meets his eyes.

"Positively delicious," she agrees, her voice indulgent.

"Well, whenever you're ready for another round, just holler." He gives Zoe a wink and moves on to the patron waving him down at the far end.

"Man, you're a hot commodity tonight, aren't you?" I tease.

"Pfft." Zoe leans her elbows back on the bar and crosses her legs to swing her foot. "You've been out of the game so long, I think you've forgotten what some harmless fun looks like."

"You're telling me he's not into you? He barely gave me a second glance," I point out.

"Well, yeah, because you've got your mom walls up."

"'Mom walls'?" I ask, taking another sip of my martini before sliding an olive off its toothpick.

"Yeah, you don't even notice when guys look at you anymore."

"I would notice!" I object, glancing around reflexively like I might spot someone looking right then. "I just don't have the time for guys —besides, I prefer to focus on being a good mom to Sarah."

"Uh-huh. How long has it been since you've gone on a date?" Zoe counters, arching a finely shaped eyebrow. "Better yet, how long has it been since you've *been* with a guy?"

"Like slept with someone?"

Zoe waits expectantly for my answer, and I feel the heat of embarrassment climbing up my neck.

"Not since the night I got pregnant with Sarah."

Zoe gasps like I've just told her some unimaginably horrible secret. "Okay, we need to fix that."

"We do not! My sex life is not something we need to *fix*."

"You can't pretend like you no longer have needs just because you have a daughter. Come on, Heidi. You deserve to enjoy life too."

Zoe's eyes shift toward the front door of the bar, and from the gust of cold air, I know someone just stepped in from outside. Her eyes follow the person for several moments, and a devilish smile curls her lips when her eyes land on me once more.

"Why are you looking at me like that?" My voice drops into a worried tone.

"Because I'm about to fix this dry spell of yours with Mr. Tall, Dark, and Handsome who just sat next to you."

"Zoe, no," I warn, leaning close to grasp her wrist.

But before I can stop her, she hops off her stool and skirts around me to tap the stranger on the back.

"*Zoe!*" I hiss as he casts an irritated glance over his shoulder at her.

"Excuse me, but my friend and I were just talking about how positively *fit* you look, and we made a bet as to whether you're strong enough to bench press her," Zoe says cheekily.

Turning, the man studies Zoe coldly, and I widen my eyes at her as I mouth for her to knock it off, but she's entirely undeterred.

"Or maybe you would prefer to just *entertain* her for the evening? My friend is a great conversationalist."

"*Zoe*, I can't stay out all night," I remind her through clenched teeth.

"Oh, but you can. It'll be good for you!" She snatches her coat from the back of her chair with a flourish and twirls toward the exit. "Meanwhile, I have a babysitter to relieve. You two have fun!" she singsongs.

Then, she flounces out the door before I can follow her.

Mortified by Zoe's behavior, I turn to apologize to the stranger, who seems even less amused by her antics than I am. But with the words on the tip of my tongue, I freeze as I get a good look at the square, masculine jaw and steel-gray eyes for the first time.

The dark-haired man is wearing a deep scowl, confirming his irritation, but that's not what steals my breath away. I recognize him immediately, and my heart stutters.

It's Maks.

And he looks as dangerous and as devastatingly handsome as ever.

10

MAKSIM

Lips parted as if about to speak, hazel eyes widening in shock, the beautiful young woman's expression wipes away my irritation in an instant. I recognize her immediately, and it only takes a second to recall her name from four years ago. Though we only spent one night together, I don't think I could ever forget it —Angel.

Just like the fleeting godsend she was to me.

I regretted making it a one-time deal as soon as she got in her taxi that night. I even went back to the club where she worked to try and find her the next day. But the club had told me she quit, and they were unwilling to give out her personal information, so I'd let it go and moved on.

But seeing her here, now, makes my heart skip a beat, and my bad mood after a terrible day vanishes as I take in her flowing honey-blonde locks and striking figure. She's wearing a fashionable long-sleeved, navy-blue dress that ties around her middle and dips into a low V neckline. Professional, classy, but just suggestive enough to hint that her breasts are fuller than I remember them. Still, she carries her curves in an entirely natural way.

Where she was still wavering on the cusp of being a young

woman when I met her, she's blossomed into a fully mature and gorgeous one now.

"It's you," she breathes, her soft, musically accented voice mirroring her stunned expression.

And though I rarely smile, I feel one corner of my mouth tug up into a crooked grin. "It's me. Were you expecting someone else?"

"Yes—I mean, no. Not really. I just . . . didn't expect it to be you."

"I can't say I expected you either." And yet, I find I'm intensely pleased to have run into her, completely by coincidence, after all this time. I'll have to remember to thank her friend for forcing me into whatever all *that* was about.

"Well, fancy meeting you at a place like this," she gushes with a breathy laugh, her eyes taking in the long bar littered with delicate martini glasses of all colors and confections.

"You mean, not a strip or sex club?" I tease, cocking an eyebrow at her.

The beautiful rose color of her blush and the way her eyes drop tell me she's just as shy and modest as I remember. And once more, I find my curiosity piqued. *Where has she been all this time?* It's not like I didn't move heaven and earth to try and find her.

"Actually, I meant it more as I wouldn't have pegged you for a martini kind of guy." The apologetic smile she offers up makes my stomach tighten. No woman should be this beautiful without even trying.

Raising my tumbler of vodka on the rocks, I swirl the glass and take a sip. "Well, I won't tell if you won't."

Her melodic laughter awakens something in my chest that I have long thought dead. A flutter of excitement at knowing a woman might find my company enjoyable—without me offering them compensation first. And that slight Southern twang that accompanies her sass has me hooked as easily as it did during our private dance.

"In truth, I come here more for the convenience of the location than their particular brand of specialized drinks," I add, leaning closer to whisper conspiratorially near her ear.

I just catch the quick intake of breath that rushes past her lips at my proximity.

"You live around here, then?" she breathes before taking a generous sip of her dirty martini. A sure sign that I'm making her nervous.

Good. I like the thought of making her tremble.

"About a block south."

"Oh, so you're livin' in high cotton," she states and purses her lips playfully.

Her facial expression would indicate that's something to be impressed by, but I have no clue what the words mean.

"Sorry?" I say, hoping she'll elaborate.

"Oh, no need to apologize to *me*." Then she gives a wink that tells me she's giving me a hard time.

Baffled, I pause, taken aback by the fact that this woman has destabilized me so easily. I'm not used to anyone leaving me short on comebacks.

"You live in The Pacific, then, I assume," she says as a way of explanation, pointing down the street toward my penthouse. "And that means you're doing more than just fine. Though I do recall that being true when we first met."

"You seem to be doing well for yourself too," I observe, giving her an obvious once-over.

Angel crosses her legs nervously and smooths her dress over her knees, but I can't quite read the expression on her face. *Embarrassment? Gratitude? Guilt?* I wonder if she feels I'm trying to take credit for her success. But I highly doubt she's been coasting on my gift to her all this time. She carries herself like someone who has worked hard to make something of herself.

"Thank you" is all she says as her lips twitch into a soft smile.

She really does look incredible, and I wonder if she might not be up for another night together. Because I know I would be. But I won't make the same mistake I did before—I'll be sure to ask for more time.

Still, she didn't seem like the kind of girl who would accept my offer back then, and now she looks like she's made it in the world. I doubt she needs the money any longer.

"Are you still dancing?" I ask casually.

Angel laughs. "No, I quit four years ago."

"I thought as much, seeing as you vanished after our night together."

"And how would you know that?" The twinkle in her eye suggests that she's about to catch me in a lie, but what I have to tell her is the God's honest truth.

"Because I went back to Lady Venus and asked for you. But they said you'd quit, and they wouldn't give me your personal address. So, try as I might, I couldn't track you down. Turns out there are more women named Angel in San Francisco than one man can meet in a month. I'm remembering your name correctly, aren't I? Angel?" Not that I could forget, but I don't need to give her the wrong impression. I already came dangerously close to sounding like a stalker.

Delicate, feminine hands press against her cheeks as she blushes profusely in apparent embarrassment. "Actually, that was just my stage name. I'm Heidi."

She bashfully extends one hand as if to shake mine, and I take it. An electric jolt of attraction crackles between our palms, making my pulse quicken.

"Maks," I say as a reminder. "It's a pleasure to meet you, Heidi." Her name is fluid and beautiful on my tongue, much more suited to her. Still, a chuckle rumbles up from deep in my gut.

"What's so funny?" she asks, though her smile widens to match my own.

"It's just . . . that explains why all the Angels in San Francisco whom I managed to hunt down weren't you." Another flood of mirth fills my chest as I recall several of the most awkward conversations that stemmed from my efforts to find this enigma I now know is named Heidi.

My admission seems to flatter her as her cheeks turn a deeper shade of crimson and her teeth capture one side of her full lower lip. "You didn't really try to find me, did you?"

"You doubt my honesty?" I cock an eyebrow in warning. "I was kicking myself after letting you walk away." Pausing, I study her face as I debate whether I dare say what I really want to. Then I plow full-steam ahead. "I should have asked for more time with you. One night was far from enough."

The soft gasp that catches Heidi's breath makes my pulse throb, and I'm sorely tempted to reach out and capture her chin with my fingers. But I don't. I haven't seen her in years, and she might not welcome the unsolicited contact. I don't want to chase her away.

But her eyes are wide with a genuine openness that would suggest otherwise, and her nearly hopeful expression makes me bold.

"It almost feels like fate is giving me a second chance. A chance to do things right this time."

"What does that mean, 'do things right'?" Heidi's head tilts curiously as she leans toward me ever so slightly. A clear sign that I've captured her interest.

She might not be saying it with her words or even intentionally telling me with her body language, but clearly, she's attracted to me—despite our age difference and even after all this time.

"What if I wanted to get to know you better?" I hint, leaning closer to lightly trap her knee between my palms. "Do you have a boyfriend or some man in your life I need to worry about?"

Heidi's eyes dilate, her breath catching in her throat, and when she answers, the words come out husky. "No, no men in my life."

That makes me smile. "Good. Then, say I give you five hundred thousand dollars to stay with me for several weeks? And after that, if we're still having fun, we can renegotiate."

I know I've crossed a line as soon as the dollar amount leaves my mouth. Heidi's countenance shifts in an instant, the color draining from her cheeks as her face falls and her back stiffens, making her draw away from me.

Blyat. I've offended her.

11

HEIDI

He's actually offering me money to sleep with him again? *Like I'm a common whore?* It took everything I had to set aside my principles and dignity to agree to his terms that night. And the implication that I could willingly spend *weeks* as his mistress, even for an outlandish sum of money, offends me deeply. Though logic dictates that if I would take his money once, I would do it again, I still find his offer incredibly insulting.

But Maks's expression holds no disdain, no indication that he considers me lesser or only worthy of serving at his pleasure. Instead, I find only a carnal desire lighting his striking steel-gray eyes.

That doesn't stop the fury from bubbling up inside me, and before I can rein it in, my sharp tongue lashes out to defend me. "What, can't you find someone to sleep with you for free?" I snap.

A flicker of amusement registers on his face, but I don't slow down to read into it.

"You're handsome, rich, clearly successful. Are you really so dislikable that you have to *pay* women to stay with you? I thought you were doing just fine with flirting right up until you implied I'm a whore by trying to buy me. *Again.*"

My cutting reply ends in a disgruntled huff, and yet, it doesn't even seem to faze him. He sits back, giving me space. And though I'm loath to admit it, my stomach knots with disappointment when his hands leave my knee.

Then I catch the briefest glimmer of the same sadness that drew me to him so inexplicably four years ago. But when he speaks, his voice is even, his tone factual, devoid of the pain that lies beneath.

"I didn't intend to upset you. I just don't do love. My fiancée was killed by my rivals years ago, not long before I met you, actually. So I choose to keep my relationships strictly physical. My brothers might enjoy love and marriage and children, but I prefer to focus on running our business and making my enemies suffer for what they've done."

My heart stutters in my chest to hear his explanation, and my shoulders drop, the defensive anger washing away as if doused by a fire hose. He just divulged terrifying facts as if they were everyday misfortunes. *Rivals who would kill his fiancée? Enemies he wants to make suffer?* Nobody but criminals and Hollywood-written Mafia bosses talk like that.

Still, as brutal as his explanation is, I'm touched because I can recall the agonizing sadness in his eyes. Knowing the cause behind that sadness makes my heart bleed for him. I understand loss like that, and more so, I can understand why he might avoid commitment if someone took away the woman he loves.

When I remain silent, Maks focuses his eyes on his rocks glass. He gives it a swirl before sipping the cold vodka. Then he continues, filling the space between us with his reasoning. "Offering cash in exchange for women's time helps keep the agreement more businesslike—a transaction rather than a relationship. Though, even then, it can be hard to avoid women catching feelings once sex gets involved."

Normally, a statement like that would sound immensely cocky, but I've spent the night with Maks, so I can see how women might fall for him once they've experienced his attentive and masterfully pleasurable touch. I can't imagine they would willingly give it up.

And despite Maks's insistence that he wants to keep emotion out of the equation, his sad tale and his openness about it tell me he's still capable of feeling deeply, even if he's unwilling to form new attachments.

Still, that wall he's built to protect himself is exactly why I need to keep my guard up. Because I have Sarah to consider. She shouldn't be exposed to that kind of emotional distance. And though I have a moral obligation to let the father of my child know he has a daughter, it doesn't feel wise to tell him if his intimacy issues are that bad. For Sarah's sake, it might be best if he remains in the dark about her.

It wouldn't be healthy for her to have a dad who's unwilling to form a bond with her. Better not to have a dad, as she's learned to live with for the first three years of her life, than to have one who is emotionally unavailable.

"So," Maks says, pulling me out of my revere.

As I look up, silver eyes scrutinize me with open desire. But they don't hold the dangerous edge one might expect of a man who could *make his enemies suffer*.

"Now that you know the reasoning behind the offer, will you reconsider?"

This time, when Maks leans forward, I manage to keep my body in check—at least audibly. But his proximity makes my pulse flutter.

I should say no. Walk away. Everything he's told me so far is reason enough to run. Especially if I want to shield Sarah from him. The safest way to do that would be to remove him from my life completely.

But Zoe's words about my abstinence ring in my ears. It's been so long since I've had sex. And despite my self-induced chastity over the last four years, I do miss the intimacy of a man's touch. I am only human, and being a mom doesn't require me to become a nun. *Right?*

The fact that Maks was the best sex I've ever had is no small determining factor. If I turn him down now, I'll be depriving myself of mind-numbing pleasure.

What could really be the harm of sex with no strings attached? That's all he's asking for. And then I don't have to worry about how he might affect Sarah. He doesn't want to be a part of my life, just to share a few weeks of nighttime fun.

I can do that.

Just . . . not for money.

"What if we compromise?" I offer.

Maks's eyebrow rises slowly, his expression intrigued. His dashing, dangerous masculinity makes my heart skip a beat. *Lord, but he's gorgeous.*

"Casual sex without an exchange of money," I offer boldly. "It would feel demeaning to accept payment. But I enjoyed the night we spent together, and I would consider it an equal exchange. We both agree to have sex, no strings attached, until one of us decides it's not working anymore."

"You think you can do that? Sex without attachment?" Maks asks, his tone playful, though his gaze heats to a silent inferno.

His fingers brush my knee once more, and a jolt of anticipation zings through my body, tightening my core. If I had any doubts about how desperately I need a man's touch, that just confirmed it.

"Why not?" I ask lightly, ignoring the heat that climbs up my neck at his proximity. "I have enough on my plate with running a business and . . . juggling responsibilities. I could use a little stress relief." My lips quirk into a cheeky smile.

Now that the offer's on the table, I'm actually on the verge of giddy about it. In the last four years, I've spent more than one lonely night thinking about Maks and our time together. Not that I would confess that to a soul.

But I want him, maybe even more desperately than I did that night. Because I know what he has to offer, and it makes my stomach quiver.

"It's a deal. Shall we seal it with a kiss?" His lips quirk in a devilish grin that tells me he knows he's using the same turn of phrase I did the night he took me to a sex club.

My breath catches as he leans in, his grip tightening around my knee as his free hand captures my chin between his thumb and finger. His eyes flick down to my softly parted lips, the hunger in them filling me with anticipation.

And when he captures my mouth in a confident kiss, it lights my body on fire. His full, firm lips caress mine, moving with them as he guides them open further. Then his tongue strokes into my mouth, deepening the kiss as he tastes me with deliberate slowness.

Core throbbing, I lean forward, melting into his embrace as my blood turns to lava, searing as it pounds through my veins. He's an even better kisser than I remembered. All the world goes quiet around us as my senses focus fully on the silky caress of his tongue, the commanding strength of his lips, the soft tickle of his five-o'clock shadow brushing my chin.

His hand travels slowly up my thigh, sending a rush of excitement to moisten my panties. But he stops before it turns too intimate for the public setting we're in.

When he finally breaks our kiss, I'm breathless, my skin flushed, my mind buzzing with unchecked lust. I don't think anyone has ever kissed me like that, and I'm desperate for him to do it again.

12

MAKSIM

The soft suppleness of Heidi's lips makes my pulse pound, and the thought of spending the night with her has me throbbing with anticipation. Kissing her was a mistake—only because I now crave her with a desperation that will be hard to contain until we get back to my place.

Releasing her chin, I turn my attention to the bartender. "Check, please. Hers as well."

Then I withdraw my credit card and send it off without glancing at the tab.

Heidi giggles softly, the musical sound a treat for my ears as I slam the rest of my drink.

"What's the rush?" she asks playfully, then captures her martini olive between her teeth and slowly slides it off its toothpick.

Standing from my stool, I place a hand on the small of her back. Leaning close to her ear, I murmur, "I've been waiting four years for another night with you. I'm not about to waste a second of it."

Heidi's eyes widen with beautiful innocence, and she swallows hard before chasing her olive down with the rest of her drink. Then she's out of her seat, allowing me to steer her softly with my hand on her back.

Outside, she barely seems to take note of my two bodyguards who fall in behind me, following at an inconspicuous distance. Instead, she walks close to me, her body heat warming my side as her proximity dulls the ever-sharp edge of the San Francisco Bay's breeze.

"You weren't joking when you said Fiasco's was a convenient location," Heidi observes as we enter the front lobby of The Pacific.

The doorman greets us with a polite nod, which I return as I guide the beautiful woman beside me toward the bank of elevators. Her heels strike the granite floor with sexy confidence, and I know she wears them with the ease of a woman who's walked in heels every day of her adult life.

Pressing the call button, I turn my attention to Alexei's men and jerk my chin toward a separate elevator. "Take the next one up," I command.

Heidi's eyes flash from my face to my men, and for a moment, she seems baffled by the order. But my guards obey without question, standing back from the elevator as the doors ding open and I usher Heidi inside.

"What . . .?" she breathes as the doors close behind us, leaving us perfectly alone.

But I don't want to waste time explaining why I have bodyguards or my reasoning behind wanting her to myself. Instead, I close the distance between us, capturing her lips once more as I back her against the wall.

She gasps as I pin her firmly between me and the mirror behind her. Then her hands travel up my chest, exploring me on their way to comb into my hair.

"God, I want you," I growl against her lips.

I swallow her groan as I kiss her passionately, my tongue stroking between her lips to tangle with her silken tongue. Cock throbbing in my slacks as it presses urgently against her hip bone, I can hardly restrain myself.

And while I want to be inside her with a desperation that's driving me wild, I also want to make this last.

With one arm firmly wrapped around her waist, I explore Heidi's body with my free hand, relishing the feel of her soft breast filling my palm and her trim waist that has grown a little since I last touched her but is still firm with muscle.

Heidi shivers against me as my hand travels lower, my fingers finding the opening of her wrap dress. I guide my hand beneath her skirt. The soft whimper she releases as my fingers brush the peak of her thighs sets my body alight.

I want to make her groan with pleasure, to cry my name as she comes.

As I cradle her lace-covered sex, I can feel how wet she is for me.

My own growl of satisfaction mingles with her soft gasp as I hook a finger around the edge of her panties to push them aside. Then I stroke between her folds, gathering her juices on the tips of two fingers.

Heidi shudders as her arms wrap more firmly around my neck, using me as a stabilizer as her legs start to tremble.

"So eager," I praise, and I press my fingers deep inside her entrance.

Heidi cries out, her walls tightening in response, and I'm awed by the realization that she's already on the verge of coming. Dear God, this woman is so sexy I might just lose my mind.

Brushing lightly against her clit with the heel of my palm, I finger her more stridently now. And all the while, I claim her mouth with my own, relishing the hushed whimpers and groans that crash against my lips.

Her hips jerk forward, her fingers tightening in my hair, and Heidi releases a euphoric moan as her pussy flutters with the first wave of her orgasm. Clit throbbing against my palm, walls beckoning me deeper inside her, Heidi gushes with the force of her euphoria, filling the small space with the sweet scent of her excitement.

Even as it turns me on, I'm amazed that she could come before we reach the top floor and my penthouse. Chuckling softly, I ease out of her, keeping my hold firm around her waist as her legs still feel too weak to hold her.

"Am I that sexy?" I tease lightly, drawing back just enough to give her a wicked smile.

Glowing with the aftermath of her orgasm, I can only tell Heidi's self-conscious by the bashful way she looks up at me through her eyelashes, her hazel gaze shy.

"It's been a long time since I've been with anyone," she confesses in little more than a whisper.

God, she's irresistible. I want her so badly it hurts. I can't wait any longer. The elevator doors ding open as I lift her off her feet, wrapping her thighs around my waist so I can carry her to my bedroom as I kiss her deeply once more.

I have a playroom, one I fully intend to introduce Heidi to, but that can wait. If she's still as inexperienced as I remember and she hasn't been with anyone in a long time, then I want to take things slowly and make sure she thoroughly enjoys her time with me.

Because I know I'm going to love every second of this.

Breasts pressing firmly against my chest, Heidi clings to me, kissing me to distraction as I palm her ass cheeks and pin her thighs between my hips and arms.

One hand moves from the back of my neck toward the tie knotted snugly at my throat. Her fingers work with confidence as they loosen the silk fabric. I'm sure that in her career as a stripper, she's removed more than her fair share of ties.

When she slowly draws it out from beneath the collar of my shirt, extracting a soft hiss of fabric, it makes me stiffen and throb between her thighs. Bursting into the bedroom, I blindly flick on the lights, eager to see Heidi naked in all her glory.

Then, I fall onto the bed with her, trapping her beneath my chest and caging her with my arms. Gasping breaths build between us as I lean back just enough to grant her access to my suit jacket. She opens it, shoving it over my shoulders a moment later as she silently tells me she wants me to take it off.

I oblige, tossing it carelessly to the floor as she gets to work on my dress shirt. But I'm too ravenous to help. Leaning in, I bury my face between her shoulder and neck, capturing the soft flesh at the base of her throat with my lips.

I suck softly and am rewarded with a quick intake of feminine breath. Once again, Heidi shoves my shirt over my shoulders, exposing my chest, and I lean back to strip that off too. Her delicate, well-manicured fingers find my pecs, tracing the intricate pattern of my tattoos.

I close my eyes, the soft brush of her touch like silk.

"They're beautiful," she murmurs, sending a shiver down my spine.

When I open my eyes once more, her gaze is soft and sultry as she admires the art on my skin. Her fingers travel lower, following the lines of my tattoos all the way down to my belt.

As she gets back to work undressing me, I do the same to her.

Tugging on the bow securing her dress, I untie the fabric and pull it free of the loop holding it closed. The edges fall open, exposing Heidi's full, black-lace-clad breasts and the soft curve of her waist. The matching black lace of her panties rests high on her hips, creating a sexy V that points me in the direction of her heavenly pussy.

I can't wait to dive in. Leaning forward, I kiss slowly down her sternum, taking my time as I reach the swell of her breasts. Her chest rises and falls more quickly now, urging me lower so I can see just how turned on she is.

As my lips reach her belly button, I look up, admiring the perfection of her soft, natural beauty, the fine line of her jaw, the thin straightness of her nose, the sheer perfection of her full, red lips.

Her explosive hazel eyes watch me with a heat that emboldens me, and I move lower, to the edge of her panty line, where I close my lips around her skin and start to suck.

"Maks!" she gasps, her head falling back as she collapses fully onto the bed.

I hum, loving how responsive she is to my touch. Then, releasing her firm skin with a soft pop, I move lower. Heidi's legs quiver as I grip her thighs, spreading them to make room for my shoulders.

Dipping down, I breathe in the scent of her delicious tanginess before pressing my lips to the lace covering her clit. Her hips roll in response, pressing her sex more firmly against my mouth. Then her fingers comb into my hair, her nails grazing along my scalp and raising goosebumps on my skin.

Gripping the waist of her panties, I pull them down, removing the slight barrier between us. Guiding them over her high heels, I leave on her shoes as I drop the skimpy lace to the floor and turn my attention to the perfection of her legs.

Taking one ankle in my grasp, I lift it to kiss slowly up the inside of her freshly shaved skin. When I get to her knee, I hook it over my shoulder and redirect my attention to her other leg. Starting where I left off, I kiss the rest of the way up her creamy thigh. As I close my lips around her clit, Heidi cries out, arching up off the bed with the intensity of her pleasure.

13

HEIDI

The feel of Maks's hot, wet mouth gently sucking my clit launches me into a euphoria that turns my body numb. Tingling pleasure washes through my veins to soothe the fire there. I can't stop my hips from bucking up into him, begging him for the release I know he'll give me.

Strong hands grip my thighs, holding me still as he lavishes attention on my slit—just like he did on our first night together.

"Lordy and hellfire!" I gasp as his tongue strokes between my folds, lapping up my arousal like it's the best thing he's ever tasted.

He hums, the low, masculine sound turning into a soft, rumbling chuckle. "Does that mean you like it when I go down on you?" he teases, his accent making him sound all the more impossibly sexy.

"Yes," I whimper.

"Good. Because I like the way you taste."

Heat radiates from my core at his daring words. The throbbing in my clit intensifies as I climb closer to a second orgasm in a matter of minutes. The only thing slowing me down is the impeccable decor of his bedroom.

It's to die for, the gray-wood furnishings stylish and expensive, the light fixtures chic and understated. Even the art is a classy collection of abstract paintings that speak of vibrant life and energy. I wonder who decorated his house, but that's a question for another time.

As Maks's fingers ease inside my entrance once more, I'm consumed by his masterful touch. He strokes my core, his fingers curling slightly to find that hidden spot that makes my mind go blank.

As his tongue circles my clit relentlessly, I cry his name before falling apart around him. He keeps playing with me, milking every last drop of pleasure from my body, until I collapse onto the bed with a shuddering sigh.

As he raises his head to meet my eyes, a slow, satisfied grin stretches his lips.

"What?" I ask, my mouth curving to match his smile.

"I've dreamed about getting the chance to do that again but never thought I would," he admits as he climbs slowly back up my body.

He kisses me deeply, the tang of my juices still lingering on his lips, and the taste of it excites me.

"Funny," I breathe between kisses, and Maks pulls back to meet my eyes. "I've had the exact same dream."

With a feral snarl, Maks claims my lips in a scintillating kiss. His hips rock forward, the cold metal of his belt pressing against my abdomen as I feel the iron rod of his arousal between the open zipper of his pants.

Reaching down, I return to my task of stripping him, shoving his pants and underwear down over his hips in one go. His cock springs free, the swollen head glimmering with a drop of precum that reminds me of the potential consequences of our actions tonight.

But right now, I'm so sex crazed, I can't bring myself to care.

He helps me, leaning forward on his muscular arms so I can push his pants lower, and when my arms won't reach, I catch the fabric with my toes, shoving them down the rest of the way.

"That's a good trick," he rumbles, his lips leaving my mouth to gently nip the lobe of my ear.

"Stick with me, kid . . ." I tease, and I can't help but giggle at my own joke. There's not a shadow of doubt in my mind that Maks has far more experience with sex than I do. All I know is that I need to feel his body against mine.

The silken skin of his erection trapped against my hips has my stomach in knots of anticipation.

"Are you going to show me a thing or two, then?" he teases, his tone daring me to back down now.

Then he grasps my hips and rolls me until I'm sitting on top of him.

Lap dances I know how to do. But this is the first time I'll be mixing one with actual sex, and it makes my heart skip a beat. His eyes heat as he watches me with anticipation, and I let the novelty of the moment fall away from me so I won't disappoint.

Closing my eyes, I sit up tall, elongating my torso as I reach up to comb my fingers into my hair. I roll my hips, relishing the way his thick erection slides between my pussy lips as I start to grind on him.

Strong fingers press into my thighs, a silent signal that Maks enjoys the sensation as much as I do. Combing my hair to one side, I peer down at him, promising him with my eyes that we're only getting started.

Then I reach behind me to unclasp my bra.

Air hisses between his teeth as I toss the last scrap of fabric aside with a flourish. His hands knead my flesh, slowly working their way up my thighs until he's following the curve of my hips, my waist, then cradling my breasts with his palms.

Placing my hands over his, I intensify his grasp until the supple flesh—softer after having breastfed my daughter for the first year of her life—oozes between his strong fingers. Again, I rock my hips, demonstrating how I would fuck him.

But not yet.

Not without protection.

As if reading my mind, Maks releases me to reach toward the nightstand beside his bed. Pulling open the drawer, he rummages blindly for a moment. Though I know from the sound of his groan that he's still fully aware of me riding him.

Retrieving a condom, he tears into it, and I snatch the quarter-sized rubber before he can object. Then, with a lascivious smile, I reach between us to slowly roll the lubricated latex onto his impressive cock.

"Watching you put a condom on me might be the single sexiest thing I've ever seen," he rasps. "Though I'm not sure if it can pass up your expression when you orgasm."

His words stun me speechless, and before I can think up a retort, he's already sitting up, one arm snaking around my waist as he rolls on top of me once again.

"I want to make you come all night long," he breathes as he lines up with my entrance.

Heat blossoms in my core as he presses inside me.

"Holy hand grenade!" I gasp as he fills me up, stretching my walls to accommodate his considerable girth.

I can hardly believe he would still feel so large after I gave birth to his daughter. And yet, after years without sex, it would seem I've reclaimed some of my original core.

"God, you feel so good," he rasps, pressing deep inside me before slowly easing out.

As we start to have sex, a primal satisfaction fills me, relieving a deep ache I didn't know was there until now. It feels so good to be with Maks, to have him claim my body in such an intimate way.

"So good," I moan in agreement. I grip his muscular back, my fingers tense with the strength of my pleasure, my body humming with the need to release.

It doesn't matter that he's already made me come twice tonight. I want more. I want it all. I never want this to end.

"Tell me what you want, Heidi," Maks purrs, his rocking motion stoking the inferno deep inside my core.

The way he murmurs my name, his Russian accent making it sound like the most beautiful song in the world, fills me with lust.

"I want you to make me come," I plead, my voice bordering on whiny, I'm so desperate.

"You want to come on my cock?" he taunts, pressing more forcefully inside me as he brushes against my clit.

"Yes!" I gasp, clinging to his broad back and relishing the way his muscles bunch and flex beneath my palms.

His pace quickens, his thrusts growing more demanding as Maks presses inside me with just enough force. Panting as I reach the brink of combustion, I lift my head off the bed to nip his lower lip.

Maks snarls, his lips slanting over mine as he kisses me possessively, his tongue claiming my mouth. And this time when I come, I can't help but scream. His driving force sets all my nerves on fire, launching them into overdrive until it feels like the euphoria is blasting through me.

Like an explosion, I burst around his cock, my walls throbbing as they grip him, urging him to come with me. My clit twitches and pulses against the base of his rock-hard erection, stimulated all the more by his urgent rigidity.

Maks groans, the sound almost tortured, and that makes my core tremble, tightening even in the aftershocks of my release.

"Christ, I love feeling you come," he rasps, his voice ragged with need.

I give a breathy laugh. "I love it when you make me come."

His rumbling chuckle vibrates through my chest, tickling my nipples. And then he's kissing me again, leaving me no time to come down from my high before he's demanding more of my pleasure.

His hands explore my body, brushing with a feather touch across my skin until he palms my breast. His thumb and forefinger pinch and roll the taut nub, extracting a whimper from me as a jolt of pain-laced pleasure races across my skin.

It brings me back to the spanking game he played with me four years ago, and my heart starts to race as I wonder if he might not punish me in some fashion tonight. I'm not bold enough to ask for it, but I wouldn't say no to exploring more of that kinkier play.

Especially with Maks.

Tightening with anticipation, my walls grip his cock more firmly, eliciting a sexy, carnal groan from his lips. In response, he captures my lower lip between his teeth, then starts to nibble and stroke it with his tongue, alternating between pain and pleasure.

At the same time, his hands travel back up my body to guide my arms above my head. His weight presses me into the mattress as he pins me down. As he interlaces our fingers, trapping my hands, I feel the intense lack of control.

Maks has imprisoned me completely, his powerful body holding me prisoner as he claims me in the most intimate way.

I've never felt so alive.

Writhing beneath him, I succumb to the strangely liberating experience. My pain, my pleasure, is now entirely in his hands. As is his. My senses heighten, brought to life by my body's instinctual urge to flee. And as they awaken, I can feel just how excited Maks is.

His heart hammers in competition with my own, his breaths ragged as he thrusts inside me. The euphoria builds in my veins as I realize he's close to his own release.

A jolt of anticipation races through me at the thought of him coming inside me, of the consequences I faced last time. I should get proactive and find a second form of birth control, just to be safe, if this is going to become a regular thing.

And I sincerely hope it will.

"Come with me, *krasivaya*," he commands.

The sexy sound of Russian leaving his lips undoes me. He is the master of my body, and I couldn't disobey him if I wanted to.

"I'm coming!" I gasp, my head dropping back and my lips parting as I give a silent cry.

His cock swells inside me, and as it starts to pulse with his own release, I fall apart around him. Throbbing and twitching, I ride the waves of ecstasy that rush out to my fingers and toes. Reveling in the momentary oblivion, I let my eyes flutter closed.

The deep, heavy satisfaction that follows relaxes my muscles until I'm nothing more than a puddle beneath him.

14

MAKSIM

The look of pure bliss that softens Heidi's face steals the air from my lungs. She's so unique in her raw vulnerability, the open honesty of her expressions, and the way she lives her life. Though I hardly know her, I feel as if we'd been together for a lifetime. Despite my determination to keep women at arm's length, I find that with Heidi, I can't resist the urge to learn more.

We still together, and I relish the sensation of her aftershocks as they twitch around my cock, still buried inside her to the hilt.

"That," she breathes, "was exactly what I needed."

A low chuckle rumbles through my chest as I press a soft kiss to the small mark I left at the base of her throat. It will be gone by the morning, but it fills me with a sense of satisfaction to know I've marked her in my own way, claimed her at least temporarily.

Then I ease out of her. Rolling off the bed, I head to the ensuite bathroom to discard the spent condom. As I return to the bedroom and rummage in one of my drawers for a pair of joggers, I admire Heidi's lean, athletic body sprawled across my bed.

She's clearly taken pains to maintain her fitness, even after quitting dance, though her curves have only gotten better with time. Her long legs draw my eyes toward the irresistible peak of her thighs.

Her cheeks color when she catches me openly appreciating her figure, and a shy smile graces her lips.

"Care to join me for a glass of wine?" I offer as I step into my gray sweatpants.

"Sure," she agrees, sitting up to collect her bra and undies from the floor as I scoop up her dress.

Her shoes litter the floor nearby, and I can't recall when they might have come off. I was so lost in the moment, I didn't even stop to think about them. Covered once again in her fine lace lingerie, Heidi steps close to accept her dress from me.

Rather than handing it over, I hold it up, making it easy for her to step into. She ties it closed before bending to collect her shoes, and my cock twitches at the proximity of her full hips proudly offered up just feet in front of me.

I can't wait for the next time.

But first, we really should discuss the details of our arrangement.

With her nude high heels hooked on the fingers of one hand, Heidi looks up to meet my eyes as I place my hand on the small of her back and guide her back out to the main living space of my penthouse.

Her eyes widen as she takes in the furnishings followed by the twinkling city lights of my view.

"You like it?" I ask, unable to keep the amusement from my tone as I note her blatant awe.

"You're going to have to introduce me to your decorator," she states, a hint of envy in her voice.

"I already have."

Her eyes flash to mine as I bring her to one of the bar stools surrounding my kitchen island. I pull it out and wait for her to sit. She does, though her gaze demands a name before she'll let me leave.

"I chose it myself," I state.

My lips twitch at the flicker of surprise that she manages to cover with impressive speed.

"Well, I love your style."

"Thanks. I like to think I have good taste." I look her up and down meaningfully and am rewarded by a humble blush.

Selecting a red wine from the wire rack, I collect the corkscrew from its drawer and open the bottle before taking two stemmed glasses from a crystal-windowed cabinet. Bringing it all back to the island, I settle onto a stool beside Heidi before pouring us each a generous portion of Zinfandel.

"Thanks," Heidi murmurs and lightly taps her glass against my proffered one before she takes a sip.

"Now that you've agreed to spending time with me, I think it's best we discuss our deal," I state, falling into my more businesslike tone so she knows I'm serious.

"Okay?" Setting her drink on the black granite countertop, Heidi gives me her undivided, curious attention.

"I have a room for you, a nice one where I will expect you to spend the night for as long as we're sleeping together. And I'll assign a security detail that will be by your side whenever you wish to leave. You'll be free to come and go as you please. It's just a precaution to ensure your safety for as long as we continue this agreement."

"Whoa, whoa, whoa, big spender," Heidi says, her expression shifting to unsettled as she leans back, her hands flying up in defense. "That is way more of a commitment than I was anticipating."

I frown, confused by what could possibly be so serious about it when she's already confirmed she's unattached and willing to sleep with me. If she likes my apartment as much as she indicated, I would think it might even be a fun change of scenery.

"Look, late-night booty calls I can work with. But I'm *not* moving into your penthouse, and I'm definitely not taking a couple of bodyguards everywhere I go. I'm an interior designer, Maks. Hauling a bunch of muscle in and out of my clients' homes would be *terrible* for business . . ." Her lips part as if she's about to pile on to her list of objections, but then her mouth snaps closed as if she feels she's said too much.

Well, that explains why she was admiring my penthouse furnishings.

And I can see her point about not wanting bodyguards. But these are the parameters I've put in place to protect any of the women I sleep with. As long as this war continues with Aleksandr Volkov, I can't just let Heidi run around San Francisco unchecked without thinking she might face serious consequences for being connected to me. Aleksandr has proven more than capable of violence against the women who matter to me and my brothers.

Frustration tightens my chest at her sudden hard-headedness. First, she won't accept my money. Now, she won't accept my protection. "It's starting to seem like you're unwilling to do any part of the agreement I've offered, though this is for your own good."

"That's not true. I'm perfectly fine with having sex without attachment. But if you don't want to be flexible and work with me, then I'm sure I'll manage on my own. I've gone this long without sex. I imagine I can go back to the way it was before you walked into my life again."

The most infuriating part about her statement is that she sounds like she means it. And the less she's willing to bend to my rules, the more desperately I want her. Releasing an exasperated sigh, I set my wine glass roughly on the counter to comb my fingers through my hair.

Then I work on a new plan that might keep her safe even if she won't stay here.

Heidi sips her wine silently, seeming perfectly at ease to let me war internally while she waits. The hint of a smile twitches at one corner of her mouth, and I'm tempted to steal her amusement with a kiss.

Instead, I force myself to focus on the resources I could use to find the compromise she's demanding.

"Alright," I grumble after several moments of intense quiet. "What if I send a driver and men to pick you up and drop you off at your house? You'll have to be discreet so people don't see you coming and going from my place. That means late nights and careful transport. But if my enemies can't connect you to me, you'll likely be safe enough."

Heidi eyes me as if considering my new offer, and I tense as she seems on the verge of shooting this one down as well. It's risky enough, and I refuse to be more lenient. I won't let her risk her life needlessly.

"I can't guarantee your protection if you won't work with me, Heidi."

She hesitates a moment longer, trapping her full lower lip between her teeth. The suspense is agonizing, and I know my need to be with her has already reached an unhealthy level. I need to keep myself in better check if I'm going to remain unattached.

Maybe it's because she's someone from back when Symphony's death was so raw and new, or maybe my attraction to her is just different, stronger than normal, but Heidi's hold on me is unlike anything I've felt since before my fiancée died.

"Okay," she finally agrees. "We can try it."

15

HEIDI

"Do I need to sign some paperwork, maybe give my fingerprint in blood or something, to make our agreement official?" I tease, poking fun at Maks for getting so frustrated with me about not following his rules.

But in truth, his original offer had me on the verge of panic, mostly because of Sarah. I couldn't possibly leave her for weeks at a time, and I'm unwilling to bring her into the equation when this is temporary, meaningless sex. So I'm grateful that he would be willing to find another solution.

My playful jab seems to have served its purpose to cover my momentary nerves, however, as Maks's gaze turns fiery, making my stomach tremble.

"I think we can make the amendment binding with another kiss," he jokes back, though the way he combs his fingers into my hair is anything but funny.

His other hand finds my hip, and in a flash, he pulls me off my chair and into his arms as he kisses me passionately. Tongue stroking between my teeth, he claims my mouth, the crisp taste of wine mingling with his deliciously masculine flavor.

Resting my palms lightly on his marble-cut chest, I melt against him. How any woman could resist this, I don't know, but I'll take what I can get because Maks might be the single most impressive specimen I'll ever have the opportunity to be with. I refuse to feel guilty or ashamed of having fun with him. Zoe's right. I need to let loose and enjoy myself every now and again.

His large hands roam over my body, up my back to unclasp my bra with a flick of his fingers, then down to grope my butt. Heat floods the peak of my thighs as he turns me on in an instant, and I gasp when his fingers travel down my thighs to lift the hem of my dress.

"Maks," I object, embarrassment crawling up my neck and pooling in my cheeks as I think about the guards I spotted in the living room. "Your men."

He pauses in his advances long enough to glance where they used to be, but when I follow his gaze, I find that we're entirely alone.

"My men know their jobs well, and that includes knowing when it's time to leave," he murmurs. Then his eyes shift back to mine, and amusement dances in their silver depths. "Now, where were we?"

"I think you were about to lay me out on your counter and have your way with me," I breathe, my heart fluttering.

Maks hums appreciatively. "I like the way you think." Then his hands travel the rest of the way up my thighs to grasp the waistline of my panties.

He pulls them down slowly this time, his eyes watching my face as the fabric whispers between my thighs, raising goosebumps along the way. My eyelids droop as a lusty shiver runs down my spine. When he drops the lacy lingerie, I step out of it.

Strong hands grip my waist a moment later, and Maks stands, lifting and depositing me on the smooth surface of the island countertop in one fluid motion. I gasp at the sudden bite of cold granite against the backs of my thighs, but before I can protest, he grabs me by the backs of my knees and pulls me roughly against his hips.

With my thighs snugly wrapped around his waist, I perch at the edge of the countertop, waiting with bated breath for what he'll do next.

"I could eat you up, *krasivaya*," he warns, the threat sounding all too appealing.

As he leans in to devour my lips, one arm snakes around the small of my back to hold me close. The other reaches between us to untie my dress once more. It falls open, and I shrug quickly out of it, eager to feel the warm, bare skin of his chest that he didn't bother to cover up after our first round of sex.

Next goes my bra as I toss it impatiently aside, and then Maks's bulging arms enclose my exposed torso, pulling me firmly against his chest as he kisses the breath from my lungs.

I can't remember a time when I craved someone as deeply as I do this beast of a man before me. He brings out a side of me that I never knew existed. I never want this to end.

Filled with a wild daring, I reach between us to work my fingers beneath the waistband of his perfectly fitted joggers and wrap my fingers around the iron rod of his cock. He groans, the sound haunting as his erection twitches in my grasp.

The sense of empowerment that floods my chest leaves me aching for more.

"I need you," I plead on a breath.

Maks digs into the pocket of his sweats and pulls out another foil wrapper. Tearing into it with his teeth, he pulls out the rubber in one smooth move, and this time, I take the liberty of shoving his sweats down over his hips as he rolls the condom on.

Then he hooks my left knee over his forearm and lines up with my entrance.

I'm still so wet from our first round of sex and the multiple orgasms he gave me that he slides inside me with ease. When he claims me this time, it's rough and demanding and sinfully pleasurable.

He fills me as if he can't hold back, can't restrain himself enough to be gentle. And I love it.

This desperate passion sets my skin ablaze and awakens a throbbing ache that leaves me begging for more.

"You like it rough?" he growls, thrusting inside me hard and fast, his hands greedy in the exploration of my body.

"Yes!" I mewl, trembling with the intensity of my rapidly building release.

"God, I can't tell if you're sent from heaven or a demon come to satisfy all my wicked ways."

The torturous ecstasy in his rasping voice lights a fire inside me, and somehow, being called a demon feels like a greater compliment than I ever could have imagined. I know just what he means. Maks could be the devil, here to tempt me with the most delicious of mortal sins, and I would gladly give him my soul for this kind of pleasure.

"Make me come, Maks. I want to come," I plead, hovering so close to the brink that I feel I might explode if he doesn't give me what I need.

Releasing my knee, Maks reaches between us to press the pad of his thumb to my clit, and it only takes the slightest pressure to send me toppling into oblivion. Arching back over his arm, I grasp his broad shoulders as I let the heavenly bliss consume me.

Black dots dance across the backs of my eyelids as relief floods into my fingers and toes. As I slowly come down from my high, Maks scoops me up off the counter and carries me into the living room. I cling to him weakly, my forehead resting in the crook of his neck as I breathe heavily, my limbs still tingling and numb.

He settles onto the pristine white couch, settling me onto his lap so I'm straddling him once again. From this new angle, I can feel just how far he's buried inside me.

My pussy throbs at the intense feeling of deep penetration, and I rock my hips, instinctually stimulating myself as I start to ride him.

"Christ, you *are* an angel," he rasps, his fingers pressing more adamantly into the flesh of my hips as he stiffens and swells further inside me.

I release a breathy laugh, relishing the way he slides in and out of me, his shaft gliding across my clit with every forward rock of my hips. Maks groans as my walls tighten around him with my laughter.

"No, I'm Heidi, remember?" I tease.

Maks smiles wickedly, his chuckle dark as he joins in my amusement.

"Tonight, you're mine, and that's all that matters," he growls, claiming my lips with hungry determination.

I find his sexual appetite positively addictive, the way he makes me feel like I'm the only thing he can see. It fills me with an excitement that dares me to let loose and be as wild and free as I want to be. And for once, I'm going to follow that urge.

Tomorrow, I can rethink my sanity.

Seemingly fully on board with this plan, Maks gropes and fondles me, his big, rough hands finding each of my sensitive points from which he can draw more pleasure from me. The confidence in his touch makes me tremble.

He knows just how to support my body to help me keep going even after my legs start to burn from the exertion. The ragged, panting breaths that pass between us only make the uninhibited sex on his couch that much hotter.

"Use me to make yourself come, *krasivaya*," Maks rasps. "I want to see just how you like it."

In truth, no one knows how I like it quite like Maks. But I love the thought of riding him to my own release, and I grind more wildly down onto his swollen shaft, pressing my clit against its base as I seek my selfish pleasure.

"Oh, holy hell," I groan, coming dangerously close to saying an actual curse word as my ecstasy consumes me completely.

My walls clamp down around his rock-hard cock, and Maks releases a string of Russian as he grips my hips. Hammering up into me as I grind down on top of him, we both find our release at the same time.

I can feel the burst of heat inside me as he fills the condom with his seed, and the sensation makes my stomach flutter with instinctual anticipation. A trickle of sweat tracks slowly between my breasts as I gasp for air, and Maks dips to lick it up, a final scintillating display of dirty pleasure.

When our eyes meet, I find it almost impossible not to get lost in the heat of his gaze. This man is otherworldly. And I'm going to be consumed by his fire if I'm not careful.

Daring to walk the line a hair further, I lean in to press a soft kiss to his lips. They're salty from my sweat and entirely too enticing. When I pull away, Maks lets me, holding my hips steady as I slowly dismount to stand.

"It's late. I'd better get going," I murmur, suddenly feeling like a teen who stayed out far past her curfew.

But Maks doesn't seem to mind. Rising from the couch, he takes my hand and guides me back to the kitchen, where we dress once again. Then he gets on his phone, speaking in low, quick Russian.

"My men will meet you in the elevator. A driver is waiting in the garage to take you home."

"Thanks," I murmur, biting my lip as I wait for my brain to catch up.

Maks has this way about him, an air that commands respect and obedience without his even seeming to try.

"Come. I'll walk you out," he offers, holding out his hand as I slip back into my heels.

As soon as my palm meets his, his strong fingers close around mine, giving me a sense of warmth and safety.

"Tonight was fun," he states as we walk, his lips quirking into a crooked grin. Then he casts a sidelong glance my way. "At least, I enjoyed it."

A giddy giggle bubbles up my throat before I realize it sounds far too girly. "I did too," I confess, feeling my cheeks heat.

"Well then, let's do it again. Soon." Maks combs his fingers into my hair, gently tipping my head to press a soft, chaste kiss to my lips.

He only pulls back after the elevator doors ding open behind me.

"Good night, Heidi."

"Good night, Maks," I breathe, stepping back into the elevator without looking away.

My pulse quickens as he watches me with unbridled anticipation until the doors obscure him from view.

16

HEIDI

Zoe left the porch light on for me, and as I make my way quickly and quietly up the pathway in my bare feet, I can feel the eyes of Maks's bodyguards following me to ensure I get safely inside.

It's nearly three o'clock in the morning, a fact I didn't realize until I checked my phone in the car and found several text messages from Zoe asking how the date was going and when I might be home.

But her last text was hours ago, so she must be asleep. Slipping inside the front door as silently as the wood boards will allow, I close and lock it gently behind me. Then I smile as I see that Zoe's left the kitchen light on for me as well. That will help guide me to the hallway and my bedroom.

Creeping silently through the house, I head for the kitchen to flick off the light.

"Holy Crayola coloring book!" I bark, pressing my hand to my heart as I find Zoe sitting at the kitchen table, her dark eyes watching me. "Zoe, what are you still doing up? It's the middle of the night, and we have work tomorrow," I scold softly.

"Yeah, I know," she says, her tone coming out cross. She scowls at her nearly empty glass of wine and finishes it in one gulp.

"Are you . . . mad at me?" I ask, confused by her tone.

"No, I just couldn't sleep. I got kind of worried after I handed you off to some stranger. It was a stupid, reckless move, and I'm sorry. He could have been a serial killer for all I knew." Zoe stands and comes to give me a hug. "I'm glad you're alive. I was really starting to debate on whether I should call the cops."

"I'm sorry I scared you, but if it makes you feel better, it turns out he's not a stranger," I say, trying to brighten her mood. "He's actually the man who paid me two hundred thousand dollars to sleep with him—you know, the one who also happens to be Sarah's biological father."

"What!" Zoe's eyes nearly bug out of her head, and her hands clasp my forearm with bruising strength. "Okay, I need details," she demands, her sullen tone vanishing.

Dragging me to the kitchen table, she forces me into a chair. Then she pulls a second wine glass from the cabinets and uncorks the bottle to pour us each a glass.

"Zoe, it's nearly three a.m. We can't talk about this tomorrow?"

"It already is tomorrow. Now dish." She plops into the chair across from me and takes a sip of wine, her eyes riveted to my face like I'm some fascinating Hollywood drama.

"Where do I even begin?" I ask, my cheeks flaming when I think about the details of my night.

Zoe might be pretty open with her sexual exploits and the stories she's willing to tell, but I don't have many of those, and I much prefer to keep the few I have under lock and key. Like my mama taught me, I don't kiss and tell.

"From the moment I walked out the door," Zoe presses. "And don't leave anything out. Did you sleep together again? What did he say when you told him about Sarah?"

"Well, actually . . ." A twinge of guilt hits me as I wonder if I might have made the wrong decision to keep that information from him. Maybe I should have led with that. *Hi, great to see you. My name is, in fact, Heidi, not Angel, and oh, by the way, we have a three-year-old daughter together. Surprise!*

It sounds ridiculous enough in my head that I'm confident that wouldn't have been the right way to tell him. Besides, if I had told him, he might want to meet her, and I don't want Sarah to wrap her sweet little mind around the concept of a father when Maks isn't interested in forming attachments.

"I didn't tell him about Sarah," I confess before Zoe has another outburst.

"Why not?" Her expression registers surprise but not disapproval, as I'd feared it might.

"Well, from the beginning, we both instantly recognized one another, and we hit it off really well," I admit, smiling as I recall the banter we exchanged. How much has taken place since happy hour is mind-boggling.

"Okay?" Zoe presses, gesturing for me to keep the ball rolling.

"Turns out he did go back to Lady Venus and even tried to track me down after I quit."

Zoe's jaw drops, her eyes bugging.

"But he only knew my stage name and assumed it was my real name—so obviously, that didn't work out too well for him."

"To be honest, I'm kind of proud of Howie to know that he stuck to his guns and wouldn't give out your information. If your hunky Russian one-night stand was willing to pay you two hundred K for one night, I imagine he tried to buy the information from Howie too."

"Huh." I sit back in my chair, considering her words. "That's a good point. Remind me to send Howie a thank-you card—even if, in this one instance, it might have been more useful to everyone involved if he'd buckled under pressure."

"Yeah, but how was he supposed to know? He probably thought your Russian was a crazy stalker you quit to run away from."

"You're really smart at three o'clock in the morning," I observe playfully.

"And half a bottle of wine in," she adds, lifting the nearly empty one sitting between us.

I shake my head, chuckling softly at my best friend. "Anyway,

Maks offered me another deal—five hundred thousand to spend a few weeks with him."

"That's a joke," she states flatly, then her brows arch as I shake my head.

"No, apparently, someone killed his fiancée, so Maks doesn't do love anymore. He pays women to stay with him, and when he's done with them, he sends them on their way." When I say it like that, it sounds even more horrible.

"Please tell me you didn't take that deal. You don't need the money, and you *definitely* don't need that kind of crazy in your life."

"I didn't," I agree, and Zoe visibly relaxes. "But we did have sex. Twice."

If jaws could literally hit the floor, my best friend's would have right then and there.

"Oh, come on! You're the one who told me I needed to get laid. And let me tell you just how right you were. Besides, if I'm being perfectly honest, Maks is a god in bed."

"So you slept with the father of your child—again—and didn't think to tell him you have a kid together?"

"No, I thought about it. And believe me, it's still plaguing me now. I don't know how long I can keep seeing him if I'm *not* going to tell him—"

"Come again?" Zoe sits forward in her chair, placing a hand on the table. "You're going to see him again?"

"Well . . . yeah. We agreed on sex with no strings attached. Both just having fun. I told him I wouldn't take the money, and he conceded to that. But he was pretty pissed when I told him I wouldn't move in with him or have his bodyguards following me around. I mean, I have clients to think about, and that would be far too confusing for Sarah—"

"Whoa, hold up. He wanted you to move in with him? And have bodyguards?"

I hesitate, wondering if I've made Maks sound way crazier than he'd seemed to me at the time. He did a far better job of conveying the significance of his choices than I seem to be doing.

"He said it was for my protection because he has enemies, and I think, he doesn't want another girl he sleeps with to end up dead because of him."

Zoe remains silent this time, taking a drink from her wine rather than offering up commentary.

"Anyway, we came to a compromise in which he'll have someone pick me up here on nights I come over for a bit of fun. And that's all it is, Zoe. But that's why I didn't tell him about Sarah. All in all, Maks is a lot of fun to be around, but I don't think it would be healthy to bring him into Sarah's life when he doesn't want to make attachments with anyone. What kind of a father would that be to her? I can't imagine growing up with an emotionally unavailable father would be better than just not knowing him at all. At least now, she won't feel that distance and think it's something she's done wrong."

Still, I worry my lip, then take a drink of wine as I wonder whether I made the right call.

"Well? What do you think?" I ask after a long moment of silence.

Zoe twists her lips in that expression that tells me she's trying to pick her words carefully.

"Oh, just spit it out," I insist, leaning forward.

"Okay, fine. For starters, I can totally get behind the idea of not telling him about Sarah. You're right. You don't want some random man coming in and insisting on being a part of her life if he doesn't care to form connections with people. And I *am* proud of you for getting some with a guy that hot. I mean, I know you told me he was old enough to be your father, but damn, that guy is a work of art . . ." She pauses there, her expression growing dreamy, as if picturing him in her mind's eye.

"Is that it?" I press when I can't wait any longer.

Zoe seems to snap out of her revere with an apologetic grin. "I'm just worried about what might happen in the long run. It sounds like this guy is a bit of a control freak, if not a dangerous person. I mean, saying he has enemies? People who hate him enough that maybe they killed his fiancée? Who says stuff like that?"

"Okay, I hear what you're saying, but we agreed that either of us can call it quits at any point. So, what's the harm in giving it a try? I'm just dipping my toe in, and if he puts me—or you or Sarah—at any risk at all, I'll end it." Funny, but usually, I'm the responsible one giving Zoe the mom look she has leveled at me right now. It's strange to have the shoe on the other foot.

Finally, Zoe sighs. "I can't say I like it—I mean, apart from your having some fun. I do like that part. But if this is really what you want to do, then I'll do what I can to support you. Just . . . promise me you'll be careful?"

"I will," I assure her, reaching across the table to give her hand a squeeze. "And seriously, Maks is not as bad as I'm making him sound. He knows how to put it so it makes a lot more sense."

"Mm-hmm. You sure that's not just because he says it in a low, sexy Russian accent that gets your hormones all in a tizzy?"

"Zoe!" I protest, and she giggles as she leans away to protect herself from my fury.

"I'm kidding. I'm kidding! I'm sure he has plenty of admirable qualities."

"It's just for fun," I reiterate. "And just for a little while."

"Okay," she agrees, flashing a white-toothed smile.

"Can we go to bed now?" I grumble, feeling like I've been thoroughly dissected, reprimanded, and teased all at once.

"Bed sounds nice," she agrees, and we stand together to head down the hall.

I might not have my head on straight when it comes to Maks, but at least I know Zoe will always have my back—even if she likes to give me a hard time on occasion. Since Mom died, she's been my rock, my best support, and I know she always has my best interests at heart.

17

MAKSIM

The sunrise breaks through the windows of my apartment, filling the modern space with the same sense of golden enthusiasm I feel after spending the night with Heidi. It doesn't matter that I got only three hours of sleep. Nothing is going to bring me down today.

I'm up early enough to finish a good workout in my home gym. Then I take a shower, get dressed, make a quick breakfast, and head to the offices of Federov Brothers Investments.

Women help take the edge off, and I always enjoy starting something with a new woman. There's a freshness to exploring a new person, understanding what makes them tick, how to give them pleasure.

But with Heidi, I almost feel like I'm on a high.

Something about her open honesty, the way she faces life with an unshakeable sincerity, makes me want to learn about her in a way I haven't cared to know a woman in years.

As I ride the elevator up to my office, a smile tugs at the corner of my lips. I can't stop thinking about her confession that she's dreamed of me, too, since our first night together. It cost her something to admit it. *Pride? Dignity?* I'm not sure, and still, she was willing to say it.

I like that about her. And I wonder if she dreamed about me again last night.

I know I dreamed of her.

Stepping out of the elevator, I'm greeted by our receptionist, Jacquie, who gives me a bright "Good morning," along with a sweet smile. Bespectacled and in her late sixties, with a halo of grayish-blonde curls, I can always count on Jacquie to do her job with a pleasant attitude.

"Morning, Jacquie," I respond, giving her a single nod in passing.

I'm at my office door before I hear Dimitri's raised tone, telling me that my brother is not in nearly the good mood I am. From the sound of it, he's giving someone on the phone a piece of his mind. Rather than go investigate, I head into my office, leaving the door open because I know Dimitri will come speak to me when he's good and ready.

Of my two brothers, Dimitri is who I would consider my true partner in the family business. He shares the burden of financial decisions, has proven a shark when it comes to laying claim to restaurants we want to acquire, and manages the banking side I find rather dull.

Our youngest brother, Alexei, on the other hand, I think would gladly never attend our family meetings to discuss business revenue again. But when it comes to security and hunting down the people who fall too far into debt to us, he's both diligent and masterful.

Except when it comes to Aleksandr Volkov. The bastard has proven untouchable over the last nearly five years of open war between our Bratvas. As hard as I've been on Alexei for failing to bring him to me, I know that I've given him a nearly impossible task.

The slimy snake is too good at hiding behind his hired lackeys, paying enough that men are willing to die in droves for his cause. But his men don't hold the loyalty of our brotherhood, and one of these days, I will find a hole in his armor.

And when that day comes, Aleksandr Volkov will face the full force of my wrath.

I'm barely in my chair before I hear Dimitri's furious end to his conversation, and he slams his phone down with an impressive crack a moment later. Stomping footsteps sound a moment later, followed by a barked order for Alexei to join us for a family meeting.

This can't be good.

Dimitri enters my office a moment later, thunderclouds darkening his expression.

"Morning," I observe with mild amusement.

Alexei slips inside the room behind him, shutting the door and making a beeline for his usual seat sprawled across my couch at the back of the room. He gives me an ironic smile on his way, a silent "here we go again" that I usually ignore. But today, I can't stop the tug of humor at the corner of my lips.

Dimitri doesn't wait for an invitation to start. Instead, he paces the open space in front of my desk, his hands clenched. "Aleksandr Volkov came into the Bay View Hotel after we left yesterday and got the owner to sign a deal—an agreement saying he will no longer take counter offers. We've been shut out of negotiations. We're dead in the water."

I watch my brother with practiced calm, though it makes my blood boil to hear Aleksandr's done it again. The greedy vulture swoops in and snipes our business acquisitions to stunt our growth and limit our hold on the city. He used to be a nobody casino owner on the outskirts of town that I wouldn't have given a second thought to. But he's made it perfectly clear that he wants our territory and he's willing to play dirty to get it.

"It's retaliation for the destruction we did to that casino of his last month. I'm sure of it," Dimitri adds, slumping into the chair before me now that he's unloaded his bad news.

I knew Frank Thompson would be a challenging fish to reel in. He's too impulsive and all but has money signs for eyes. Still, it irritates me that he would shake my hand and turn to my enemy with an open palm within hours.

Sure, his hotel might be worth more than I've offered him so far, but from where I stand, he's lucky we aren't just taking it from him. We could, and I'm reaching that point with him now. If he doesn't want to work with us, then there are other ways of acquiring his hotel.

"I'll send some muscle. See if we can't get that contract torn up. I'm sick of dancing with Frank. It's time he understands the bottom line," I state coldly.

When our father began building our empire, brick by brick, he had to be far more brutal than we have in years. My brothers and I have been lucky in that regard. He handed this business to us on a silver platter. But that doesn't mean I failed to learn everything the old man had to teach.

"I'll handle it," I state, closing the discussion as my frustration turns my words curt. Jerking my chin toward the door, I silently excuse my brothers.

"Well, that was a fun pow-wow. We should do it more often," Alexei mutters under his breath as he rises from his chair.

Dimitri only scowls at him, giving our youngest brother a light shove as they both exit my office. As soon as the door clicks shut behind them, I release a low growl. Good mood obliterated, I take up my phone to make the call, but my frustration constricts my throat, and the building tension in my chest gives me only a few seconds' warning.

Slamming the office phone back into its cradle, I snatch the stress ball off my desk and launch it across the room. It hits the standing lamp in the far corner of the room with such force that the glass torchiere shade shatters, exploding in a burst of shards.

"*Blyat,*" I hiss under my breath, irritated that my temper has only created another mess for me to clean up.

But rather than do that—or make the call to show Frank we mean business—I pick up my cell phone and dial Heidi.

She answers on the third ring, her cheery hello instantly bringing me back to the seemingly unshakeable good mood I woke up in. It would seem she hasn't had a heap of bad news dumped on her head just yet.

"I'm sending someone to pick you up tonight. Be ready at eleven,"

I state. After the way my day is unfolding, I'm going to desperately need some stress relief.

"Well, good morning to you too. I slept fine, thanks for asking. Though it was a bit shorter than usual. Now that we've covered the basics of polite conversation, would you care to ask nicely if I'm available to come over tonight?" Her tone is mild, pleasant, laced with a teasing laughter that lets me know my bad mood won't be welcome in her day.

And though I grumble a protest, like a brilliant ray of sunshine, her playfulness cuts right through the gloom of my frustration. "I'd like to send someone to pick you up tonight. Are you free to come over at eleven?" I ask, forcing my tone into a cordial, businesslike tone.

"I would love to. I'll see you tonight," she says, her smile carrying through the phone line.

And despite myself, I find my lips curving into a grin. "I look forward to it."

As I hang up, I'm shocked to find how quickly Heidi can put me back in a good mood. Setting down my phone, I stare at it for a moment, impressed that any woman could have that kind of impact on my emotions.

That's never been true before.

Pushing the thought aside, I collect myself, compartmentalizing my anticipation for tonight as I return my focus to the office phone. Picking it up, I dial Iosif Pachenko, the *avtoriyet* I send in to make a point. When it comes to intimidation, he knows just the right amount of pressure to apply.

"*Gospodin,*" Iosif greets respectfully.

"I need you to speak with a Frank Thompson today," I say, falling into our native tongue. "Owner of the Bay View Hotel." I give him the address where he'll most likely find Frank. "He has a contract with Aleksandr Volkov that I would like you to watch him tear up."

"Consider it done," Iosif says.

"Call me as soon as you're finished with him."

"Yes, *Gospodin.*"

18

HEIDI

Bubbles of excitement fizzle in my chest as I glance toward my phone, sitting on the drafting table throughout the morning. I'm giddier than I should be about receiving a booty call, but I can't seem to help myself.

In truth, I didn't sleep a wink last night. I couldn't when my body kept reliving my time with Maks, the spell he puts on me every time he touches me.

He's like a drug.

And I'm happily addicted.

I know I need to keep things in perspective, that this is just a temporary high, and eventually, our time together will come to an end. But I'm determined to enjoy every last second of it while I can.

And afterward, I'll go back to being the responsible, disciplined, chaste mother Sarah deserves.

Though I can't get Maks's phone call out of my head, I refuse to stop working until I've put in a full morning of research and layouts. I need to stay on top of my work if I'm going to rise to the challenge of decorating one of the Painted Ladies.

As soon as the morning is done and my clock informs me it's time to get lunch and collect Sarah from daycare, I'm up out of my chair in a flash. Biting my lip to calm my smile, I head to my office door.

"You want anything while I'm out?" I offer Zoe as I reach the reception desk, where she sits diligently, waiting to answer any calls.

"I'm all set," she says, holding up her to-go salad she must have had delivered.

"Hey, do you think you could keep an ear out for Sarah tonight if I'm gone? She should already be in bed and asleep by the time I leave. But just in case she wakes up and needs anything."

Zoe quirks an eyebrow, her lips curving slightly.

"I have plans . . ." I say to answer her silent question. But I'm confident the warm embarrassment that pools in my cheeks gives me away.

"You know, I'm starting to think you took my advice a little too literally when I said you needed to have more of a sex life," she teases, her eyes dancing.

"Zoe!" I object, my cheeks burning now.

"Of course I'll be there for Sarah. You don't have to worry about a thing."

"I'll be back before morning," I promise, flashing her a grateful smile.

Then I head toward the door.

"You'd better not be late!" she calls in her best mom voice. "Be safe! Play nice with the other kids!" she tacks on, making me laugh.

As I step out into the sunny spring day, her admonishment to be safe reminds me that I want to pick up a second form of birth control—just to be proactive. Glancing at my watch, I determine that if I skip lunch, I'll have enough time to stop by the doctor before collecting Sarah.

Loaded up with my first birth control shot, I head to Sarah's school, collecting her from her classroom, where she hops up from her seat at the art table to show me the colorful crayon drawing she's made.

"Look, Mommy," she says, her broad grin showcasing pride in her work.

"We've been working on drawing our favorite animals today, haven't we, Sarah?" Miss Irine says with a kind smile.

Sarah nods, watching closely for my reaction as I kneel beside her.

"What did you draw, Sarah?" I ask, studying the rainbow-colored animal with four legs, three ears, a long, skinny neck, and a tail.

"A unicorn, silly!" she says, giggling as she leans against my leg.

"Oh, there it is!" I agree, tracing her adorably thick outline of a body that tells me she put all her strength into keeping the line straight. "What a colorful unicorn," I admire.

"It's magic," she explains solemnly.

"We'll see you again Friday, right, Sarah?" Miss Irine confirms, waving goodbye to my little girl as I take Sarah's hand and straighten.

Sarah gives her signature wave, holding her palm out and rotating her entire arm from the shoulder in her best impression of a princess wave.

"What did you learn today?" I ask as we head out to the little white BMW I bought to replace my old Honda Civic just this year.

"I learn to count!" Sarah says, her steps turning into skipping hops of excitement.

"Really? Will you count for me?" I love how much Sarah enjoys learning.

She's proven a quick learner and an attentive student, from what her daycare teachers have said. Not that she's in an intensive program. Mostly, the children spend their days learning social skills, arts and crafts, and playing. But the school offers a fair amount of basic educational instruction that will prepare her for preschool.

"You count too, Mommy," she insists as we reach the car and I open the back door.

Sarah climbs in, determined to put herself in her car seat because she's as stubbornly independent as I am. I watch her carefully, ready to lend a hand if she gets stuck. Then she plops into her car seat and watches as I lock the buckles in place.

"Okay, I'll count with you," I agree.

"Oone, twooo, thweeee . . ." Sarah holds up a finger for each number she says, though the fingers don't necessarily match her words.

And I say the numbers just a hair behind her because I want to hear how high she learned to count. She makes it to five before the numbers start to escape her. Then she takes a long pause, her eyebrows pressing together in determination.

"What comes next, Mommy?" she asks when she can't recall.

"Sssi—"

"Siiiix, niiiine, *ten!*" she finishes with a triumphant shout.

Breaking into applause, I beam down at my little girl. She might have skipped a few numbers, but clearly, she knows her end goal, and the numbers she remembered, she even kept in the right order.

Pressing a kiss to the crown of her head, I close the car door and round the back of my sedan to climb into the driver's seat.

"Are you ready to go to the park?" I ask.

I often take Sarah to the Koret playground in Golden Gate Park if we have a free afternoon, and with the sun out today, I thought it might be a perfect opportunity to enjoy the rare bit of warmer weather.

"Yeah!" Sarah says, her hazel eyes growing wide with excitement.

She watches out the car window with the enthusiasm only a toddler can have for colorful plastic slides and jungle gyms. She's not big enough to do the long cement slides some of the older kids race down. They still scare her. But she's getting better and better on the short slide, and she's a natural climber.

As soon as we pull into the parking lot, Sarah's bouncing in her seat, ready to get on a roll. She's going to sleep well for Zoe tonight. I can guarantee it.

But she's still a good girl, taking my hand and walking with me until we reach the sand footing. Then she's off like a rocket, heading straight for the tiny rock wall, her black curls bouncing as she toddles through the deep footing.

She's going to have a pile of sand come pouring out when we empty her shoes before we leave. But I don't care, and neither does she. The park is one of her favorite places to go, and I wouldn't deprive her of it for a second over the grains of sand that make it through my front door.

Some messes in life are worth cleaning up after, my mom used to say, and I smile as I hear her warm, loving voice in my head. That's what she used to say about Sarah when my seven-month-old baby was still pouring pasta noodles over her head instead of eating them.

God, I miss her.

But it means the world to me that I got the extra time with her that I did. The money Maks gave me for our one night together helped prolonged her life by nearly a year—or so the doctors believed—because, for a time, the alternative treatments did manage to slow the cancer down. But nothing was going to stop it.

And now, if I want to spend time with my mom, I have to visit her in my memories.

"Come play, Mommy!" Sarah calls over her shoulder, her tiny hands clinging to the colorful knobs that serve as rock ledges.

"I'm here," I agree a few seconds later, coming to a stand behind her. Not that the rock wall is tall enough that I would need to climb it, but I know Sarah likes it when I stay nearby.

She babbles happily to me as she climbs—her version of playtime with me.

After the rock wall, we have to hit the swings, followed by the slides, and ending with the park's very own carousel, which Sarah has to ride at least three times to ensure that all of her favorite animals get the proper amount of attention.

Standing beside her ostrich, as Sarah holds tightly to its neck, I pull my phone out of my pocket when it starts to ring.

"Hey, Zoe," I greet, loving this day more and more.

"I have a craving for Le Fleur. Want to meet me there for dinner with Sarah?" she suggests.

"Sure. You just leaving the office?"

"Yep, you have five new calls from potential clients waiting on your desk. And the Eriksons left a message gushing over the new dining room decor that went in yesterday. I think they're in love with the light fixture you chose."

Smiling, I suppress a chuckle. They've been a particularly hard-to-please client, but now that the job is wrapping up, I think I might have won them over. "Thanks, Zoe. Sarah and I are just finishing up at the park. We'll see you soon."

"Meet you there in fifteen."

"Sure thing." Hanging up, I slip my phone back into my pocket and turn to Sarah. "Hungry for Le Fleur?"

"Yeah!" she squeals excitedly.

The cute little French restaurant right off Pier 39 is one of our favorite spots owned and run by a young female chef who has made a massive splash in the culinary capital of the West Coast. We try to support her business every chance we get, often eating there every week or so.

Just thinking about it makes my mouth water.

As the carousel slows, Sarah offers up her arms to me, and I help her down off her ostrich. It's days like these that make me so grateful I'm a mother. I have much to thank Maks for, and a small part of me twinges with regret that I can't share this with him. I don't see how anyone could fail to fall in love with our little girl.

But I have to respect his choice not to make strong connections, and I won't put my daughter through the feelings of loss and abandonment that would come from having a father who can't love and adore her.

Right now, she has two women who would do anything for her. While Zoe, Sarah, and I might not make up a traditional family, I'm confident that we're enough for my little girl. She's so incredibly cherished, and that's what I care about most.

19

MAKSIM

After a rough day, it's all I can do to wait until eleven. Several times, I contemplated pushing the time up so I might have more of Heidi to myself. But her safety takes precedence over my desires—especially after Aleksandr spent the day rubbing my face in his blatant schemes against my family.

He's trying to provoke me into doing something rash, and I refuse to be baited.

I pause my agitated pacing in front of my picture windows that look out on the San Francisco skyline as a soft *ding* sounds in the foyer, announcing Heidi's arrival.

Finally.

She's here promptly at eleven fifteen, and secretly, I'm thrilled to know she must have been ready and waiting for the driver I sent to fetch her. She couldn't have gotten across town so quickly otherwise.

Soft clicking steps precede her, then Heidi enters the living room wearing chic feather-and-pearl-studded high heels and a dressy, belted, knee-length white trench coat with two rows of stylish black buttons running down the length of the front. She looks stunning with her hair pinned away from one side of her face to cascade down the other shoulder in a waterfall of honey waves. The subtle makeup that accentuates the striking color of her eyes and her full lips tells me she went all out tonight.

I wonder if she might not have expected me to take her somewhere nice if she's dressed like that.

"Thanks, fellas," Heidi says, glancing over one shoulder to offer my bodyguards a flirtatious wave of her fingers that subtly excuses them from the room.

They both fade silently into the shadows as she redirects her gaze to me.

"You look beautiful," I state, giving her a generous once-over and noting the way her long legs look particularly sexy working those thin stilettos and fishnet stockings.

"Thanks." Her smile is coy, almost shy as she approaches. "I decided to dress up for tonight."

A twinge of unexpected guilt tightens my stomach at the realization that I've disappointed her. Somewhere along the line, I must have misdirected her about our arrangement in some way. Because what I have in mind requires very little clothing—of any caliber.

But as my lips part to explain that to her, Heidi reaches for the belt wrapped snugly around her waist, and she unbuckles it with a flourish. Her fuck-me eyes kill the words on my lips, and I watch as she slowly, intentionally undoes one button of her designer coat at a time.

When she shrugs out of it, letting it slide sensually down her arms to pool on my floor, I think I might just be in love.

She's wearing nothing but lingerie, lacy white lingerie. A bra that cups her full breasts and just hints at the outline of her pert nipples, a practically see-through lace thong that guides my eyes toward the peak of her strong thighs, and a garter belt that connects to the top of her knee-high stockings with thin bow-capped ribbons.

It looks shockingly similar to the outfit she wore four years ago, and it brings me back to that strip club and laying eyes on her for the first time. Even in my pain-clouded stupor, I could see she was beautiful. And tonight, I can't wait to put my hands on her.

"Is that . . . ?" I don't even want to finish the question because there's no way she would have remembered what outfit she was wearing that night, let alone have chosen to put it on for me tonight.

"The outfit I gave you a private lap dance in?" Heidi traps her plush lower lip between her teeth in an adorably shy expression, her chin tipping down so she can peer up at me through thick, dark lashes. "I might have stolen it when I quit. As a keepsake of our night together."

Closing the distance between us, I stand before Heidi, burning to touch her and yet wanting to play whatever game she has in mind.

"Do I have to pay to get a lap dance when you wear it?" I murmur playfully, my lips hovering mere inches from hers.

I know it's a risk, tempting her with payment. She got mad enough at my offer last night that I wouldn't put it past her to walk out on me for teasing her. But I can't help myself.

"I take payment in pleasure," she breathes, tipping her chin to close the distance even further. "And I expect payment in full. Tonight."

"Done," I rasp, and I brush my lips across hers in a delicate kiss that makes me throb with need.

Heidi's lips part slightly, air rushing between them. Her artist's hands find my chest as she presses firmly against me, guiding me back toward the living room couch. I let her, following her lead as I allow her to take the reins—at least for now.

"Well, Mr. Federov, are you ready for your dance?" she murmurs.

Placing her hands delicately on my shoulders, she presses down, silently commanding me to sit. Though I could easily refuse her, I'm caught up in her spell, enraptured by the sensual way she moves and speaks.

Lowering onto the couch, I find myself at eye level with her perfect breasts. All I want to do is pull her to me and close my lips around the taut nubs straining against the fabric.

As if sensing my desire, Heidi adjusts her palms to guide me against the couch's back. Then she steps away from me.

"Music?" she asks, her eyes hypnotic as she waits, her legs spread just wide enough, her hip slightly cocked in a sexy pose.

"Hey, Google," I say. "Play something slow . . . and sexy."

Heidi's lips curve into a coy grin as the song trickles through the surround-sound speakers. Then her hips start to sway in rhythm. Perhaps it's been four years since she's danced professionally, but the way she moves is a gift no amount of practice can change. It's pure talent.

Eyes locked on mine, Heidi stalks closer once again, her hands roaming from her hips, up the curve of her waist, and over the swells of her breasts as she touches herself exactly how I want her to.

"Do you want to touch me, Mr. Federov?" she teases, her eyes hooded, making her expression lusty and inviting.

"Yes," I rasp, clearing my throat as my excitement has left me hoarse.

"But you know the rules," she teases, placing a hand on either side of my shoulders and leaning close to my ear.

A low, rumbling growl issues from my chest, a warning that I might not be capable of behaving myself when she's teasing me so boldly.

"You can look, but you can't touch," she warns. Then she places one knee on either side of my hips and slowly lowers herself onto my lap.

Rolling her hips in time to the song, Heidi dances on top of me. Her body brushes against me in the most tantalizing of ways, her breasts just grazing against my pecs, her thighs sliding along mine as she slowly rises and falls.

My fists clench convulsively at my sides, my thumbs brushing her calves, and the silky softness of the fishnet covering her skin makes my cock twitch inside my joggers.

"You smell divine," she breathes, her hot breath washing across my skin as she tips her head, allowing her hair to form a curtain on the far side of her face. Then her lips graze my ear lobe a moment before her teeth give it a playful nip.

I groan, throbbing with need, and though I know I'm not allowed, my hands seem to have a will of their own. Wrapping around her ankles, I slowly guide my palms upward to grasp and massage her calves.

"That's against the rules," she scolds softly, bringing her lips close to mine as she continues to dance on top of me.

"Oh. My apologies," I tease, but I let my hands travel higher until I find her knees.

With fire in her gaze, Heidi gives each of my hands a sharp slap across the back of my knuckles to punish me. Then she takes my hands and removes them from her legs, guiding them behind my head.

"Interlace your fingers," she commands, her fingers weaving mine together so my hands are clasped at the nape of my neck.

Then she reaches for the bottom of my T-shirt and guides it slowly up my torso. She's stripping me, a playful glimmer in her eyes. I love the way her fingers ghost up my sides, tickling the sensitive skin along my ribs.

All the while, her hips rock and sway, grinding against me with gradually increasing pressure until I can feel the heat of her pussy against the back of my throbbing erection. She pulls the T-shirt over my head and tosses it aside.

Pressing her full breasts against my chest, Heidi leans in to steal a slow, achingly soft kiss.

Then her fingers travel down my chest, tracing the contours of my muscles as she works her way to the waist of my joggers.

"I didn't think stripping the client was a part of the job description," I observe mildly, my hands falling back onto her calves. "Let alone kissing them."

"Do you want me to stop?" she teases, drawing back so her hips come to rest between my knees.

"No," I growl, the sudden and intense need to claim her making my fingers tighten behind her knees. I pull her firmly against my hips.

Heidi releases a startled gasp, her sexy stripper persona falling away for only an instant as she feels the steel hardness of my arousal.

"Well then, Mr. Federov. You'd better behave yourself," she scolds, her words breathy.

Again, she removes my hands from her legs. Only this time, she guides my hands back to her hips, and she fits my palms firmly around her supple ass cheeks.

"Christ, woman," I groan, my grip tightening until my fingertips press into her creamy flesh.

Heidi moans, her hips rolling against me in the sexiest display of excitement. Then one hand falls onto my shoulder to steady herself as she reaches between us with the other hand. Slipping her fingers between the waist of my joggers and the flat plane of my abs, she finds my swollen shaft and grasps it firmly.

"*Fuck*," I hiss, unable to control my language as an intense wave of arousal crackles through my core. My hips press forward, lifting Heidi off the couch slightly as my need to be inside her skyrockets.

"That's exactly what I was thinking," she purrs, her hand stroking me, slow and strong.

"You know, I have a keepsake of my own—in a manner of speaking—from that night together," I growl, my hands gripping and kneading her ass as she gives me a tantalizing hand job.

"Oh?" she asks. "What's that?"

And while I never want her to stop what she's doing, I'm also very eager to show her just what I had in store for her tonight.

"My turn?" I suggest playfully. Then I capture her lips with my own, kissing the breath from her lungs.

Almost reluctantly, Heidi releases my cock, withdrawing her hand as she nods against my mouth. With a feral snarl, I spring into action, rising off the couch and hoisting her over my shoulder in one smooth motion.

Heidi squeals, squirming in my grasp at the sudden shift in balance, and I give her round ass a sharp spank.

"Jam on a cracker!" she squeaks, bringing a wicked grin to my lips as I carry her toward my playroom.

20

HEIDI

Teasing Maks with a lap dance was both liberating and exhilarating. I love that he let me get away with it. More than that, I think it genuinely pleased him to know that our night together four years ago was so memorable to me. Not just because of the money.

And hearing that he kept something from that night as well made my heart do giddy flip-flops.

But the sudden shift in power and equilibrium as Maks hoisted me over his shoulder like I weigh nothing at all? That was beyond sexy. It doesn't matter that my pulse is roaring in my ears from being carried like a sack of potatoes. I'm throbbing with anticipation to find out what he's talking about.

Even as my ass cheek burns from where he spanked me, I silently hope he kept the fur-tipped riding crop.

Slick arousal dampens my panties at the thought, and though I was already excited by the feel of Maks's hard cock in my palm, I'm suddenly pulsing with need.

"You think you get to play with me, *krasivaya*, without facing consequences?" Maks growls, making my heart flutter.

He slaps my other ass cheek, drawing another squeal from my lips, and I squirm in his iron grasp.

"What do you think you're *doing*?" I protest, though the heat flooding my body would indicate I want more of it.

"I'm taking you where naughty strippers go to be punished," he threatens.

Then he's opening a door and carrying me unceremoniously across the threshold.

He deposits me on my feet a moment later, catching my hips and steadying me before I have time to stumble. At the same time, he kicks the door closed behind him. Then his hands spin me to face the spacious room.

My eyes widen at the sight. It's a private playroom—very similar in design to the sex club he took me to, but with a muted red glow to the air and stylish furnishings that match the grandeur of the rest of his penthouse. This room is pristine. And it makes my heart pound.

Fingers press into my hips as Maks pulls me firmly against his body. One arm snakes around my waist to pin my back against his chest.

"Look around, *krasivaya*. See anything familiar?"

I do as I'm told and gasp when I recognize the frame he tied me to at the sex club. Or at least a contraption that looks very close to the same thing.

"Are you ready for that payment in full?" Maks teases, carrying my little strip-tease game into this playroom that holds every sex toy and erotic piece of furniture I could imagine—and plenty I couldn't too. It even has a bed, like the sex club. Though the sheets look like the finest quality of black silk.

My mind flashes to our conversation last night—his initial intention to have me stay at his house for the duration of our time together—and I can't help myself. I have to ask.

"Is this the room you would have had me sleep in?" My voice is breathy, with just a hint of incredulity.

Maks chuckles, the soft sound vibrating against my shoulder blades and down my spine.

"No. But I'm perfectly willing to tie you up and keep you here for a few days—or longer," he murmurs in my ear.

A jolt of anxiety hits me as I worry that he might not be teasing. *Would he keep me here against my will?* It's difficult to say. After all, when it comes down to it, I barely know the guy.

Tension raises my shoulders ever so slightly as I consider what I should say. I can't be trapped in his sex room for days at a time. Not only would my business suffer, but more importantly, I couldn't leave Sarah like that.

Maks instantly seems to pick up on my distress, and his hands knead my flesh, almost as if to comfort me.

"This room is intended to be used to explore desire, different ways to stimulate the body and activate pleasure. You should never genuinely feel scared or trapped here, Heidi. That includes keeping you here longer than you want."

Hearing that releases the air trapped in my lungs, and the tension slips from my shoulders.

"Now that we're on the topic, you should pick a safe word," he says, turning me to face him. "You're to use it if I ever take things too far. If you do use it, I will stop whatever I'm doing immediately."

"Like a fail safe?"

Stroking a finger down my cheek, he lifts his silver eyes to meet mine, and his lips quirk into a slight smile. "Something like that," he agrees. "Just pick a word you're confident you wouldn't say accidentally unless you want me to stop."

I rack my brain, unsure of what word that might be.

After several moments of deliberation, I still don't have one that I'm confident I won't use. Maybe that's because I don't use words when I can't think of them. This is harder than I would have thought.

Maks releases a chuckle as he runs his fingers softly over my tresses. "Would you be willing to curse as a safe word?"

"That won't work. I curse plenty!" I object, planting my hands on my hips.

His laughter intensifies. "I mean a real curse word."

"Well . . . yes, I suppose I would." I certainly know them, even if it makes me cringe to use them. But then again, that does seem like a safe word. "How about the F-word, then?"

My voice drops when I say it, a habit built in from having a three-year-old who is sometimes more similar to a parrot than a human child.

Maks's rumbling chuckle intensifies. "Perfect," he says a moment later. Then he leans in to place a slow, scintillating kiss to my lips.

I lean into him, my pulse quickening as we shift back into the spicy moment.

As we kiss, Maks's tongue softly exploring the seam of my lips, he starts to walk me backward toward the frame I spotted when we came into the room. His hands travel from my hips up to my back, where he unhooks my bra with familiar ease. Then his fingers trace up between my shoulder blades to slip the straps down my arms.

"Give me your hand," he commands softly, dropping the lacy bra to the floor.

His low baritone raises goosebumps across my flesh, hardening my nipples. I do as he says, lifting my right hand, palm up, for him to take. Strong fingers encircle my wrist, and he brings the soft flesh to his lips, brushing a kiss there, his facial hair tickling lightly.

Then he guides my hand up over my head and curls my fingers around the bar, silently indicating that I should hold on. I do, gripping the cold metal as he gets to work tying a knot around my wrist with nylon rope. He attaches it to the corner of the frame and gives a firm tug to ensure I'm secure.

Then he holds out his hand for my other wrist.

Repeating the same process, Maks draws a gasp from my lips when he kisses and then sucks the tender skin against his lips. The sudden, intense pressure makes my core throb as my breath quickens.

As he lifts my arm, forcing me to stand tall in my heels, I'm more than ready to further explore with Maks. He gave me a small taste of his world four years ago, and despite the fact that I'm at his mercy now, I find myself at ease—if intensely exhilarated.

He heads to the table displaying various whips, rods, chains, and devices, and this time, he collects several, making my pulse flutter. One is a delicate chain with what look like miniature rubber-coated chip clips on either end. The second is a small, simple rod that easily fits in the palm of his hand, and the third is a mean-looking whip I can only classify as a flogger. Though the strands attached to the handle look like soft leather, there are enough of them to make it look like a horse tail of sorts.

I can't tell which one I fear most.

But despite Maks's assurance that this room is for exploring pleasure, they look rather pain-inducing to me.

As he stalks toward me once more, his eyes brilliant with anticipation, my heart stutters. With his tattooed, muscle-bound chest on full display and several torture devices in hand, he looks dangerous, even deadly.

Still, heat coils in my belly at the magnificent sight of him.

"Tell me, pet, did you have fun teasing me?" He prowls a circle around me, his eyes scanning my body hungrily, like a predator that's isolated its prey and is waiting for the right time to pounce.

His question feels like a trap. *I know the answer, but if I say yes, will he punish me?*

My momentary hesitation brings on a quick snap of the leather flogger across my behind. I gasp as stinging pain sears across my flesh, followed by a warmth that makes my stomach tremble.

"Yes!" I gasp, the flash of pain driving me to speak. "Yes, I liked teasing you."

Maks comes around to face me, one finger hooking beneath my chin so he can tilt my face toward his. "You might not say the same thing after I'm done with you," he murmurs.

I shiver, my knees starting to quake from the dark promise in his tone.

"Let's play a little game, then, shall we? And we'll see if you like being teased as much as you like handing it out."

Heart hammering against my ribcage, I wait with bated breath to learn what he could possibly mean by that. I'm used to teasing men. I was trained to do it, and do it well, when I was working at Lady

Venus. That's what men came to experience at a strip club. The promise of sex without the follow-through.

I hadn't even considered whether a man could tease a woman.

"I'm going to play with you, and the only rule you have to follow is that you won't come," he states.

Releasing my chin, he tucks the whip beneath his arm so he can twist the small rod until it makes a low buzzing noise. I gasp as he brushes it across my nipple a moment later and a jolt of euphoria flashes through me.

It's a vibrator. The silicon covering is like silk across my sensitive nub, and he gently circles each one, making them pucker more intensely.

Then he plays with the silver chain, running it through his fingers in front of my face. When his fingers find the small clip at the end, he opens it and deliberately latches it onto one of my hard nipples.

"Hollyhocks in May!" I whimper, the pressure pinching the tip of my breast intensifying the pulse in my nipple and at the same time making my core ache for relief. It almost hurts, but mostly, it floods me with fresh heat.

He does the same to my other nipple, connecting them with the fine chain. Then he gives it a light tug, igniting a fire in my belly and urging a groan from my lips.

Taking up the vibrator once more, he slowly traces it down my stomach to the peak of my thighs.

I have no clue how I'm supposed to stop myself from coming once the toy finds my clit over my panties and Maks starts to circle it with expert accuracy. Gasping, I twitch convulsively, my hips jerking as intense pleasure crackles up my spine. There's no way I'm going to be able to hold off for long.

"I can't!" I cry, my wail verging on panic.

I'm so turned on that I'm at the edge of release within a matter of seconds.

And to my relief, Maks removes the vibrator.

He leaves a throbbing pulse in its wake.

In an instant, my relief turns into devastation, and again my hips jerk forward, seeking the pleasure from a moment ago.

"You can't what?" Maks purrs, his lips capturing the lobe of my ear to end his sentence.

"It feels so good," I whimper, trying to explain without having to say something so exceedingly intimate.

"This?" Maks places the vibrator against my clit once more, drawing a euphoric moan from me.

"Yes!"

He hums appreciatively as my breaths grow ragged, my chest heaving with the intensity of my pleasure. All the while, the clamps leave my nipples throbbing, and the chain lightly taps against my stomach.

Running the vibrator slowly over my panties and along my folds, Maks stokes my arousal, awakening in me a reckless sense of abandon. And this time, though I know I'm dangerously close to climax, I bite my lip and try to hold on.

The burst of tingling magic that explodes through me a moment later leaves me breathless. I'm coming hard and fast before I even know what hit me. I cry out with the intense pleasure, my knees buckling with sudden weakness.

Shuddering, I ride wave after wave of ecstasy, my mind too overcome with relief to fear that I've broken Maks's rule.

"Did you just come?" he asks, his voice carrying a note of lethal warning.

"Y–Yes," I stutter, a knot of cold anticipation tightening in my stomach.

"And what did I tell you about doing that?"

His voice is steady, even patient, and that makes my agonizing anticipation multiply exponentially.

"That it's against the rules?" I try to add a silent apology into my response.

"And do you know what happens when you break the rules, my pet?"

I don't know why that term of endearment makes my heart race. But it does.

"I get spanked?" I suggest, catching sight of the flogger out of the corner of my eye.

"Very good."

The leather strips clap against the backs of my thighs a moment later, catching me just beneath my butt cheeks. I yelp at the stinging punishment. Then a familiar heat starts to pool in my belly as my panties grow wet with fresh arousal.

It's a very similar game to the one Maks and I played four years ago—though perhaps pushing my boundaries a bit further—and just like last time, my body responds with a fiery pleasure unlike anything I ever would have imagined.

"Shall we try again?" he says, coming close to place the vibrator against my clit once more.

And this time, on the tail of my first orgasm, I'm so intensely sensitive that it almost feels like an electric shock as he awakens my excitement once more.

If I thought it was going to be hard to resist coming before, now, it will be nearly impossible. But that doesn't stop Maks. It doesn't even slow him down. Instead, he pushes aside the skimpy fabric covering my pussy and sets the vibrator directly against my flesh.

Within seconds, he has me on the brink of climax, the vibrator swirling my slick arousal over my clit in the most tantalizing way. All the while, Maks's strong hand kneads my ass, explores the expanse of my torso, and teases my nipples by tugging lightly on the delicate silver chain.

"Please," I whimper, hoping he'll take mercy on me because I can't hold on much longer.

"Please what?" he murmurs against my neck.

"Please let me come?" I moan.

He hums a low, enticing sound. "Since you asked so nicely..." he teases. Then he removes the vibrator from my skin completely.

An agonized groan rips up my throat at the aching loss that follows.

Shortly behind it is an intense frustration as my muscles tighten, seeking the relief that I was so close to obtaining.

"Maks!" I whine.

"You want more?" he teases and brings the vibrator back to my clit.

I think my brain might just explode from the way he's torturing me with pleasure. I would do just about anything to come right now, and he's deliberately withholding it from me.

"*Yes!*" I beg, grinding forward against his hand and the vibrator.

And again, he brings me within moments of release before removing the toy.

"Frustrating, isn't it?" he growls. "Having someone show you the gates of heaven and tell you not to go inside."

I nod, my body humming with need.

"Now, let me teach you a fun little secret," he breathes, enfolding me in one strong arm as he comes to stand behind me.

The heat of his rock-hard chest against my back sears into my flesh. I melt against him, panting and eager for his touch.

"Edging—exciting you without letting you come—makes the eventual climax that much stronger," he murmurs.

And this time when he places the vibrator against my clit, I nearly jump out of my skin. Fireworks explode through my core, heating my chest to an inferno as my body twitches and trembles with unbridled pleasure.

"Please let me come. Oh, hellfire. Please, please, please, *please*," I whimper, on the verge of tears I'm so overstimulated.

And then he whispers the sweetest words I've ever heard. "Come for me, *krasivaya*."

The euphoria rips through me like a hurricane, turning my body into molten lava. I cry out, so consumed by my release that I don't care how loud I am. All I can think about is the pleasure blasting through my veins.

"Good girl," Maks praises, his arm an iron support around me as he eases the pressure on my bound wrists.

As I ride wave after pulsing wave of my orgasm, he reaches up to untie me from the frame. My legs are too weak to hold my weight in the wake of the most powerful climax I've ever experienced, but Maks seems to know that before I even start to fall.

Scooping me up in his muscular arms, he carries me like a bride to the bed.

21

MAKSIM

I love playing with Heidi, exploring what gives her pleasure, discovering what turns her on. Her genuine, unhindered response to my touch is dangerously arousing, her natural sensuality intoxicating.

Something about her awakens in me a deep protective urge. I'm being far more careful with her than I usually would be with the girls I sleep with because I find I don't want to cross the hard line that might frighten her away.

I'm not sure if it's her endearing Southern accent and the fact that her version of cursing entails stringing complete nonsense into a phrase or if it's because I met her when she was still so young and innocent. Maybe it's her scared doe eyes combined with her willingness to trust me. But I want to make sure she feels safe, that she can rely on me.

Whatever this new instinct is, I find giving her pleasure far too exhilarating, and the more of her I claim, the more I want. She smells vaguely of cinnamon and vanilla, a warm combination that envelops me as I carry her to the bed.

Laying her down, I settle on top of her, spreading her knees with my hips as our bodies align. My need to be inside her is almost agonizing, and yet, I want to take my time, to thoroughly enjoy every second of her.

Kissing her deeply, I tangle my tongue with hers. Heidi sighs, her arms wrapping around my shoulders as her fingers comb into my hair. Tingles race down my spine as her nails graze lightly across my scalp.

Running my hand down her thigh to the tops of her stockings, I grasp her knee and raise it, spreading her legs further as I fold her in half, exposing her lace-clad pussy. She mirrors the motion with her other leg, and my cock throbs dangerously as the heat of her excitement presses against my erection.

"I need you," she whispers, her hips rocking forward to demonstrate exactly what she means.

God damn, this woman is sexy as hell. I need her too, so desperately I'm about to blow my load. Instead, I give myself a moment of reprieve. Sitting up, I shove my joggers down, releasing my swollen, aching cock.

Heidi bites her lip, her eyes combing down my body to take in the sight of my arousal as her fingers brush across my pecs and abs.

I don't have the patience to take off her garter belt and stockings. Instead, I grip the waistline of her white lace thong and give a forceful jerk.

Heidi yelps, her eyes flying wide as I rip the lingerie from her body. Her breasts, still caught in nipple clamps, heave as awe transforms her face. A deep satisfaction fills me. Reaching between her thighs, I stroke my fingers along her slit to see just how wet she is from my display of strength.

"*Blyat,*" I groan as my fingers come away slick. Then I guide them to her lips. "Taste," I command, my voice low and hoarse.

Her lips part, and she lifts her head off the bed just enough to wrap them around my fingers. Her tongue strokes lightly across the tips, and my balls tighten at the sexy way she sucks me clean.

"You are so *fucking* sexy," I growl.

Then I redirect my attention to her nipples. They've been in the clamps for as long as I should let them. It's going to be a wakeup call for Heidi when I take them off. I do, starting with the right.

Heidi gasps, and when I close my lips around the taut nub a moment later, soothing the ache with gentle circles of my tongue, she whimpers. "Hallelujah!" she breathes, her back arching so her full breast presses into my face.

I repeat the process with her other nipple, taking the time to massage her exposed breast at the same time.

"Good *night*," she whispers, her breath hitching. "I think I'm going to come."

Rumbling approval, I reach down to press my fingers to her clit, circling it as I continue to suck her nipples each in turn. Then I ease my fingers inside her wet entrance.

Heidi cries out, her body tensing as her walls clamp down around my fingers. Then her pussy starts to flutter as she comes once again.

I can't wait any longer.

Seeing her in the throes of passion, her body writhing with ecstasy, completely undoes me. Sliding my fingers out of her, I replace them with my cockhead and the feeling of heavenly bliss as her warm, slick walls wrap around me and drive all reason from my mind.

I shove inside her, relishing the way she takes me deep inside her glorious depths. Heidi cries out, her aftershocks still fluttering around my rock-hard girth. Her fingernails dig into my back as I brace my forearms on either side of her shoulders.

Then I start to thrust. Hot, panting breaths burst from our lips, mingling in the air around us as my face hovers just inches from hers. I slant my mouth over hers to claim it for my own, the same way I'm claiming her pussy.

"You feel incredible," I growl against her lips, my cock aching with the sinful sensation of her slick arousal so silky and her warm, wet depths so enticing.

I shouldn't have started without putting on a condom because now I never want to stop. Heidi seems fully on board with the plan. Our rhythm is desperate, almost punishing, and yet that only intensifies the euphoria.

"Come for me, *krasivaya*," I command as the familiar pressure starts to build at the base of my spine.

She cries my name as she obeys me, and it's pure agony not to come inside her. As her walls clamp down around me, milking my throbbing cock, red sunbursts explode behind my eyelids. I drive into her for as long as I can.

As she unravels beneath me, her muscles relaxing as her orgasm consumes her, I pull out. It takes one stroke as I grip my shaft, aiming for her perfect breasts, and I release my load in several powerful bursts, sending pearly cum across her chest.

Heidi's breasts heave, her flushed cheeks darkening with color as she looks down at the aftermath of my release. Then her gaze travels upward to meet mine with a smoldering heat.

"Okay, why was that so sexy?" she asks, her tone baffled.

I chuckle low in my belly. "I'm glad you think so." Leaning forward without smearing the cum between us, I reward her with a passionate kiss. "I'll get something to clean you up," I murmur.

Then I rise from the bed and head to the sink to soak a washcloth in warm water.

Heidi's striking hazel eyes watch me as I approach once more. Though her breathing has calmed some, her cheeks are still the most exhilarating shade of rose.

"Did you like our game tonight?" I ask as I settle onto the bed beside her and gently wipe her breasts clean.

Her eyelids sink closed, her face taking on a deeply relaxed expression. "Yes," she confesses, her coloring intensifying yet again.

"And that embarrasses you?" I ask, intrigued.

A nervous giggle escapes her. "No. Just . . . it's very new to me. I never thought I'd enjoy being punished. I guess I never even really thought about being punished until I met you. I feel . . . inexperienced? Maybe that makes me more self-conscious."

"But you're not self-conscious when you dance," I observe, catching her meaning.

"Right."

"Hmm." Finishing her ablutions, I stand to toss the washcloth in the sink and collect my joggers.

Heidi pulls her knees up to her chest, crossing her ankles at the same time to cover herself better, and the position, with her heels still strapped to her feet, is an appealing blend of modest allure. "Hmm?" she repeats. "What does that mean?"

"I suppose I like the way your inexperience makes you so . . . open. I enjoy exploring with you."

Trapping her lower lip between her teeth, Heidi gives me a shy smile. "Thanks. I like exploring with you too."

"Would you care for some wine?" I offer. Once again, I find I'm not ready to let her go home yet, and since she won't be staying the night, I hope I can entice her with a glass.

"That sounds nice." Then Heidi's eyes dart down to her stocking-clad legs, as if she's only just realizing she doesn't have clothes.

Since I destroyed her undies in our passion, she doesn't have anything to cover her.

"I'll get you a shirt," I suggest.

"Thanks," she breathes gratefully.

When she doesn't move to stand, I leave her in the playroom to find her something appropriate. I grab a casual button-down from my closet and return, tossing it to her where she still sits, her knees drawn up, on the bed.

Only then does she stand, slipping her arms through the sleeves and closing several buttons before she rolls the cuffs up to her elbows. She looks sexy as hell in my shirt, the hem falling just below the curve of her ass so her long legs are on full display.

Scooping her hair over one shoulder, Heidi leads the way to the kitchen this time as I hold the playroom door open for her. As she leans against the center island, I pull out two wine glasses and open a bottle, then I collect them all in hand and jerk my chin, gesturing for Heidi to follow me into the living room.

As soon as my eyes fall on the couch, the image of her straddling my lap fills my mind, and though we've only just finished, I could easily be ready for round two just by the memory.

"So," Heidi starts as she settles onto the seat beside me, "what kind of business do you and your brothers operate?"

"Banking and investments, mostly. We have a special focus on restaurants in the Bay Area." That's a very simplified, PG version of what my brothers and I do, but confessing that I have shady dealings that often involve illegal business and money laundering might not be the best information to hand out to a fling.

I prefer to keep the girls I sleep with at arm's length. Then they have nothing on me when we go our separate ways.

"That's really neat. And you have . . . enemies because of it?" Heidi's lips quirk in a wolfish grin that tells me she's not so easily fooled.

"The restaurant industry is a cut-throat business," I joke, passing her a glass of wine before taking a sip of my own.

Heidi laughs, the musical sound carefree. She takes a sip of her own wine and delicately sets down the glass. "Are you and your brothers close?"

"We work in the same offices, so my brothers are constantly underfoot."

Again she laughs, her eyes sparkling as she leans back into the plush couch. "You make them sound like children."

"Sometimes, they are. No, I'm kidding—mostly. At times, they can be infuriating, but I'm blessed to have the opportunity to work with my brothers. It creates an unshakeable trust and confidence in our business. There is no loyalty like family loyalty."

Heidi nods thoughtfully, her smile taking on a melancholy edge that piques my curiosity. But I don't ask. Better to keep the conversation light. This kind of arrangement tends to take a more serious turn when I let questions get too personal.

"You're an interior decorator, is that right?" I ask, diverting the conversation to avoid digging deeper.

"Yeah. I've always loved home magazines and learning the new trends in decor, so it seemed like a good fit. And my business has really taken off in the last few years—once I finished my degree."

"Is that how you used the money I gave you?" I ask, enjoying the thought that I might have made a small contribution to the career she wanted. "Paid off your student loans or something?" I could see how a college-aged girl might be tempted to relieve herself of that financial burden if the offer was right.

"Oh, um . . . well, in a way, I guess." Heidi takes a sip of wine as if to mask her discomfort.

I frown. "You guess?"

"Well, I was actually paying my way through school as I went. I hadn't taken out any loans. But then my mom got sick with cancer, and since she didn't have insurance, I had to quit school to help with her medical expenses."

Understanding hits me at the same time I register a deep sadness in her eyes—the same sadness that I'm all too familiar with, the haunting kind of emptiness that only comes with terrible loss.

I know I shouldn't ask, but I can't help myself. "And your mom?"

Heidi's head hangs as her gaze drops to the floor, and she shakes her head slowly. "The brain tumor was too aggressive. They couldn't stop it. She died just over two years ago now." She sniffles softly, staring at her hands as she picks at her nails. "I still miss her every day."

Deep, echoing empathy squeezes my heart, and my chest suddenly feels tight with emotion. "I'm sorry. I know what it's like to lose someone so close."

Heidi's chin lifts so she can meet my eyes, and a single tear rolls down her high cheekbone. Before I can think about it, I reach out to cup her jaw, brushing the tear away with the pad of my thumb.

Then we both seem to realize the intimacy of the gesture. Heidi draws herself upright, squaring her shoulders and quickly pulling herself together as I clear my throat, retrieving my hand.

At the same time, I fight to shove the emotion down, forcing it into a small, dark chamber of my heart. I don't have room for emotions like that in my life. I need to remember to keep my objectivity.

"Anyway," Heidi says, brushing off her momentary vulnerability, "my night with you ended up paying for her chemo—and the alternative treatments that followed when chemo proved ineffective. It also covered my last year of college tuition and helped me get my business up and running."

Somehow, this revelation hits me deeply. I'm glad my selfish offer that night made such a difference in her life. But I keep that to myself.

Heidi's lips part, as if she's about to say more, but then she doesn't, and I don't press her because I'm walking a thin line of developing genuine feelings for her, and that's not allowed. I need to shut this conversation down before I get myself in deeper trouble.

"Are you ready to go home?" I ask, the question coming across as rather brusque.

But Heidi doesn't seem to take it that way. Instead, she gives a small but warm smile and nods, as if I've suggested the best remedy for her grief.

We rise together, and Heidi collects her trench coat from the floor. It is quickly becoming my favorite item of clothing in her wardrobe.

"Keep the shirt," I offer as she moves to unbutton it.

That seems to disarm her. "You don't mind?"

"I have more than enough."

Again, Heidi smiles, this time the gratitude burning away some of the lingering sadness. "Thanks." She shrugs into her coat a moment later and buttons it all the way up to hide the scandalous wardrobe she's hiding underneath.

I walk her to the elevator, my hand coming to rest instinctively on the small of her back, and the doors ding open a moment later. Pyotr and Sev appear wordlessly in the entryway as Heidi turns to face me, and they step inside the elevator to hold the door until she's ready.

"Tonight was fun," she confirms, her eyes taking on a mischievous twinkle.

"Yes, we should do it again sometime," I tease.

Rising onto her tiptoes, Heidi brushes a soft kiss across my lips. Then she steps back into the elevator.

As the doors close, I find it unacceptably hard to watch her go.

22

HEIDI

Standing in the living room of the Painted Lady I've been hired to furnish, I snap several pictures of the current layout, getting it from several different angles. Then I move on to the kitchen. I spend some time brainstorming in each room, jotting down ideas based on what the owners are interested in and how I might incorporate that into their home.

It's a beautiful home, one I'm eager and excited to be working on. This is every interior decorator's dream challenge. But today, I find my thoughts particularly preoccupied.

By a particular Russian businessman with the body of a god and the sexiest voice of temptation. As I work alone, surrounded by silence and the din of my own thoughts, I find it particularly challenging to focus on anything but him.

Something about spending time with Maks just feels right, so right that I almost decided to tell him about Sarah last night. It was on the tip of my tongue after confessing how I put the money he paid me to use. Because the truth is that his generosity also helped me get my feet on the ground as a parent.

But that doesn't mean I should tell him about our daughter. Saying anything would be a mistake because Maks doesn't want to be a father. He said it himself—he doesn't want a family. And I don't want to force that upon either of them.

Most importantly, Sarah doesn't need to experience the kind of loss or rejection that would come from his walking away. No, Sarah is mine, and I can love her enough for both of us.

I can't lose sight of what I am to Maks, and I have to keep repeating it until it's thoroughly engrained. What we have is just a contract, a brief respite from reality. He told me that from the start, so it would be unfair of me to expect more.

He can't help that he's gregarious, charming, gorgeous, and far too good at sex.

But that's all it is. Sex. I just have to keep telling myself that.

My phone rings as I enter the master bedroom, and I pick up without checking the caller ID. "Turner Interior Design."

"When will you be heading back to the office?" Zoe asks, her tone warning me that she's up to something.

"Why? What's happened? What have you and my daughter gotten into this time?" Zoe and Sarah never fail to get into mischief when I leave them alone together for too long.

"*Nothing*," Zoe says, her tone guiltily defensive. "But she, ah, may have left you a surprise on your drafting table."

Though I know Zoe can't see me, I can feel one eyebrow creeping toward my hairline.

"I know! I know!" she says as if she's reading my exact expression. "I lost track of her for, like, two seconds. How was I supposed to know she has a bloodhound's nose for sniffing out markers and a penchant for drawing on tables?"

That sounds like Sarah. She loves drawing, and few things can deter her from putting her art skills to the test—regardless of the medium. Zoe knows it too. We've already painted the living room twice and still can't figure out where Sarah's getting the markers—or stashing them.

In truth, I find it rather adorable. I love that she has a passion for creativity, but it won't be good when she turns her focus to the walls at school. Fortunately, so far, they seem to understand that crayons are the only way to keep their environment safe from my artistic terror.

"Well, thanks for the heads up. I should be back within the hour."

"I'll try and clean it off before you get here."

Releasing a soft chuckle, I let Zoe off the hook. "Take a picture before you do?"

"Yes, ma'am."

Hanging up with Zoe, I get to work taking pictures of the last few rooms in the house, brainstorming for my meeting with the couple this afternoon. Then I pile back into my BMW and head toward the office, picking up lunch for us on the way.

"I brought sandwiches!" I call as I open the swinging glass door.

"Mommy!" Sarah calls, hopping up from the colorful little table where she works on a coloring book as Zoe taps away at the computer.

"How was your morning?" I ask them both as Zoe greets me with a bright smile and stands to help with my armful.

Sarah beats her to me, wrapping my leg in an adorable bear hug. This is my kind of greeting. Zoe arrives a moment later to showcase my daughter's handiwork on the drafting table in my office.

She's done an adorable mockup of a home—two outside walls, a roof, and the insides divided into four rooms. But what I love is that Sarah actually decorated each room like I would on a proper mockup. The top left corner is a bedroom with a bright-purple bed that sits opposite a purple dresser. The dining room has a table with three chairs around it. The living room, a couch and a TV. Sarah put serious thought into the home's layout, and even if she used the marker directly on my table, it warms my heart to see her inclination to practice my profession.

Wordlessly, Zoe and I share a smile. Then she collects the food, and I scoop Sarah up and plant her on my hip.

"Do you have something to tell Mommy?" I ask her.

Sarah plucks at the collar of my shirt, her eyes decidedly avoiding mine. "I colored on your table. I'm sorry, Mommy." She sniffles slightly.

"Thank you for apologizing. Will you draw me another house on paper? Then I can keep it. That's the nice thing about paper."

Sarah meets my eyes now, her smile sudden and brilliant. "Okay."

"Good girl. Now let's wash our hands so we can eat."

We share lunch together, and then I get back to work, pulling up available furniture and applying colors, flooring, and light fixtures into the computer program I use to offer customers a visual of my intended layout.

I put together three different suggested options so I can get a better feel for what they want. Sarah plays quietly, some alone at her table, some with Zoe. My best friend and my daughter are two peas in a pod—adorable and absolute troublemakers—and I don't know what I would do without either of them.

Zoe makes it possible for me to bring my daughter in to work, and I know that means the world to both me and Sarah. Over the years, Zoe has become more like a sister than my friend. And after Mom died, she's been the single best support in my life.

My meeting with the Hansons starts promptly at three, and miraculously, though Maks continued to infiltrate my thoughts right up until their arrival, I managed to put together a solid presentation of the vision I have for their home.

"We love it," Mrs. Hanson says after discussing quietly with her husband.

"You're sure? You haven't even seen my alternate suggestions."

"No, you've really nailed our vision," Mr. Hanson says. "I love the way you've opened the space between the living room and dining room, and this classic lighting throughout? That will really fit with the soul of the property."

My shoulders relax slightly knowing that my newest and most challenging clients to date are happy with my mockups. "That's great. I'll start ordering the materials today. I can have the painters in as early as tomorrow, if that works for you. Looks like the kitchen appliances are the only thing on backorder, but they should be in shortly after the flooring is done."

"How long do you think the project will take?"

"Total? I think we can get this done in three months. The bathrooms and kitchen will take the longest. But my contractors are the best, very good at sticking to a schedule. And if you're happy with the tile I've chosen, we shouldn't have any supply setbacks. I've checked to make sure they're in stock."

They share a look and grin.

"That sounds perfect," Mr. Hanson says.

"Wonderful." Rising along with the Hansons, I shake each of their hands in turn.

"We have several friends we'll be recommending you to—friends in search of a high-end interior designer," Mrs. Hanson adds. "You've been such a pleasure to work with, and the quality of your vision only makes me more confident we made the right choice putting our trust in you." She beams, her red-painted lips stretching across her round face in delight.

"Thank you so much. I can't tell you what that means to me and my business. I look forward to getting started!"

The Hansons exit my office a few minutes later, and Zoe and Sarah give them a collective goodbye from behind the front desk as the smartly dressed couple head out the glass front door.

Only then do I feel like I can breathe. Something about showcasing my vision to a client for the first time is always so nerve-racking. Even after years of designing concepts that my clients have loved.

My phone buzzes in my back pocket, and I pull it out. Maks's name flashes across the screen, and my heart skips a beat. After thinking about him all day, I wonder if his ears must have been burning.

"Hello?" I answer, a smile tugging at my lips before I even hear his voice.

"What are your plans for later tonight?" His tone today is much more amicable—not commanding like yesterday.

I wonder if that means he's in a better mood or if he took my words to heart. Whatever the case, his question makes my stomach do an excited flip-flop. Glancing out at the front office, I watch Zoe talking with Sarah, and I hope she'll be okay keeping an ear out once again.

"Hmm, I was hoping I might find a playroom and a man who knows how to use it."

"Good," he rumbles, his deep voice sending a giddy ripple through my chest. "Then my car will pick you up at ten."

"Great."

I bite my lip as we hang up, aware that I'm ridiculously excited over seeing him for a third night in a row. Rather than satiating my craving for him, the more I see Maks, the more I seem to want him. I don't want to think about what that will mean when our time together comes to an end.

For now, I intend to just enjoy it.

23

MAKSIM

Sitting in the leather-clad interior of my sleek, black Escalade, the engine purrs softly as my brothers and I wait for the car to pull to a stop. The midday sun blazes overhead, casting a harsh light on the upscale hotel we're about to close on. Its modern glass façade glints with the promise of lucrative returns.

But even with victory within reach when it comes to out-maneuvering Aleksandr Volkov on this closing, my mind can't help but stray to Heidi. The corner of my mouth twitches into the shadow of a grin as one of her ridiculous, nonsensical phrases enters my mind unbidden.

Apparently, it's a Southern thing—to toss together a random string of words that vaguely sound like the curse word she's thinking of. After remaining baffled by her expressions for too many nights, I had to ask. She'd been shocked that I wouldn't know about the tradition. It's one I find I'm swiftly becoming a fan of, even if I don't understand it in the least.

But the woman I associate them with has piqued my interest and satiated something inside me no one else has these last four lonely years.

Heidi's been over nearly every night since our chance meeting at

Fiasco's, and after almost two weeks of seeing her, I have to admit I'm in a better mood than I have been in years. She's a breath of fresh air amid the constant anger that has gripped me since the day Symphony died. The day Aleksandr took her from me.

From the corner of my eye, I catch Dimitri and Alexei sharing a knowing glance. Their smirks alert me to the fact that they've held some discussion outside my knowledge and something I've done has just confirmed their conclusion.

"What?" I demand, turning my eyes on them as the Escalade pulls up to the curb.

"Have you finally decided to take our advice and start dating a girl, Maks?" Alexei quips, a mischievous glint in his eyes.

"What gives you that idea?"

"Oh, come on," Dimitri steps in. "We've heard your phone calls in the office. Setting up late-night rendezvous with someone named *Heidi*. And you've been . . . chipper for days. You've got a girl in your life, and not just the usual fuck toy you're so hellbent on keeping. Admit it."

Neither make a move to exit the car, even though we're at a standstill and the meeting's due to start any minute.

Cocking my eyebrow, I try and fail to keep the touch of amusement from my tone. They're so desperate to see me settle down. But it's not going to happen. It doesn't matter that I've found someone who can actually lift my mood when she's not even around. "Don't get your hopes up. Heidi's just another 'fuck toy', as you two insist on calling them. But she doesn't mean anything to me."

It feels wrong saying that about her, and the words leave a sour taste in my mouth. Funny, because I haven't really cared about my brothers' nagging term for the women I sleep with. But I can't picture Heidi as a toy. She's too *alive*, too independent and full of personality.

Alexei and Dimitri share another look. They seem to have noticed it, too, the way I cringed when I put the offensive term so close to Heidi's name. Momentary silence fills the car.

Then I clear my throat. "Ready to buy the Bay View Hotel?" I ask, abruptly redirecting them.

"More than." Dimitri gives a wicked grin, his steel gaze matching my own. Any opportunity to undermine Aleksandr Volkov is a victory in his book. Mine too.

Alexei gives a more noncommittal shrug. "Ready to screw a certain Bratva bastard over. That's for sure."

Stepping out of the car, we straighten our crisp designer suits and head through the front doors of the luxury hotel we all but own. The grandeur of the hotel's lobby welcomes us as we stride in, our demeanor drawing the attention of both guests and staff alike. Polished marble floors reflect the elegant chandeliers above, and the scent of fresh flowers wafts through the air.

I lead the way, my confident stride exuding authority, followed closely by my brothers, who wear expressions that radiate a sense of quiet power. Behind us, our small contingent of bodyguards finish the commanding entrance, one meant to intimidate, should Thompson be thinking about backing out last-minute.

"Mr. Federov," a woman greets me before we reach reception. She strides forward in high black pumps and a pencil skirt as sharp as her expression. Then her eyes dart to my brothers as her composure falters just a hair. "And . . . Mr. Federov, Mr. Federov." She acknowledges them each in turn with a nod. "Mr. Thompson and his lawyers are already waiting for you upstairs. I'll take you to the conference room."

Gesturing to the elevator bank, she escorts us, pressing the call button and stepping into the elevator with me, my two brothers, and the three guards accompanying us.

Mr. Thompson stands as we enter the room, his shoulders appearing slumped in defeat. He knows that he has little left to bargain with, and the deal is now inevitable. Greed might have helped us get him to this point, but I detect a hint of regret in his face now.

Considering the price we're offering for the Bay View, he should be anything but disappointed. Even if he's selling against his will. But that doesn't stop a hint of guilt from trickling into my gut, as it does every time I snap up a deal that will expand our family's empire and strengthen the claim on our territory.

"Gentlemen," he says with a weary smile, his voice carrying the weight of resignation. "Welcome back. I believe my lawyers have drawn up the appropriate paperwork, so we are ready to sign and make this deal official."

I offer him a nod of acknowledgment as I silently note the toll our negotiations have taken on the hotel owner. I wonder how much pressure Aleksandr must have put on him after he found out that Mr. Thompson physically ripped up the noncompete contract Aleksandr had made him sign.

Relief joins the resignation in his eyes as we settle into the chairs around the conference table. I wonder if he's not grateful to be handing over the rope in this metaphorical tug-of-war between Bratvas.

After I exchange polite nods with his lawyers, they slide several thick contracts across the polished wood.

"It's been a pleasure doing business with you," Thompson says, though his words ring hollow.

Leveling him with a piercing gaze, I study the hotel owner for a moment longer, then I offer a thin, almost imperceptible smile. "Likewise. Shall we proceed?"

He gives a nod, and I drop my eyes to the paperwork.

Dimitri and I take our time, each reading through the contract from front to back to ensure nothing in the language might attempt to disrupt our acquisition. Though neither of us went to law school, our father taught us the importance of understanding the contracts we sign. After decades in the business, I know all the tricks and loopholes that business owners might try to use to cling to their companies.

But not Mr. Thompson. It seems that our added pressure—compliments of Iosif—has paid off, and the contract looks nearly pristine.

"Very good, Mr. Thompson," I praise, signing the paperwork

before passing it on to Dimitri, who follows suit before handing it to Alexei.

Thompson is the last to sign, and he only hesitates a moment before definitively pressing the pen tip to the paper.

Next comes the cashier's check, which I slide back across the table toward the nervous business owner. Mr. Thompson takes it with shaking fingers. He swallows hard as he counts the zeros, making sure they're right.

Only then does he seem to grasp that the deal is done. He's now millions of dollars richer—and no longer the owner of the building around us, the business within its walls, or even the chairs we sit on.

Standing from the conference table with set determination on his face, he silently extends his hand to shake a final time. His once-confident, almost cocky demeanor has been tempered by the weight of the documents he just signed. No longer does he own the hotel he poured his life's work into. And for a fraction of a second, I could almost feel bad.

But not in light of the victory we've won against Aleksandr.

Rising from my seat, I accept his hand, shaking it firmly. "Thank you for your trust, Mr. Thompson."

He nods, his gaze dropping to the floor. "It was a difficult decision, but I believe this is for the best," he admits, though parting with the hotel was not entirely by choice.

"Rest assured, we have plans to bring this hotel to new heights," Dimitri assures him. "Your legacy will live on in the success of this place."

He and Alexei shake hands with Thompson as well.

Mr. Thompson forces a smile, though it doesn't reach his eyes. "I hope so."

As we leave the conference room, contract securely in hand, the weight of our newfound ownership hangs heavily in the air. The successful purchase is a testament to our strength and determination, but it also marks another step on our relentless path toward vengeance against Aleksandr.

He tried to undermine us and failed—a more and more common

occurrence now that we know his game and will stop at nothing to beat him. And I plan to shut him out completely.

It feels good to have such a big win under our belt. The Bay View Hotel is a significant landmark to the city that will bring in major income and allow us significant freedom with the business we run.

We've dealt Aleksandr some pretty massive blows lately, but I won't call it quits until he's dead. I couldn't care less if his business or Bratva survives, and though we're no closer to accomplishing the physical goal, figuratively, we are tightening the noose around his throat.

Surprisingly, though, as we exit the Bay View Hotel, I find that the unbridled rage I've felt for so long when I think about killing Aleksandr isn't so strong anymore. I still want the man dead. I will see it done for the safety of my family if nothing else.

But something about Heidi's presence in my life has started to soothe that wrath that has completely consumed me for the last four years. Where once, my sole goal in life was to take Aleksandr's head for killing my fiancée, that might no longer be the force that drives me.

24

HEIDI

My heart never fails to skip a beat when I see Maks's name pop up on my phone's caller ID. We've spent all but two nights together over nearly the last two weeks, and the more time I spend with him, the less I want it to end.

Trying to hide the giddy anticipation that quivers in my chest, I answer the call. "Hello?"

"Hello, *krasivaya*." Maks's voice comes through the phone as smooth as a saxophone, his tone demanding respect even in his greeting. "Are you available for dinner tonight? I'd like to take you somewhere nice."

The request hangs in the air, and I can almost hear my heart skip a beat. This isn't just one of our late-night trysts. This is more personal. Dinner. And while that seems like such a simple first step in a relationship, my mind races with a mix of anxiety and anticipation.

The request puts my stomach in knots as I wonder how this might shift the dynamic of our very narrow parameters on a relationship. What we have in place is supposed to be strictly business—well, very pleasurable business.

Dinner might permanently change that dynamic in a way I can't possibly begin to fathom. And yet, the prospect almost excites me.

The pause is agonizingly long before I finally manage to stammer a response. "Dinner? Like ... a date?"

Maks chuckles softly, a deep, resonant sound that sends shivers down my spine. "Something like that."

My heart flutters as I think about the possibilities, the uncharted territory this could lead to. I've tried to keep things in perspective between us, but Maks's commanding presence has a way of breaking down my defenses in a way I didn't expect.

"I'd like that," I say, trying to keep my voice steady.

But before I can finish with a "let me check my schedule," Maks cuts in.

"Great. I'll make the reservations. Can you be ready for the car to pick you up by seven?"

"Uh, can you hold on just one sec?" I ask, reeling from the speed with which he's changing gears.

"Of course." He sounds exceedingly relaxed, as though this is a perfectly normal request.

Perhaps it would be if it weren't me and Maks, two people who haven't shared a single meal together but have had sex nearly twenty times in less than two weeks.

"Thanks." Quickly muting my phone, I stand from my desk and head to the frosted glass door separating my office from the main office.

Poking my head out around the door, I spot Zoe sitting at the front desk, working diligently on my schedule for the week. "Hey, Zoe?" I ask tentatively.

"Yeah, Boss?" she asks, knowing full well that I hate it when she calls me that.

I take a deep breath, trying to find the right words to explain the situation. "Maks just called. He wants to take me out to dinner tonight."

Zoe's eyes widen with surprise, and she abandons her work to give me her full attention. "Dinner? That's a big step up from your . . . casual arrangement. Are you considering it?"

I nod slowly, my thoughts still swirling. "Yes, I am. But I need your help."

She leans in, her curiosity piqued. "Sure, what's up?"

"Sarah," I say, my heart sinking a little when I think about skipping a meal with her. I haven't since she was born. "Obviously, I can't take her with me, and I don't want to impose on you, but . . ."

Zoe flashes me a reassuring smile. "Say no more. I can take care of Sarah for the evening. We'll stay up late eating popcorn and watching PG-13 movies. It'll be great."

"Zoe," I scold, my eyebrows buckling.

"Only kidding. Of course I'll watch her. You have fun on your date." Zoe gives me a cheeky wink.

Relief washes over me. "Thank you, Zoe," I say, my voice filled with gratitude. "You're a lifesaver."

She waves it off with a chuckle. "No problem at all. I've got your back. Just promise me you'll spill all the juicy details about your date tomorrow."

I laugh, feeling a bit more at ease now that the babysitting situation is sorted. "Deal." Then I take a deep breath, feeling a mixture of nerves and excitement as I step back into my office and unmute my phone. "Yes, seven sounds perfect," I tell Maks, my pulse quickening.

"Wonderful. Then I will see you tonight. Wear something . . . nice." He sounds genuinely pleased I accepted, and the way the word "nice" rolls off his tongue makes my skin flame. "And, Heidi?"

"Hmm?"

"I know you do not normally wish to spend the night, but I have something special in mind for this evening. May I keep you until the morning? I promise you will make it to work on time."

I hesitate for a moment, my mind racing as my mouth goes dry. Spending the whole night with Maks feels like a bold move, especially considering Sarah, but something about his request tugs at my heartstrings. I want to take the plunge. "Yes, that should be fine." *Hopefully. I'll check with Zoe as soon as I'm off the phone.*

"Excellent. See you tonight." Maks sounds pleased, and I can almost picture the satisfied smirk on his face.

As I hang up the phone, my heart is racing with a mixture of excitement and uncertainty. Once more, I poke my head out of my office to catch Zoe's attention. "Soooo, I might have just agreed to spend the whole night with Maks. Is that alright? If not, I can call him back."

Zoe grins, her eyes sparkling with mischief. "I think Sarah and I can manage just fine, don't you worry. I'll bring her to the office in the morning."

Relief washes over me once again as I thank Zoe profusely. She's always been my rock, my confidante, and this is no exception.

With my plans in place, we decide to call it an early day at the office. Zoe, Sarah, and I head home together, a sense of excitement filling the air. Once we arrive home, the reality of the evening ahead sets in.

I haven't been on an actual date in so long, I can't even remember the last one. Definitely back in college, before Mom got sick. My nervous excitement sends me rushing to get ready, my heart pounding with anticipation. Full of boundless energy and curiosity, Sarah follows me around, watching with wide eyes as I select outfits and lay them out on my bed. After a half hour of indecision and second-guessing myself, finally, Zoe steps in.

Always the fashion voice of reason, she picks up two dresses—a rich forest-green silk cocktail dress and a black sheath dress with an open back and a glossy gold collar in place of a halter top. "Alright, Sarah, it's dress-up time. We need to make sure Mommy looks her absolute best for her special night out. Which dress should she wear?"

Delighted by the prospect of getting to choose my pretty dress for the evening, Sarah bounces excitedly across the bed. But when she reaches the dresses, she seems to realize the gravity of her responsibility, and she studies both dresses gravely before saying, "The green one."

Zoe and I exchange knowing glances, both of us sharing a

moment of silent amusement. Of course she picked the colorful dress. But I don't blame her. It's a striking shade of green, one that Zoe demanded I buy because it brings out my eyes.

"Thanks, sweetie," I say with a soft chuckle. "That's such a pretty dress. I love your choice. And now, I'll think of you while I wear it."

Sarah beams with pride and strokes the soft dress as I lay it on the bed beside her and put away my other options. Then it's time for hair and makeup. Sarah follows me into the bathroom, climbing up onto the vanity stool to watch as I lean over the counter to apply eyeshadow.

"Pretty," she observes as I add a thin wing of eyeliner at either corner of my eyes.

"Did you want to try some makeup on tonight?" I ask her, a smile splitting my face.

Sarah nods in wide-eyed wonder then scrambles to sit on the vanity stool.

I carefully select a few child-friendly makeup items from my own collection, including a purple eyeshadow, some blush, and a touch of lip gloss.

"Close your eyes for me," I instruct, bending with my eyeshadow brush in hand.

Sarah does as she's told, trying to hold perfectly still and watch me even as she tries to keep her eyes shut. But the task seems fairly impossible, and I barely manage to get a swipe of color onto each lid before she's peering at her reflection in the mirror.

Next comes the blush, and Sarah watches with rapt attention as I apply a small amount to her rosy cheeks. Her giggles fill the room, and I can't help but feel a surge of maternal love as her shoulders creep toward her ears.

"Does that tickle?" I ask.

"Yeah!" She giggles, wriggling harder as I use the brush to tickle her nose and neck.

Zoe watches from the doorway, her shoulder pressed against the door jamb as she makes a valiant effort not to laugh. When we finish

Sarah's look with a swipe of lip gloss, she turns around to show off to our patient witness.

"Auntie Zoe, look. I'm pretty like Mommy," Sarah says, her voice filled with awe.

I nod in agreement, my heart swelling with affection.

"You look absolutely beautiful, sweetheart," Zoe agrees.

Disinterested in the styling of my hair, Sarah gets Zoe to make her a snack before dinner, and I focus my attention on curling my hair into gentle waves. Then I slip into my green cocktail dress.

It fits me like a glove, the soft fabric like water over my curves as it follows the lines of my body and tapers into a subtle train. My favorite part of the dress is the back. The silk is cut low, stopping at the base of my spine, but a delicate green lace forms an elegant diamond-shaped panel that starts where the silk leaves off and rises to form something of a racer back that showcases my shoulder blades.

With the final touches in place, I check my reflection one last time, and a newfound confidence washes over me. Tonight is just dinner. I can do this. I can have fun and keep it casual. I want to because I'm not quite ready for my time with Maks to end, and he's made it very clear that catching feelings is a sure way to end our agreement fast.

Stepping out of my bedroom, I head to the kitchen and am rewarded by a soft gasp from Zoe. Her eyes sparkle as she admires my outfit—all the way down to the strappy black heels that I lift my skirt to showcase.

"He's going to love you in that," she observes.

"Who is?" Sarah asks, making my stomach drop uncomfortably.

Zoe cringes, her eyes apologetic as she hands the reins over to me.

"Mommy's having dinner with a friend tonight, Sarah. So you and Auntie Zoe can have a very special sleepover together. Just the two of you."

Sarah's eyes widen in shock, and she forgets all about the tangerine on her plate as she bounces excitedly. "We're having a seepover!" she informs Zoe, though Zoe has been sitting next to her this whole time.

Zoe chuckles, her eyes twinkling. "That's right. We'll have so much fun."

"And I'll be there to pick you up from school tomorrow. Okay?"

"Okay!" Sarah agrees, seeming far too excited about the new adventure to be thinking about missing me.

Smiling softly, I walk across the room to press a kiss to the top of her head. I only hope *I'm* ready to spend an entire night without my daughter. I sure hope so.

25

MAKSIM

The evening air is crisp as I step onto the rooftop of my apartment building, my chest full of an excitement I haven't felt in a long time. The helipad stretches out before me, its surface gleaming under the soft glow of the city lights. The helicopter blades whir above, casting long shadows across the concrete.

I don't often take my women on dates—dinner here and there, yes. A weekend getaway of spa treatments if I'm feeling stressed and know they might enjoy the pampering. But this will be a first with Heidi, and somehow, with her not living in my penthouse, it feels more significant.

I know she was teasing when she asked if it was a date, but the question sits in the back of my mind now, all the same.

The roof access door opens, and my breath catches in my throat as Heidi walks out in a green silk cocktail dress, the likes of which I've never seen. The stunning fabric hugs her curves until nearly down to her knees, where it expands into a flowing foot-long train behind her.

And she has on the same classy white trench coat as she did the night she came to my penthouse wearing only that and lingerie. My body responds to the triggered memory, my cock coming to half mast in an instant.

Heidi really is breathtaking, her honey-blonde hair cascading around her oval face and over her shoulders in loose waves. My eyes linger on her figure. Her eyes shine with a mix of surprise and wonder as she takes in the sunset on the city skyline before tracking to our transportation for the evening. It's a sight that never gets old for me, and I find I'm grateful for the privilege of sharing it with her tonight.

"You look beautiful," I say, my voice low and filled with heat as I put my lips beside her ear so she can hear me over the helicopter's whirling blades.

Heidi blushes, a warm, rosy hue spreading across her cheeks. "Thanks. This is . . . wow." Her voice trails off as she continues to take in the surroundings.

I offer her my arm, and after a moment, she takes it with a smile.

"Shall we?" I gesture toward the waiting helicopter.

She chuckles nervously, her hand gripping my arm a little tighter. "I can't believe we're taking *that* to dinner."

Grinning cheekily, I guide her toward the waiting chopper. "Well, it comes in handy sometimes. Have you ever been in one before?"

She simply shakes her head as I help her inside. As she precedes me, I can't help but admire the way the dress accentuates her curves. I'll have to take her to dinner more often, just so I can see her in outfits like this.

The helicopter doors close, and we lift off the rooftop, the city lights disappearing beneath us as we head south, the sunset glowing gold and pink and brilliant orange to our right.

Heidi takes it all in, her hazel eyes wide, as if she doesn't want to miss a thing. "This is amazing!"

I chuckle, a sense of satisfaction spreading through me at her joy. "I'm glad you like it. I thought it would be a unique way to start our evening. But I have plenty more surprises planned for tonight."

Heidi nods, her gaze fixed on the cityscape below as we soar down the coast. The cool breeze tousles her hair, and I can't help but steal glances at her throughout the flight. She was the right person to bring tonight. I want to celebrate my victory over Aleksandr Volkov. Closing on the Bay View Hotel today was a major statement, and tonight, I want to enjoy it by treating myself and the girl who has lifted my mood so effectively.

The helicopter lands smoothly at our destination, Prime, one of my family's many restaurants that just happens to be attached to a luxury spa. As we disembark, I offer her my hand, and she accepts it with a radiant smile.

The car is already waiting for us at the helipad, ready to transport us to dinner. As we settle inside, Heidi finally seems to find her voice once more.

"Where are we?" Her eyes continue to follow the landscape outside, tracking the coast that gives way to rolling hills and palm trees.

"Caramel."

The blunt response raises Heidi's eyebrow, and she sinks back against the seat to study me further. "And why did we fly all the way down to Caramel for dinner?"

I shrug but don't quite manage to contain my smile. "You'll see."

Heidi's eyebrow creeps higher up her face, but she seems to decide to drop it a moment later as the luxurious spa hotel comes into view.

The restaurant's ground-floor entrance through a garden at the side of the building is adorned with elegant golden doors. As I offer Heidi my arm once more and escort her up the walk, the doors open to reveal a warm, dimly lit interior. Soft jazz music fills the air, creating an atmosphere of intimacy and sophistication.

"Ah, Mr. Federov," the host greets us, his sleek black tux as professional as his demeanor.

I can feel Heidi's eyes on me as if to say, *They know you by sight?* But they should, considering my family owns this establishment and I frequent it.

We're led to a private corner table with a view of the ocean. A crystal chandelier hangs above us, casting a gentle glow on the pristine white tablecloth and fine glassware.

The menu is a work of art, one I never grow tired of, as the chef changes it seasonally, and the excitement sparkles in Heidi's eyes as she peruses the options.

"Evening, ma'am, Mr. Federov," the server says as he steps up to our table.

Once again, Heidi's eyes flash up to meet mine before she turns to give a charming hello.

"We took the liberty of selecting a bottle of 1992 Screaming Eagle's cabernet, as we know it's your favorite." The server showcases the bottle, ensuring I'm pleased with his choice.

"Wonderful." I gesture for him to proceed, and he swiftly uncorks the fine wine with practiced ease.

Then he pours it into a decanter—one of the reasons I appreciate this restaurant so highly. They treat their expensive wine the way it ought to be.

"We'll also take an order of the oysters," I inform him.

"Very good, sir." Our server gives a slight bow and departs.

"So . . . you've been here a few times?" Heidi guesses, her tone cheeky.

I chuckle. "A few," I agree. "My family owns this establishment, and I find it's a wonderful way to . . . unwind."

Heidi's cheeks color as she looks around the room with fresh eyes. "You own all this?"

"We own many restaurants, several in Caramel. And yes, we happen to own this one."

Heidi releases a low whistle. "Color me impressed."

Silence falls between us once more as her eyes revert back to the menu. "So, what's good here, Mr. Federov?" she asks teasingly as she adopts the same professional tone with which the staff have addressed me.

"I would highly recommend the lamb."

"Mmm."

Her nod of acknowledgment is just cheeky enough that I could spank her for it, and I just might do that later tonight. But her eyes flash back to the menu to read about my suggestion, so she doesn't quite catch the subtle warning look.

"Your oysters," the server states a moment later as he arrives to set the tray of oysters on the half-shell in the center of the table. "And some champagne to accompany them."

A sparkling flute is set before each of us, and as soon as the waiter departs, Heidi raises hers in a toast. "To a beautiful night."

"*Tvoyey krasote.*"

"So, is this something you do with girls?" she asks, her lips curling into a smile before she takes a delicate sip of champagne.

"Dinner?" I ask, preparing an oyster.

"Yes. Dinner."

"Sometimes," I admit. "Just because I don't do relationships doesn't mean I don't enjoy dating."

"Really?" Heidi looks baffled. "I always thought that dating was the worst part about relationships, going out to eat with random people until you find the right one."

"And then what? You stop going out to eat with them once you are sure you enjoy it?" I tease, arching an eyebrow.

Heidi laughs, her face flushing. "Well, when you put it that way..."

"I believe a married couple should date as often, if not more than, the single man. How else can you keep the spark alive?"

"You know, for someone who doesn't do romance, you certainly seem to have romantic notions."

I know it's meant to be playful, but something about Heidi's observation gets under my skin. "I never said I don't do romance. That is very different from commitment."

Swallowing her oyster, Heidi falls silent, her warm hazel eyes studying me with unnerving perception. "It's too bad you quit the idea of love. I bet you would have made someone very lucky."

"Or dead," I point out flatly.

Her face falls, and I almost feel bad for being so cynical. Twice in a day, I find my conscience coming out unexpectedly, an urge to be a better person, and I wonder if that might not be a bit of Heidi rubbing off on me.

Perhaps I've been spending too much time with her.

"I'm sorry. I shouldn't have said anything," she says, her eyes dropping as her cheeks color.

"You're fine. Mine was a poor attempt at humor." Not entirely the truth, but I like the thought of Heidi's discomfort even less than lying.

She gives a grateful smile, her eyes lifting to mine, and I can read it in her face—she knows I'm just saying it to put her out of her misery.

"Are you ready to order?" our server asks, his timing impeccable as he helps the transition out of a heavy topic.

"Yes, I'll take the lamb," Heidi says, this time her smile coy as she throws me a glance.

"And I will do the same," I agree, handing over my menu as Heidi does the same.

"Excellent choice."

Our server disappears as seamlessly as he arrived, and I turn my attention back to Heidi as she eats another oyster.

"Do you like them?" I ask.

"Mm-hmm," she confirms, swallowing her bite.

"Did you know they are meant to be wonderful aphrodisiacs?"

I get the reaction I'm searching for as Heidi snorts and nearly chokes on the sip of champagne she chased the oyster down with. Coughing as her eyes water, she presses a hand to her green-silk-clad chest.

Try as I might, I can't help but chuckle.

"Are you pulling my leg?" she demands, her voice raspy from having inhaled her bubbly.

"I would never."

Her eyes narrow as she scrutinizes me, then she releases a giggle. "So even when we're having dinner, this is really about sex?"

"When it comes to you, Heidi, it's all I can think about," I confess, leaning forward to murmur the confession in a low tone.

The excitement that ignites in her eyes fills me with intense satisfaction. Beneath the tablecloth, I brush her crossed knee with the tips of my fingers, and Heidi gasps, her blush darkening further.

And in that moment, all the tension from our earlier conversation vanishes, replaced by a new, electrical connection that I look forward to exploring early into the morning hours. Our conversation remains light and playful, teasing the line of flirtation for the remainder of dinner and into dessert.

Another thing I like about Heidi. She knows how to keep things casual, even if she occasionally strays into deeper emotional territory, and she doesn't seem to mind backing out when I give her a clear signal.

After our meal, we make our way to the spa, where I've arranged for us to receive professional foot massages. I soon discover it's another first for Heidi, and she reclines in the comfortable chair with a contented sigh as the skilled masseuses work their magic. Her eyes meet mine, and she smiles, the gratitude evident in her expression.

"I can't believe you put this all together today. Thank you for inviting me," she says, her voice soft.

Something about the way she looks at me, her hazel eyes so open and genuine, makes my pulse quicken. "You're welcome."

I'm tempted to lean in and capture her lips with mine, but I hold back, wanting to savor every moment of this evening. Instead, I focus on the way her eyes flutter closed as she loses herself in the bliss of the massage.

At the end of our spa treatment, I feel like a new man, and Heidi looks as though she's on the verge of falling asleep. But I'm not nearly done with her for the evening.

The fun's only just begun.

I take her to our room, where our overnight bags already sit neatly on the luggage holders near the door. I like that she's packed light—little more than an oversized purse. Somehow, knowing she doesn't feel the need to pack a suitcase for a single night away from home appeals to me.

She's not one of those high-maintenance beauty queens who has an hour-long regimen to follow before she goes to sleep. Symphony always did . . . Then again, her livelihood demanded that she remain young and beautiful forever, so the earlier she started on maintaining her appearance, the better odds she had of lasting as a model.

But Heidi seems to do just fine without all the masks and creams—more than fine, really. She's stunning, her skin nearly glowing, her makeup so subtle, I don't doubt she would be beautiful without it.

"Are you ready for your next spa experience?" I tease, loosening my tie and hanging it over the back of the hotel room's leather chair.

"There's more?" she asks, her eyes bugging with disbelief.

"I hope you remembered to pack a swimsuit," I tease.

"You didn't tell me I would need one!" she objects.

"Hmm." Eyeing her dress up and down, I scrutinize her appreciatively. "Well, then. I suppose you'll just have to go naked."

"I can't go to a spa naked!" She gasps, appalled.

A low chuckle rumbles up my chest. "Not even if I join you?"

Heidi bites her lip, her expression tentative but surprisingly tempted, and it only makes me want to ravish her more. But first, I should put her out of her misery. "We have our own private hot tub."

Laughing outright, Heidi drops her shoulders, her discomfort vanishing. "Oh, well in that case . . ."

Rather than giving me the okay, she reaches up behind her neck and undoes the two crystal buttons I've been wanting to release all night. The top of her dress trickles down the front of her in an emerald waterfall, slowing only as it nears her hips.

I groan as I realize she hasn't been wearing a bra all night.

Her nipples stand out, delicate rose-colored nubs against creamy flesh, inviting me to cup and cradle them. But Heidi doesn't stop there. Hooking her thumbs into the shiny silk, she guides the fabric the rest of the way over her hips, allowing it to pool around her feet.

"Christ, woman," I hiss, stepping forward involuntarily when I realize she hasn't been wearing a stitch of underwear all night.

"Ah-ah," she scolds lightly, her fingertips finding my chest to stop me from pulling her into my arms. "You said you would be joining me."

Releasing a growl of frustration, I resume taking my suit jacket, then shirt, off. At the same time, Heidi slips out of her heels. Before I can fully remove my slacks, she's already heading toward the glass door of the patio.

Her hips sway seductively, inviting me to join her as she slips confidently into the inky night.

Like a small swimming pool built directly into the floor of our balcony, the hot tub is illuminated, casting a soft blue light on the steam rising from its surface. I find myself spellbound for a moment as Heidi slowly descends the steps into the luminescent water.

"Coming?" she asks, glancing over her shoulder at me as I hesitate in the doorway.

I follow her into the water, only stopping when she's within my reach. Then I pause as something catches my attention from out of the corner of my eye.

I had arranged for a bottle of champagne and a platter of ripe strawberries to be brought to us ahead of time, and my eyes shift to them now, already sitting in wait, the glasses of bubbly freshly poured.

Suddenly, the ambiance feels more intimate than I had intended, passing beyond romantic to something more intentional. Keeping my tone casual, I suggest, "Champagne?"

"Sure," she agrees, flashing me a smile as she accepts the delicate crystal flute.

Then we settle onto the seat, submerging our bodies up to our necks, our knees brushing as we sit close together. The burbling water is warm and inviting, and for a moment, we silently soak in the luxurious surroundings.

I catch Heidi studying me from the corner of my eye, her soft hazel eyes sparkling with curiosity. "Maks, this is incredible," she says when I meet her gaze. "But what's the occasion? Why are you pampering me so thoroughly?"

I'm glad she seems to understand without saying that, as romantic as this night might seem, it's not an attempt to make our situation more than what we initially agreed upon. Leaning close, I murmur, "I closed on a very big deal today, and I wanted to celebrate."

"Congratulations!" Her smile widens, and she clinks her champagne glass against mine. "I'm honored to be a part of your celebration."

"You are definitely that," I agree, unable to resist her any longer.

Wrapping an arm firmly around her waist, I pull her onto my lap so she's straddling me on the hot tub's bench seat. Her soft breasts find my chest, trapping the warmth between us, her flesh as silky against my skin as the dress she just took off.

Wrapping one arm around the back of my neck so her champagne flute rests behind me, Heidi places her other palm over my heart. Then she leans in slowly, her eyes shifting down to my lips.

With my palm spreading between her shoulder blades, I trap her to me as I close the distance between us, stealing a fiery kiss. Heidi melts into me, her tongue dancing out to tangle with mine in a deep and passionate embrace.

In an instant, my cock is swelling beneath her, ready to feel her from the inside. Her quick intake of breath tells me she can feel it pressing up between her ass cheeks, and her hips rock softly on top of me.

This is what I've been building up to all evening.

Now that we're alone once more, the real celebration can begin.

26

HEIDI

The way Maks kisses me turns me molten with desire, and I don't hesitate to eagerly return his attention. It relieves me to know he considers tonight a celebration. It's not intended to be more than that. And I like that Maks would choose to celebrate closing on a business deal with me when he could have chosen to grab drinks or go all out with his brothers instead. They're business partners, after all.

But he chose to spend time with me, and somewhere deep inside, that gives me confirmation that he feels the connection between us that has drawn me to him from the very beginning.

Without breaking our kiss, Maks sets aside his champagne flute. Then his strong hands travel down my sides, exploring my flesh on his way to my hips. His fingers press into my hips, and I groan, rocking forward instinctively as he triggers a fresh wave of arousal.

I can feel his silken cockhead pressing against me, ready to slide inside me as soon as I lift my hips. Combing my fingers into his hair, I deepen the kiss at the same time, tipping his head back as I rise off his lap.

As I sink back down, Maks guides his thick erection to my slick entrance. Something about the heat of the water, the crisp coldness of the champagne, and the dark night enveloping us in a small, blue-lit world sets my senses alive. I feel every inch of him pressing inside me as I lower myself onto his cock.

A grumbling growl issues from low in Maks's throat, and his arms snake around my waist, forming an iron cage around me. The warmth and security of it makes my heart pound, and I rock on top of him, slowly riding him as our make-out session turns into something far more erotic and sensual.

I've never done anything like this—sex outside, in a hotel hot tub, trying to be quiet in case anyone else is enjoying their patio as well. Thankfully, each room's deck seems to be thoroughly enclosed, so no one would even know we're here—as long as I can stay quiet.

But it feels so good, the way Maks and I are intertwined, his tattooed skin brushing against mine and creating a tantalizing stimulation. The water only seems to intensify the feeling, and as he slides in and out of my depths, I can hardly catch my breath.

"I hope you hadn't planned on sleeping tonight," he rasps against my lips, "because I intend to keep you very busy."

The warning sends a delicious shiver down my spine, making my nipples harden despite the intense warmth, and I roll my hips more forcefully. His rock-hard excitement presses deeper inside me, hitting that spot that drives me wild.

I like that we have no deadline—no time that we need to call it quits. We haven't yet explored whether there is an end to this insatiable hunger, and I'm more than ready to find out.

"Good," I breathe, and I start to ride him harder.

Powerful arms keep me on rhythm, guiding my weightless body as Maks gives as good as he receives. Tingling excitement raises goosebumps across my shoulders, and the contrast of my body's response and the hot water enveloping my taut breasts only increases the pleasure.

Whimpering with the intensity of my need, I keep our lips locked, trying to muffle the sound. But even though we're not using toys and bondage, I find myself hovering dangerously close to climax just from the euphoria of Maks inside me.

His grunting breaths sound so loud over the soft, roiling bubbles of the jacuzzi, and that, too, sends excitement zinging through my veins. Though I'm fully protected against pregnancy now, it still fills me with nervous anticipation to think of Maks coming inside me.

The thought of it is all it takes to launch me over the cliff. Crying softly against his lips, I come on top of Maks, my walls clamping around his hard cock, my clit throbbing against him. A shudder ripples down his body, and he groans, the sound pained.

Slowly, I come to a stop, my panting breaths crashing between us as I melt against his chest. Tingling euphoria ripples through my body, making my fingers and toes deliciously numb. Then a giddy sense of lightheadedness takes over as the heat overwhelms me.

As if sensing my shift in energy, Maks eases out of me and shifts my body until I'm cradled like a bride against his chest. Then he lifts me from the water to carry me inside. The cool air washes over me, raising goosebumps on my flesh once more as it provides me with immediate relief.

It doesn't matter that we're both dripping wet. As soon as we're inside the room, Maks lays me on the bed, falling on top of me a moment later. His strong arms envelop me in the perfect amount of warmth, his chest a sturdy blanket pinning me to the earth. The world stops spinning as my pulse calms.

Maks's lips explore my body, starting with my throat and traveling down my chest to my navel. "Stay," he commands, and a moment later, his weight shifts off the bed.

I watch him drowsily, my brain foggy with the perfect cocktail of pampering, wine, and sexual relief. Rolling onto my side, I watch him with hooded eyelids, admiring the way his muscles flex and bunch as he stalks across the room.

He vanishes onto the patio once more, and I'm half tempted to follow him. But he told me to stay put, so I do, fresh anticipation bubbling in my belly. A moment later, he comes back in with the open bottle of champagne resting in its ice bucket.

His eyes take in my casual position, my head propped on my palm as I recline on my side, and his fiery gaze combs appreciatively over the curve of my hips. I love the way they light with a renewed appetite.

He sets the champagne bucket next to the bed, and only then do I notice his tie folded in the palm of his hand. Leaning in, he steals a kiss, taking my breath away as he guides me gently onto my back.

Then his hands find mine, and he guides them up over my head. Silky fabric encircles my wrists, and Maks turns his attention to tying me up, and my stomach flip-flops at the intent expression on his masculine face.

This is when the fun really begins.

The fabric tightens with a hiss as he attaches me to the thick wooden corner post of the luxurious four-poster bed. Then a devilish smile stretches across his lips.

"Are you ready, my pet?" he growls, tracing a finger between my breasts and giving one nipple a light pinch.

My stomach clenches. "Yes!" I gasp, my back muscles tightening with the pain-laced pleasure.

Maks hums a low note of approval. Then he reaches into the ice bucket and withdraws a cube. Slipping it into his mouth, Maks keeps his silver eyes trained on mine as he slowly dips toward my breasts.

Then he wraps his mouth around one puckered nipple. Frigid cold hardens the taut nub and makes me gasp. It's a shock to my system, and I squirm as the intensity of the temperature raises goosebumps across my chest.

"Hell in a handbasket!" I gasp, my wrists jerking against their restraints as Maks's strong hands pin my hips in place.

I can't move more than a few inches, but the extreme cold makes me quiver with the need for relief.

Moments later, Maks grants it, removing the ice cube from my breast as he slurps it back between his teeth. Cool water trickles down my ribs, and I breathe heavily. Then Maks's warm, callused palm cups my breast, sending heat radiating into the tortured flesh as he kneads it.

My core tightens at the delicious contrast, and I moan, my eyes fluttering closed as the sharp chill fades away.

Only to be jolted from my stupor as Maks applies the ice cube to my other nipple.

"*French!*" I gasp, my back arching off the bed.

I can't decide if I like the biting cold, but the promise of relief afterward helps me hold out because *that* feels amazing.

And when he draws a frozen line down my torso, my nerves start to tingle. He deposits the nearly melted ice cube in my belly button, and I'm shocked at how the frigid temperature radiates through my core.

His eyes find mine, traveling slowly up my body with a hunger that sets my soul ablaze. In his gaze, I can see the promise of ecstasy.

Strong hands grip my hips, and I gasp as he flips me over as if I weigh nothing. Then his knees press between my thighs, spreading my legs so he can find my slick entrance from behind. One hand snakes between my body and the fine cotton sheets, traveling lower until his fingers find my clit.

At the same time, he presses inside me. My body ignites, heat radiating through my core as he satiates an ache I hadn't known was slowly building. The way he fills me makes my spine tingle.

My clit throbs against his fingers, my arousal so intense that I can't help but beg for relief.

"You want me to make you come, *krasivaya*?" he purrs in my ear, his chest pressing me softly into the mattress.

"Please!" I cry, desperately trying to buck beneath him. But I'm so thoroughly restrained that I can't move an inch.

It doesn't matter that we left his playroom behind. Maks is just as good at finding props and using his body to stimulate me. I'm practically humming with the need for relief.

He rocks inside me, his thrusts strong and deliberate while his fingers tease my clit, circling it relentlessly. I can feel him swell further, his cock hardening as he reaches the brink of his own release, and I can't hold on any longer.

"Come for me, Heidi," he rasps, his voice low and commanding.

I cry out, my hips jerking back into him as my orgasm blasts through me, tightening my core. Maks snarls, thrusting deep as he comes at the same time, pouring his seed into me. We pulse together, the intensity of my release compounded by the deeply satisfying sensation of our simultaneous relief.

Gasping for breath, I slump onto the bed, my muscles relaxing as my ecstasy leaves me weak and exhausted in the best possible way. It never ceases to surprise me how consistently and frequently Maks makes me come. His touch is addictive, and the more he gives me, the deeper I crave it.

Slowly, he eases out of me, then presses a soft kiss to my shoulder blade. After a moment, he reaches up to release my wrists with a light tug. My arms go limp, and I hum contentedly as the euphoria leaves me with a tingling calm.

I roll onto my side once more, meeting his eyes, and a lazy smile spreads across my lips. He smiles back, slow and sexy as he takes the time to massage my wrists, bringing the circulation back to my hands.

Then, without a word, Maks rises, heading to the ensuite bathroom and donning his boxer briefs along the way. I hear the sink turn on, a toothbrush go to work. And while I would love nothing more than to languish in my bliss, the thought of brushing my teeth is too tempting.

Groaning, I rise from the bed. I collect my dress from the floor, hanging it in the small closet. Then I take my toiletries from my overnight bag and head to the bathroom.

Maks's eyes meet mine in the mirror, and I smile, suddenly and inexplicably shy. To mask my insecurity, I turn my attention to my dental hygiene.

We work in tandem, each of us using our own sink but standing close enough to the other that our elbows occasionally touch as we perform our nighttime rituals.

Strangely enough, getting ready for bed, brushing my teeth, and taking off my makeup with the intention of spending the night together feel far more intimate than what we've been doing for the past few weeks.

As I follow Maks back into the bedroom a few minutes later, dressed in a set of striped pajama shorts and a tank top, I realize for the first time that we've never actually fallen asleep together. In truth, I've never spent an entire night with any man.

In an instant, I'm a hundred times more nervous than I should be.

27

MAKSIM

The sight of Heidi in her adorable pink-and-white striped outfit—dressed for sleep rather than a steamy night between the sheets, no makeup to mask her natural beauty—makes me pause as she enters the room.

I knew she would be pretty even when dressed down, but what astonishes me is that she might just be even more stunning now than when she stepped out onto the roof of my penthouse at the start of this evening.

Her hair is a wild mess of waves after our last round of sex, and she looks just rumpled and innocent enough to be cute rather than her usual sophisticated elegance. But the natural color of her complexion and full nude lips is radiant, even captivating.

"What?" she asks, her bare feet hesitating in the bathroom doorway as he catches me watching her.

"I like your pajamas," I observe, flashing her a smile.

"Well, not all women like to sleep with a thong shoved up their booty and wire cups poking them in the ribs," she states, her tone halfway between playful and defensive.

"Why would they when this is an option?" I look her up and down once again to confirm my approval with a glance.

Heidi bites her lip, seeming to wonder whether I'm poking fun at her or actually giving her a compliment. But I can't stop smiling, and after a moment, she relaxes, returning my grin as she heads to her side of the bed.

Only after she climbs beneath the covers do I turn off the bedside lamp.

The electric energy that follows takes me completely by surprise.

I've taken women places overnight before, slept in the same bed with them without it feeling like a big deal. Then again, those women had stayed at my house, if not in the same bed as me, for weeks leading up to our getaways.

Perhaps it's the novelty of knowing Heidi will have to completely let down her guard in my presence. That she must trust me enough to fall asleep in the same bed as me. But suddenly, the situation feels more intimate than I had anticipated.

And what concerns me most is that I'm not sure I mind.

I'm intensely aware of the sound of her breathing, soft and shallow beside me. An indication that she might be nervous.

I sense every little shift she makes in the bed, and I'm consumed by an uncommon need to feel her body warmth. I want to close the distance between us once again.

It's well past midnight already. We both have work in the morning, and yet I find I'm not ready for the night to be over.

Easing over to Heidi's side of the bed, I lean on my forearm to look down at her in the dim light. Her eyes peer up at me, the color leeched to nearly gray in the soft moonlight. But they twinkle with unspoken excitement.

As I lean in to kiss her, her thick lashes flutter as her eyes close. Our lips meet with a soft caress, the contact tantalizingly sensual. Heidi hums, wriggling closer until her body perfectly molds to mine.

My heart swells with a sudden and intense desire to hold her, and rather than teasing or punishing, I want to just experience the perfection of her body. It's not something I've craved before—even with Symphony.

I've always had a dark side when it comes to sex and seeking pleasure through testing women's lines. But not with Heidi. I find her soft edges and willingness to trust too alluring to risk it. Instead, I'm drawn toward bringing that out in her. Right now, I want to see what she's like without all the toys, the bondage, the punishment.

I kiss her slowly, tracing the soft pad of her lower lip as I stroke the line of her jaw with my fingers. The groan Heidi releases makes my stomach flip and my pulse flutter. She likes soft and sensual. I can feel it in the electricity crackling between my fingers and her body.

And though I adore the cute pajamas she brought for our night together, I need more skin-to-skin contact. Easing my hand down over the soft cotton of her tank top, I find the hem with my fingers and slip them beneath the edge.

Then, my palm grazing the soft satin of her stomach, I guide her shirt up over her ribs.

Heidi willingly complies, arching her back to help me and raising her arms over her head so I can take it the rest of the way off. Then her supple breasts press against my pecs once more, the taut nubs of her nipples against my skin.

"You are so beautiful," I murmur against her lips, taking the liberty of exploring her silky skin as my hand travels freely over her body.

"I love it when you touch me," she breathes, her voice airy with swiftly growing arousal.

"Good, because I don't intend to stop," I rasp and kiss her deeply.

Running the backs of my knuckles up the length of her arm, I stroke her skin, relishing the goosebumps that rise along my path. As I round the corner of her shoulder, I release her lips to kiss the delicate line of her clavicle.

Each kiss is feather light, my lips brushing across her flesh, my tongue licking the salt from her skin as I make my way slowly across her chest to her sternum, worshiping the beautiful lines of her body.

My hand travels down the flat planes of her stomach to the waistband of her night shorts, and I slip beneath the elastic until my fingers find the peak of her thighs. She gasps as I stroke along the slick seam of her pussy, and I groan at how wet she is.

Easing my fingers between her folds, I press inside her entrance. Heidi moves beneath me, her hips rolling to intensify the penetration, and my palm presses against her clit. This eager excitement and insatiable desire feeds my own, and I finger her, relishing in her soft gasps from my penetrating touch.

Her body undulates, her breasts rising with each deep breath, her legs quivering with need. And all the while, I trail kisses across her flesh.

I can feel her walls tightening in anticipation of her climax, and I love how responsive she is to my touch. Even the soft, slow way I play with her now turns her on, and feeling her arousal makes my cock throb with anticipation.

I want to feel her pussy pulsing around my cockhead, soak in the sultry juices that slick her folds. But first, I want to make her come with my fingers.

Burrowing my chin between her ear and shoulder, I find the tender flesh of her throat and kiss it, working my way up to her earlobe.

"Oh, heck!" she gasps, her voice quivering with excitement. "Oh, Lord, I . . . mmm." Her words trail into a groan as she finds her release, her pussy clamping onto my fingers before breaking into a frantic pulse.

Gasping with her release, Heidi shudders against me, her fingers pressing into my skin as if she's holding on for dear life. And when I can't stand it any longer, I remove my hand, sliding it back out of her shorts so I can remove them as well.

We're naked beneath the sheets in a matter of moments, and I settle between Heidi's knees, spreading her thighs as I align our bodies.

Hovering with my forearms braced on either side of her, I lean in to steal a slow, scintillating kiss. Her palms travel up my body, her fingertips following every line and groove in my muscles as she kisses me with equal passion.

It's not the fierce, desperate pace with which we normally devour each other.

This time, we're taking our time, each step intentional, each touch exponentially electrifying. And when my cockhead presses against her sinfully wet entrance, it takes all my strength and restraint not to shove inside her.

Instead, I ease in, inch by inch, relishing the way she tightens with anticipation, her walls fluttering around my thick head.

"You feel so *fucking* good," I growl. I've thought it a hundred times before, but this time, I'm fully enraptured by how perfect Heidi's pussy is, how gloriously her warm depths take me in. Like she was made for me.

She nods, as if unable to speak through the euphoria written across her face.

Head tilted slightly back, her lips parted, eyes closed, Heidi looks as if she's lost in a world of pleasure, consumed by the bliss of our bodies becoming one.

And I can't help but join her.

It feels so incredible, every sensation setting off a million explosive bursts of pleasure that have me quickly building toward a powerful release, though I've only just begun.

28

HEIDI

The way Maks moves inside me, slowly, as if savoring every second, cherishing every caress—it feels dangerously close to making love. And though I'm trying desperately to cling to the logical side of my brain that reminds me that this is just sex, this time, I can't stop the wave of infatuation.

My chest is a confused muddle of emotion, and what frightens me most is that I know I'm falling for him. It doesn't matter that Maks made his intentions clear from the start. I can't help it.

I've never met a man so in tune with my every want and need.

Yes, he's commanding and can sometimes be overly controlling. But when he touches me, it's as though all that transforms into an iron will to please me. It's intoxicating, addicting. I find I can hardly breathe with the intensity of attraction that overwhelms me now.

His lips caress my skin with a tenderness that not only sets my skin alight but ignites the very depths of my soul. *This* must be what love feels like. The romantic kind of love. It's this deep, earth-shattering connection that turns two bodies into one, not just physically but by joining their very spirits in heavenly bliss.

I know my parents had that before my dad died. And somewhere in my heart, I always believed I would find it too. Then Sarah came along, and I put all thoughts of a romantic relationship on the backburner.

But when it comes to Maks, I can't help but catch feelings.

I've been fighting it for weeks now, since the moment we reconnected, really. And for the most part, his proclivity toward punishment and hardcore sex has made it easier to think of what we have as purely physical.

But as he goes soft and slow, almost worshiping my body rather than teasing or punishing me like I'm used to at this point, I find it painfully hard to keep my perspective.

It doesn't help that we spent an incredible evening together.

And while I still know little about Maks's personal life, what I have learned is the kind of man he is. This, the way he's treated me tonight, confirms all the suspicions I've had over the past few weeks.

Try as he might, Maks can't avoid the fact that he's incredibly empathetic.

And passionate.

He has so much love to give. If only he would risk it.

But after his response at dinner tonight, I know that's not a path he's willing to explore again. And I can't make him. So, instead, I close my eyes and try to focus solely on the ecstasy of his touch. The way his kisses release bursts of tingling pleasure across my skin and zinging excitement up and down my spine.

My heart pounds an agonizing beat against my ribs, launching into overdrive as he slowly eases in and out of me, his thick cock silky smooth as he penetrates me deeply before withdrawing.

I can feel myself building to another orgasm, and I wonder just how many times I might be able to come in one night. It seems that my body is eagerly responsive to his touch regardless. As his pelvis grazes my clit in a tantalizing release of endorphins, I can't recall how many times I've already come.

All I know is that I never want this night to end.

His arms wrap around me, holding me close to his chest as he maintains a sinfully slow pace. When his lips find mine once again, I can feel the passion seeping through his kiss.

I've never felt so close, so connected to anyone, and it leaves me vulnerable in a way I'm not prepared for. Because suddenly, I'm not so sure I can do casual with Maks any longer.

I waited too long to figure that out.

Now, I'm in trouble.

I'm just like all those other girls he mentioned he let go of because they got too attached. I can recall his words clearly in my head now. *It can be hard to avoid women catching feelings once sex gets involved.*

He's right. Because I gave my heart away without even knowing it, and now I'm not sure how I'm supposed to get it back.

But that doesn't stop my body from responding to him like a junkie desperately in need of a fix. If anything, the realization that I'm falling for Maks only sends my euphoria into a sharp spike.

Despite my intense confusion, I'm overwhelmed by an orgasm that rips through me like a tsunami. It hits me with such force that I can't even catch my breath to make a sound. Instead, my lips part in a silent cry as my body twitches and convulses beneath him.

Maks continues to rock inside me, his rhythm slow and steady as he coaxes every drop of pleasure from me. When I finally dare to open my eyes and look at him, his strong jaw is rigid, the tendons popping along his cheeks, his expression near agony.

Capturing his temples between my palms, I smooth the lines of his brow, and Maks's silver gaze finds mine. The intensity there takes my breath away, and before I can ask what's wrong, he leans in to claim my lips in another passionate kiss.

I can't resist him. I don't want to.

He makes me feel so good. I never want it to stop. As he presses inside me, drawing out the aftershocks of my release, I tremble with the strength of my feelings for him.

Shifting on the bed, Maks rises onto his knees, pulling me up with him so I'm straddling his thighs. With one arm wrapped around my hips, the other supporting my back, he finds a new, somehow more intimate angle as he maintains his deep thrusts.

Panting, I cling to his broad, muscular shoulders. I know he's close to coming, and the anticipation stokes my excitement, regardless of the fact that my clit is still twitching from the last orgasm.

I'm so sensitive after having come as many times as I have that I know I won't last long this time. Crackling electricity dances up my spine every time he sinks into me, and the way he kisses me leaves my mind blank, my heart sprinting.

"Come with me, *krasivaya*," he murmurs against my lips.

Nodding, I comb my fingers into his silver-flecked hair, my arms tightening around the back of his neck to bring me closer still. As Maks grunts with the power of his release, I feel the first burst of hot cum pour inside me.

That's all it takes to launch me into my own climax.

Coming together, Maks and I pulse and throb in sync. My body milks his cock as he releases his seed with deep, erratic thrusts, and all the while, he holds me close, his lips imprisoning mine in an erotic kiss.

Our ragged breaths crash together, and Maks gives my lower lip the softest of nips that sends a jolt of pleasure to my core. Then he eases me back onto the bed as he settles on top of me like a weighted blanket.

"Okay, wow," I breathe, my chest heaving as I try to catch my breath.

Maks chuckles low in his throat, the sound vibrating through my chest. "Agreed."

After a moment, he eases out of me to roll onto the mattress beside me. One arm falls above his head as the other remains extended beneath my neck. I know I should lift my head and let him move it, but I'm too consumed by my thoughts. Or my emotions, really.

I don't know what to do.

I don't want to stop seeing Maks, but if I keep going down the path, it won't end well for me. I lie with my eyes open, staring at the ceiling for several long minutes, and gradually, our breathing calms, his growing deep and steady.

He still hasn't even tried to move the arm from beneath my neck, and while I find it exceedingly comfy, I imagine it's putting his fingers to sleep. I start to sit up, glancing in Maks's direction as I do to see what state of mind he might be in.

And I'm shocked to find he's already fast asleep. A soft snort issues from his nose, and I can't help but smile. He looks shockingly younger in his sleep, as though years of stress and responsibility have slipped away to show me what he must have looked like at the height of his youth. The silver at his temples is the only reminder of the age that separates us, and even that just makes him look more distinguished.

Why is he so impossibly gorgeous? And smart? And funny? And far too good at sex?

Not to mention he's kind.

He might not know that, but I do. I've been the benefactor of that kindness more than once. But I can tell he doesn't see it that way.

God, I'm a wreck. I need to get my emotions in check.

Maybe agreeing to an overnight was a bad idea. The dynamics have shifted so drastically—or at least my emotions have. Before, I had a firm grip on the reality of our situation. Now, I can't help but wish things might have been different between us.

That he might have wanted to date me for real.

Biting back a sigh, I roll to face away from Maks, trying to give myself a bit of space to clear my head.

But as I settle onto my side, Maks turns, one strong arm snaking around my waist as he pulls me close in his sleep. His other arm drapes over my body, lightly trapping me against his solid chest. It makes my heart throb to realize we fit together perfectly in more ways than sex.

I know he's probably completely oblivious to the fact that he just pulled me into his arms. He's out like a light, and I doubt he even knows it's me.

I should stop it. Walk away. Find another bed—maybe even sleep on the leather chair. Anything to keep these growing feelings in check.

But I can't bring myself to extricate my body from his arms.

It just feels so right. So warm and safe and relaxing.

I haven't had someone hold me like this in so long, I can't even remember the last time. When I'm near Maks, it just feels right.

Despite the emotions running rampant through my body, I find the drowsy contentment that had consumed me earlier once again seeping into my limbs. Though I know I shouldn't let it happen, I start to drift off in the warm, comforting embrace.

Tomorrow, I can deal with the reality of my situation and the impact my feelings might have. Right now, I'm fully prepared to sink into a deep and dreamless sleep.

29

MAKSIM

The soft glow of the early morning sun filters through the curtains, casting a warm and gentle light into the room. I slowly stir from my slumber, the hazy remnants of a dream fading away.

As my surroundings come into focus, I feel an unfamiliar weight on my chest. The realization dawns on me with a mixture of warmth and dread—Heidi is in my arms.

I typically avoid cuddling. It's a slippery slope toward emotional attachment. But last night, it seemed impossible to resist the gravitational pull of her presence. And now, as I look down at the peaceful expression on her beautiful face, I'm paying the price.

Scarcely daring to breathe, I slowly try to extricate myself from beneath her without jostling her awake. I don't particularly want her to wake and find we've been snuggling. That would definitely send her the wrong message. But as soon as I shift, Heidi gives a soft moan. I freeze, hoping she might fall back asleep. But it would seem I'm out of luck.

Heidi's eyes flutter open, and she offers a sleepy smile, her voice soft and warm. "Good morning."

It's a simple greeting, but it carries the weight of significance. I expected some level of awkwardness, a moment of hesitation or uncertainty after we crossed a boundary we'd both been avoiding. Yet, Heidi seems perfectly at ease with what happened between us, as though the line we crossed isn't a point of concern for her.

"Morning," I mumble, releasing her to sit up, and she willingly lets me go.

She stretches languidly, her fingers grazing my chest as she arches her back, and I suppress a shiver at the sensation. "Last night was . . . fun," she says, her eyes meeting mine with open sincerity.

A pang of unease lances through me at the simplicity of the word. "It was."

She props herself up on one elbow, studying my expression. "Did we celebrate your successful deal properly?" she asks, and a hint of insecurity slithers into her tone.

"It was perfect," I acknowledge, leaning in to brush a gruff kiss across her lips. Regardless of my inner conflict, I don't want her to feel like she did something wrong. I'm the one who messed up. And now I'm kicking myself. "We'd better get going. I promised I would get you to work on time."

Heidi gasps, her eyes flying to the clock.

"Your business hours start at eight, yes?"

Momentary surprise flits across Heidi's face, as if she didn't think I would look something like that up to ensure she gets to work on time. "Yes?"

"You'll have time to go home and change," I assure her.

I, on the other hand, will have to skip a shower. I'm expected in the office at seven for the weekly family meeting.

Heidi's shoulders settle, and she gives me a grateful smile. Then she slips out from under the covers, giving me a glimpse of her perfect naked body. Her adorable pajamas are strewn around the room, discarded during our last round of sex that culminated in my poor decision to cross a line of intimacy I shouldn't have.

She collects her PJs on the way to her overnight bag and packs them neatly before pulling out a pair of leggings and a flowing white tunic. As she dresses, I tear my eyes away to get ready myself.

We move around each other in a space somewhere between awkward silence and quiet companionship, and by the time I call for our ride to the helicopter, my tongue is so tied, I don't know that I could speak even if I knew what I wanted to say.

Yesterday was a mistake. I know that now because I'm treading dangerously close to having feelings for Heidi, and our connection last night has only further clouded my judgment. I unintentionally managed to create a tangled web of emotions in a single night.

So as we ride out to the helipad, I keep my hands to myself, not placing one on the small of her back to guide her like I've grown accustomed to. The chopper's intense hum fills the air as it ascends from the helipad, carrying me and Heidi away from the hotel Prime and Caramel.

I stare out the window, my mind a whirlwind of conflicting thoughts and emotions. I messed up. I took it too far, and now I'm not sure I can reel my feelings back in. But I must if I'm going to continue to see her.

And if I can't, it's time to cut her loose.

The thought of ending things with Heidi is beyond painful. But we had an agreement, one I intend to stick to—no attachment, just sex.

Normally, that works just fine for me. It's the women who tend to want more. But with Heidi, it's different. *I'm* different. She seems perfectly capable of managing a casual relationship, like she said she would be. Yet, I find myself falling deeper for her, feeling emotions I swore I would never mess with again.

How did I let myself get into this situation?

As the chopper carries us up the coast, I steal a glance at Heidi, sitting beside me. Her profile is serene, a stark contrast to the turmoil inside me. She peers out the window at the skyline, seemingly caught up in the view.

I try to find some of that same composure, but the war within me is too powerful. By the time the wheels touch down in San Francisco, I'm more lost in my thoughts than I was when I woke to find her in my arms.

Walking Heidi to the elevator, I ride it down to the garage, where my men are waiting to take her safely home. Before she climbs into the car, she turns to face me.

Something in her gaze catches my attention, a guardedness that I haven't seen before. Suddenly, I realize how quiet she's been this morning. I was so wrapped up in my own thoughts, I hadn't wondered if her silence might not mean something more. The tension in the air is palpable, and I can't help but wonder what's going through her mind.

In an instant, I'm troubled by the possibility that she might recognize the signs of my feelings and want to end our agreement now.

"I'll see you again soon?" I state, though my tone makes it sound more like a question.

"Okay." She offers up a smile, but this one is weaker, almost trembling at the corners of her lips.

Our lips meet in a soft, almost absentminded kiss goodbye. I can tell something is definitely amiss. She pulls away too quickly, and her gaze shifts from mine as if she's mentally miles away.

I want to ask her where she went, but I stop myself. If she's trying to put some distance between us again, it's probably for the best. My probing into her thoughts and emotions will only further contradict the parameters I very carefully have laid down in our relationship from the start.

That doesn't make it any easier to watch her car whisk her away.

Releasing a growl of frustration, I head straight to my car, my guards following me wordlessly.

My morning doesn't improve when I arrive at the office. As I step out of the elevator, I'm greeted by the sight of my brothers already occupying my office, the door open to indicate they're waiting for me to begin.

"Sorry I'm late," I state, straightening my suit jacket uncomfortably.

It's the same one I had on yesterday evening, but it doesn't look too rumpled, and I only wore it for a few hours. But that doesn't stop me from feeling slightly like I'm doing an uncommon version of a walk of shame.

Dimitri and Alexei greet me with knowing smirks and raised eyebrows.

"Did hell freeze over? You're never the last one in the office," Dimitri observes drily.

"Ha-ha," I respond humorlessly, shrugging out of my jacket and folding it neatly over the back of my chair. "I might have gotten a little carried away celebrating Aleksandr's most recent loss."

"I'll say," Alexei pipes in, though the glint in his eye tells me he's not talking about Aleksandr. "You must have gone all out with your newest fuck toy. You still smell like her perfume. Didn't you have time to take a shower?"

I glare daggers at him as I slump into my chair, then scrub my face with my palms.

"Can we just get this meeting over with?" I growl. Their teasing grates on my already frayed nerves, making my tone gruff.

"Sure thing, Boss," Dimitri says, and I just catch the amused look he shares with Alexei before continuing. "We don't have much to go over, seeing as our big deal just closed yesterday and we don't have much more in the lineup for this month's acquisitions."

I nod.

"My men kept a close eye on Aleksandr after the closing yesterday. Sounds like he had his own . . . bender last night. One with less sex and a lot more violence, I guess," Alexei adds. "He's on the move a lot right now, though. We might just find our window of opportunity."

My eyes flash to Alexei's as a spike of anticipation lances through me.

He knows how much I want the man dead. We all do for one reason or another. And it's been years of trying to get to him, but Aleksandr keeps a tight contingent of guards around him at all times, so it's been nearly impossible to find that window of opportunity Alexei's talking about. We share a moment of loaded silence.

Finally, Dimitri shrugs. "That's all we have. And considering your contribution would be closing on the Bay View—which we were all present for—I think we can consider the meeting adjourned."

"Good," I agree, and I watch as my brothers rise and exit as one.

Alexei closes the door behind them, and in the silence of my office, I take a deep breath, trying to focus on my day ahead. But as I look over the list of potential acquisitions Dimitri wants to put on my radar, my mind keeps drifting back to the night I shared with Heidi.

The memory of her laughter over dinner, the warmth of her eyes as we talked and joked, the feel of her soft, beautiful body snuggled close to mine, it all haunts me. I broke all the rules, and now I'm paying for it. The weight of my feelings for her presses down on me, and as loath as I am to admit it, I need to break it off with her. I can't let this spiral any further out of control.

Despite my best efforts, I find myself staring at my phone, contemplating sending her a message, ending this before it gets even messier. But as my finger hovers over the *Send* button, I hesitate, thinking of all the things I enjoy about spending time with Heidi. Breaking it off with her is easier said than done.

Frustrated, I toss my phone aside and turn my attention back to work, determined to put her from my mind.

Time passes slowly, but I refuse to lift my head—until finally, my phone vibrates, pulling me from my restless thoughts. My first thought is that it might be from Heidi, and I immediately quash the idea, furious that I almost wish she'd decided to text me first.

I've always been the one to instigate our nights together, and that's how it should be. I shouldn't want her to bother me at work.

Still, when I check the text, it's from an unknown number. My disappointment only lasts a moment, though, as I open the photo someone sent me. In it, Aleksandr Volkov stands with Heidi, both of them smiling as he's taking the selfie. Her company's logo, Turner Interior Design, is visible in the background.

Look *who I had the pleasure of meeting today,* the words accompanying the picture say. *Looks like your girlfriend and I are going to hit it off just fine. I wonder if I might not be able to work out my own little agreement with her... unless you'd care to weigh in on the matter.*

I CLENCH MY JAW, trying to contain the storm of emotions brewing inside me. *How did Aleksandr find out about her? What might he do with the information?* My mind races, and I feel a knot forming in my chest.

I can't let Heidi get caught up in our crossfire. Not like Symphony. Never again.

30

HEIDI

Zoe knocks lightly on the glass door of my office before peeking her head inside. "I have a man out here to see you, Ms. Turner," she says, using her polite business voice that would indicate a potential client just walked through the door. "A Mr. Cherny."

"Wonderful. Thank you, Zoe. Please, send him in."

Zoe gives a polite nod and swings the door wide, gesturing for the tall rail-thin man to enter. He looks to be in his mid-fifties, his too-black hair slicked back with enough product that it shines in the overhead lights. He's dressed in a midnight-blue designer suit and wears a smooth smile that looks like he's hiding some mischief that he can't wait to talk about.

"Hi, Mr. Cherny? I'm Heidi Turner," I say cheerfully, rising to offer my hand.

"It's a pleasure, Ms. Turner. I've been dying to meet you." Accepting my hand, he gives it a quick shake, and his smile broadens.

"You have?" I ask, surprised by the intensity with which he says it.

"Oh, yes, I've heard nothing but praise about your work."

He must be here on a referral, which is wonderful. I prefer earning business by word of mouth. "Oh. Why, thank you. I provide only quality work and do my best to ensure each customer is completely happy with the end product." Flashing him my warmest grin, I try to calm the sudden wave of nerves. I've never gotten comfortable with the sales part of marketing my business.

And for some reason, selling to Mr. Cherny feels even more nerve-racking than usual. Maybe it's because his accent reminds me of Maks, and right now, my body doesn't know up from down when it comes to my Russian companion.

"Well, I'm sold," he says, his smile oozing confident charm.

"And what is it that I can do for you today, Mr. Cherny? Are you looking to redecorate your home?"

"A few of my newly acquired restaurants, in fact," he says, toying with the nameplate on the far side of my desk. "They're in dire need of rebranding and a facelift." At the end of the explanation, he drops his hands, folding them in his lap and looking at me directly with his dark, steady gaze.

"Restaurants?" I've done businesses before—usually corporate offices and such. But never a restaurant, and I wonder which of my clients might have recommended me for such a task. But I don't want to ask and hint at my surprise or inexperience. Because, frankly, I would love the opportunity to decorate a restaurant, and if Mr. Cherny wants to put his faith in me, I don't want to place any doubts in his mind.

"Are you up for the challenge?" he asks, as if he somehow heard my thoughts.

"Of course! It would be my pleasure. If you'd like, we can set up a time for me to come look at the floorplans. If you have any stylistic preferences you'd like me to work with, I'm happy to include them in my mockups. Once I have a feel for the space and your personal preferences, I can put together a few suggested plans, and we can go from there."

"That sounds great," he says and pulls out his phone. "Before we start that, can I get a picture with you? My friends are going to be thrilled when they learn that I intend to work with you."

"Oh. Of course," I agree, caught off guard by the request but flattered all the same.

"Great." Mr. Cherny turns, raising his phone as I lean across my desk to ensure we're both inside the screen.

Trying my best for a polite smile, I hold the pose long enough for him to take the picture. Then I straighten once more, smoothing my pencil skirt before I reclaim my seat.

Mr. Cherny dabbles with his phone for a moment, a broad smile stretching across his face. Then he returns his attention to me. "Sorry. I had to. They're going to love that. Now, let's set up a good time for you to come by."

"Do you have the addresses of the locations you would like me to look at?" Pulling up a notes page on my computer, I wait patiently for him to say.

He gives me three different addresses, all within the confines of San Francisco. They'll be easy to visit within a day or so.

"I'm hoping you can start with the Landmark. It's the one I want to put back on the map as quickly as possible."

"Great," I agree, typing in my notes. Then I pull up my calendar. "It looks like I have some time midmorning tomorrow for that one. The other two, I should be able to take a look at around noon on Friday. Will that work for you?"

"Perfect."

"Do you have any designs in mind, any concepts you would like me to use as inspiration?" I pause my typing to give him direct eye contact and show I'm listening.

"I want to see what you have locked away in that pretty little brain of yours. Feel free to get creative."

Heat tracks up my neck and into my cheeks, and I try not to think too hard about the demeaning language. It's not the first time a big businessman has talked to me like a little Southern lady rather than a professional businesswoman. Until my client roster is full, I can't get too particular about who I'm working with. Besides, if he's a referral, he must not be all that bad. I just have to suck it up and remember that this is part of the job. *We can't always love everything about our clients, right?*

"I'll see you tomorrow, then," I agree, reaching across the desk to shake his hand once more.

He takes my hand in both of his, giving my arm a thorough shake, and the enthusiasm with which he does it helps put me at ease once again. "It's been such a pleasure meeting you. I look forward to speaking with you soon, and I can't wait to see you in action."

Mr. Cherny rises from his chair and heads toward my office door a moment later. In the wake of his departure, I stare after him in confusion. *Who could possibly have referred me?*

I almost wonder if he might not somehow be associated with Maks. After all, Maks is deeply involved in owning restaurants, and perhaps he and Mr. Cherny have a past, considering they're both from Russia—or so Mr. Cherny's accent would indicate.

I push the notion aside.

I doubt Maks would send such big business my way. Especially when we rarely talk about our careers. More likely, Mr. Cherny has an association with one of the corporate businesses I worked with.

I finish typing out my notes and get the walkthroughs scheduled into my calendar. Then I glance up at the clock. It's past noon. I'm supposed to be at the Hansons' Painted Lady to ensure the work is staying on schedule.

Turning off my monitor, I reach under my desk to grab my purse, then I stand.

I'm heading out the door of my office a moment later, and as I step into the reception area, I find Sarah and Zoe in a heated debate over which Bluey character is the best one. I try not to chuckle as I approach and plant a firm kiss on my daughter's temple.

"You ladies having fun?" I ask, smoothing Sarah's dark curls away from her face. The soft, silky texture of her hair is just like Maks's, and it both thrills and pains me to know that my little girl is so much like her father in some ways.

It means that I will always get to keep a part of Maks with me—regardless of when our agreement ends. At the same time, it makes me sad to think of how Maks will never know the beauty of having a child and loving them more than life itself.

I can't believe how much I missed Sarah after just one night without her. And though she and Zoe seemed perfectly content and were having fun when I came home, it still warmed my heart to see Sarah so excited for me to be home, the way she jumped up from the kitchen table, abandoning her cereal to give me a big hug.

I'm sorely tempted to take her with me now on my field work, solely because of how good it feels to be back with her. But I can't bring her to the Painted Lady. The construction is already underway, and I find it best not to bring a little girl into a potentially hazardous construction area. Even if they're just starting with the paint, a toddler tends to find ways to contribute creatively that owners might not always appreciate.

So instead, I release her after several moments and promise, "I'll see you both in a few hours, alright?"

"Okay," Sarah agrees, seeming perfectly content to remain behind with Zoe.

Giving Zoe a grateful smile, I'm rewarded by a supportive wink.

"Bye!" Zoe calls as I turn and head out the front door.

31

MAKSIM

In a full-on panic about the text from Aleksandr and what he might do to Heidi, I race to her office. She hasn't answered her phone, which only intensifies my anxiety, and the horrible, crushing fear that I've failed her—that I might lose her too—has me on the brink of losing my mind.

The drive to the office feels like an eternity, every second stretching on as I grapple with what the text might mean. My hands grip the steering wheel so tightly that my knuckles turn white.

My heart is racing as I throw my car in park at the curb outside her office. Barking a command for my men to keep watch outside, I make a beeline for the door. I need to see Heidi, to talk to her, to know that she's not been harmed. I also need to stress the importance of why she needs my protection. That text was like a bolt of lightning, jolting me out of my complacency.

Though I tried to do it her way, though we have been painfully careful about sneaking her in and out of my penthouse, Aleksandr knows. Which means it's too late. She needs my protection now, whether she wants it or not.

As I push open the door to Heidi's interior design office, my eyes dart around the room, searching for her familiar face. Instead, what I find is the same petite, dark-haired pixie-cut girl who reintroduced us at the bar. Heidi told me her name is Zoe, I believe—Heidi's coworker, roommate, and best friend.

She sits at the reception counter, a phone to her ear as she speaks politely with whoever is on the other line. *Heidi, maybe?* I'm desperate for some small shred of proof that she's okay. But now, as Zoe signs off, she tells the man to have a wonderful day. Then she sets the phone back in its cradle, her dark-lined brown eyes meeting mine with warm welcome.

"How can we help you, sir?" she asks.

Only then do I notice the beautiful little raven-haired girl with hazel eyes beside Zoe. She straightens from her coloring book to greet me with a winning smile. I assume she must be related to Zoe. They look enough alike for Zoe to be her mother.

Their polite greeting reminds me that, to them, I'm just another customer, and I do my best to rein in my panic so as not to frighten them. I must appear a bit disheveled, I realize, with my hurried entrance and the worried expression on my face.

Forcing the tension from my shoulders, I comb my hair back into place and smile as I step up to the reception desk. "Hello," I manage to say, though my voice is strained slightly.

"Do you have a 'pointment?" the little girl adds, and despite myself, I'm immediately taken by her.

She doesn't look like she can be more than two or three years old, and she's already working on three-syllable words. I have enough nieces and nephews at this point to know to be thoroughly impressed.

"No, actually. Do I need one?" I ask, unable to brush aside the question she so clearly put effort into learning.

"No," she says with an exaggerated shrug of the shoulders. "We take all kinds here."

I can't help but snort at the offhand comment. I don't think she fully knows what she's saying, but from the way Zoe gasps, I can guess the little girl must have overheard her say as much at some point.

"I'm so sorry," Zoe cuts in, her apology profuse.

"That's alright. From the mouths of babes, right?" With great effort, I suppress the urge to laugh, which I know will only increase her discomfort.

Zoe releases a breathy huff, relief flashing across her face since I don't seem offended. "How can I help you today, Mr. . . . ?"

"Federov. I'm looking for Heidi. Is she around?"

"Oh, of course," Zoe replies, but I can't help but notice a slight flutter of anxiety in her expression when she hears my name.

Clearly, she knows about me. I wonder what Heidi might have said about me to her friends to make her respond in that way.

"Heidi went to oversee one of her projects, but she should be back soon. You're welcome to wait for her in her office." Her voice is polite but guarded, and I can't help but feel a little uneasy.

It's evident she doesn't like me. But at least it doesn't sound like Aleksandr dragged Heidi from the building against her will. I'm tempted to press further, but I don't want to create more stress for Zoe when my presence is clearly upsetting her enough.

The little girl, on the other hand, peers up at me with an open warmth that I can't help but smile at.

"Thank you for your help," I say to her.

"Welcome!" she says back with such casual friendliness that it fills my chest with warmth.

This little girl is something else. I adore my brothers' children and tend to like kids in general, but I've never met such an intelligent, gregarious little toddler before.

"What's your name?" I ask her.

"Sarah," she says, her voice almost growing shy. "Do you like my drawing?" She holds it up for me, her hazel eyes round with innocent expectation.

It's a culmination of crayon blobs, each less distinguishable than the last. But she has clear intent, as several colored blobs have patterns drawn on them and they come in a variety of shapes and sizes.

"I love it. What's this?" I ask, pointing to one of the long yellow-and-brown blobs.

"A giraffe, silly!" she squeals, releasing a giggle like my question had the most obvious answer in the world.

I can't help but chuckle with her.

"My mom told me we can go to the zoo for my next birthday!" she explains, and suddenly, I can see that she's drawing each of the different zoo animals.

"That sounds like so much fun! I'm sure you two will have a fantastic time."

She nods eagerly, her hazel eyes sparkling with excitement. "I want to see the lions and the zebras and maybe even an elephant!"

"That sounds like a great plan," I say, genuinely delighted by the little girl.

My eyes flick up toward her mom, and once again, Zoe's expression borders on anxious. Though as soon as she sees me looking at her, she quickly rearranges her face into a pleasant smile.

"Heidi's office?" I ask, disturbed by her discomfort and wanting to give her the space she would clearly prefer.

Zoe gestures to a frosted-glass wall to her right, and I give a polite nod.

"Thank you." Without another word, I walk toward the glass door, glancing back at little Sarah, who is engrossed in coloring her picture once more.

Once inside Heidi's office, I settle into a chair, trying to calm my racing thoughts. The room is filled with her familiar scent of vanilla and cinnamon, and her design sketches are neatly organized on the desk. She's left her sport coat behind, a reassurance that she won't be gone long. I can't help but feel a sense of comfort in her presence, even when she's not here.

As tempted as I am to start pacing, I'm sure Zoe would see me through the frosted glass. So instead, I pull out a chair and settle into it. I place my elbows on my knees and clasp my hands, but the need to jiggle doesn't allow the position for long.

Minutes stretch into what feels like an eternity, and I can't help but steal glances at my watch every few seconds. I wonder what's keeping Heidi and whether I might not have made a bad judgment call. Perhaps Aleksandr did take her and she's in need of help, but if so, I imagine he would be sending me more taunting images.

Still, the uncertainty gnaws at me, making my anxiety flare.

I suspect the bastard is getting exactly what he wants right now, the reward of having something to hold over my head. I doubt he's taken her—yet. But the threat is there. And I intend to take it seriously. Her safety is my priority now. I don't care what she has to say on the matter—her clients will just have to understand.

I'm not letting Heidi dictate the terms this time.

Because no job is worth risking her life over.

We can figure out where we stand in our personal relationship after things are settled with Aleksandr. Hopefully, that means he'll be dead within the week. But in the meantime, her safety is what matters most.

32

HEIDI

As I walk back to the office, the cold San Francisco breeze cuts through my shirt, reminding me once again that my sport coat is still sitting on the back of my chair, where I forgot to grab it. Entering from the small parking lot behind my office building, I push open the hallway door and round the corner into the reception area.

Before I can greet Sarah or Zoe, my friend stands from her desk, her face a mask of anxiety.

"What?" I ask, immediately picking up on her concern.

"Sarah, would you mind getting me a bag of nuts from the welcome basket?" Zoe asks, forcing her lips into a smile as Sarah's gaze shifts from me to Zoe.

"Okay!" she agrees, sliding down from her seat to head to the seating area where a carved-wood basket holds snacks for any customers who might have to wait to speak with me.

She toddles off, seemingly oblivious to Zoe's worried expression.

Zoe takes a deep breath, her words coming out in a hurried whisper. "Maks is in your office, waiting for you."

The mention of Maks's name sends a jolt of apprehension through me for two reasons. I've managed to keep Sarah a secret from him for this long. But if he's here now, he must have met her. After all, Sarah's been sitting behind the reception desk with Zoe all morning.

But the second reason for my anxiety is that Maks's presence at my place of work can't mean anything good. For an instant, I wonder if he might be here to break things off with me. *But then why would he have asked if he would see me again when we parted this morning?*

He was certainly withdrawn and quiet on the trip back to the city. Something's troubling him, and it makes my stomach quiver. And now I have the larger concern of whether he's found out about Sarah.

Panic begins to unfurl in my chest, tightening its grip with every passing second. "Does he know about . . .?" I give a subtle jut of my chin toward my daughter without saying her name.

Zoe shakes her head, her eyes shifting nervously. "No, but it was a close call. They talked about her birthday plans on where you intend to take her. He knows her name, her age . . ."

My stomach knots as I think about my loquacious little girl and how easily she could say something out of innocence that would reveal exactly who she is to Maks.

Making a flash decision, I reach across the desk to give Zoe's hand a reassuring squeeze. "You did a great job of handling the situation. Thank you. Will you take Sarah home for the day? I'll talk to Maks, so you can be gone by the time he leaves."

Zoe's relief is palpable. "Sure. Call me if you need me?" Her eyes flash toward the door to my office, concern lingering there.

"I'll be fine," I reassure her. Then, with a smile, I turn toward the office to face the man I'm falling for.

Nerves tighten my stomach as I consider, once again, the possibility that he's here to end things. I knew it would happen eventually. And it's probably best if he does it now, before I fall any harder. Still, my heart pounds as I make my way to my office door. Taking a deep breath, I push it open.

Maks is standing by the blueprint sketch of my mom's house—now my house with Sarah and Zoe—that I drew in college. He studies it carefully, his tall, imposing figure still, his hands clasped behind his back.

He turns as I enter, his silver eyes intense and searching as they lock onto mine. He's dressed in the same tailored suit he had on last night, and I wonder what could have happened in the time since I left him.

I close the door behind me, trying to maintain my composure. "Hi," I say, unsure of how else to start.

Maks doesn't waste any time on pleasantries. "Heidi, you're in danger. I know how you feel on the matter, but you need to accept my protection. I'd prefer if you let me hide you away for a week or so until I can be sure you're safe."

The gravity of his words sinks in, and a shiver of fear crawls up my spine. "What happened? Why do I need your protection?"

Maksim sighs, running a hand through his dark hair. "I received a threat. My enemies know who you are to me, and they know how to get to you."

His enemies. The revelation turns my body cold. The knowledge that I'm a target because of my association with Maks jars me from my happy state of denial. I thought that our strategy to keep our relationship hidden would be enough. I was kidding myself. I never should have taken the risk. And now my daughter, my precious Sarah, could be in danger too.

Instantly, I'm furious with myself for succumbing to my attraction and ignoring my better sense. I can't accept his protection without having everything blow up in my face. Because if I accept his protection, I'll have to tell him about Sarah. And he may or may not agree to house my daughter if he finds out I've been keeping Sarah a secret. That's a risk I'm willing to take. I need to figure out a way to keep us safe without involving Maks.

But how?

The thought hits me like a bolt of lightning. If his enemies realize I'm as meaningless to him as the metaphorical contract we signed, maybe they won't consider me a target. I take a deep breath, trying to sound resolute. "Maks, you don't need to hide me away. That will only put a bigger target on my back. The answer is simple. We need to stop seeing each other."

It's harder to say than I imagined it could be, and as soon as the words leave my mouth, an aching sadness grips my chest. But I forge on, determined to convince him. "This was just a business contract anyway, right? If you make it clear that it's over between us and that I'm not the leverage they think I am, I'll be far safer than if you do anything to prove you care—like spiriting me away."

His expression darkens, and I can see the frustration building in his eyes. "That's not an option," he growls. "If they don't believe it, then you would be left completely exposed."

"Well, then, make it convincing. It's the truth, isn't it? You've said it yourself. You don't do love. And if they're watching you closely enough to know about me, then they must know that about you. I'm sure they've seen all the other girls you've slept with and let go. So, this, now, is the perfect opportunity for you to make a convincing show of breaking it off with me. Then we'll go our separate ways, and you won't have to concern yourself with my safety anymore."

I can tell he's unconvinced, and I sense the storm brewing as his anger simmers beneath the surface.

"Why can't you just do as you're told, for once?" he demands, his voice laced with frustration as he steps close to me.

His proximity alone makes my heart flutter, and I suddenly hate the power he has over me. I'm helpless against his charm, unarmed when it comes to defending my heart.

And after a sleepless night of fighting the emotions he's triggered in me, I can't handle the roller coaster anymore. I never imagined I would not only have to endure the pain of losing him but also have to convince him that leaving me is the best thing for all of us.

The pain that sliced through me at having to tell him goodbye gives rise to a sudden burst of anger. And before I can control the urge, I shove him, my voice rising as it fills with indignation. "Why should I? You're just an arrogant ass who thinks he can just tell women what to do and they'll obey your every command. You boss everyone around and expect them to just blindly follow orders. But I have a mind of my own, and I intend to use it."

Maks's eyes narrow, his anger intensifying. "Is that what you've been telling your friend, Zoe, to make her dislike me? That I'm an arrogant, controlling ass?"

Caught off guard by the accusation and shocked that he's aware of Zoe's feelings toward him at all, I'm momentarily stunned into silence. But as I scramble for an excuse to explain Zoe's discomfort, he brushes his question aside with a dismissive wave.

"You know what? If you want to paint me as the bad guy, I might as well play the part," he threatens, his voice taking on a dangerous edge.

Anger seethes from him, making me tremble as I really face for the first time that Maks has the potential to be a dangerous person. And while I'm fairly confident he won't hurt me when this entire display of temper is about protecting me, that doesn't stop my body's very real, visceral reaction to his size combined with the heat of his wrath.

"When it comes down to it, I don't need your permission, Heidi. I can *make* you come with me if you won't agree." He closes the distance between us in an instant, his intent clear as he grabs for my arm.

Instinctual fear hits me with a surge of adrenaline, and I lash out, slapping him across the face. The sharp sound of skin meeting skin echoes through the room, and Maks's head snaps to the side. His gaze returns to me slowly, a mixture of surprise and fury in his eyes.

And for a moment, we both freeze.

Shocked by my unexpected response and entirely uncertain of how he might react, I panic. Before he can make a move, I dash for the door as quickly as my heels will carry me. I can't believe I hit him. I've never done that before, and I'm as mortified as I am terrified.

A strong hand catches my upper arm before I can reach the exit, jerking me back toward Maks, and using the momentum of my sudden direction change, he shoves me up against the wall. He pins me there, one strong hand on each of my arms, restraining me.

Heart hammering in my chest, all I can do is stare up at him with wide eyes. He looks furious, the heat of his gaze blasting through me like a laser. A violent shiver runs up my spine, and my lips part to apologize.

Before I can utter a sound, he's kissing me, his lips crashing down on mine with frenzied passion. Heat blasts away the cold fear inside me, turning my core into a blistering inferno in a matter of seconds.

All that tension, anxiety, and hidden pain behind my angry words transforms into a desperation unlike anything I've known before. As Maks kisses me, hard and deep, I lean forward, kissing him back with equal fury.

33

MAKSIM

I can't control myself around Heidi. Even when she's pissed off, she's sexy. And though she's entirely infuriating because she's so damn hard-headed, as soon as I touch her, I know I've lost the upper hand.

Because now I have to have her.

Two seconds ago, I'd had half a mind to overpower her, throw her over my shoulder, and take her where I know she'll be safe. But the instant I had her in my grasp, all the frustration and anxiety transformed into molten desire. I need to feel her alive and warm and fierce in my arms.

And I know she feels it too.

Because in an instant, she's kissing me back just as violently, her body leaning desperately into mine. Thoughts of trying to run from me seem to vanish from her mind. As I release her arms, my hands traveling up her shoulders and neck to cup her face, her fingers hook in my belt loops, and with a meaningful jerk, she brings my hips forward to grind against hers.

I groan, my throbbing desire overcoming my rational mind. I'm vaguely aware of the fact that someone else might still be in the other room, but I can't find it in me to care. Unapologetically, I claim Heidi's mouth with my own, devouring her as I keep her pinned to the wall.

Then I reach down to pull her dress shirt out of her pencil skirt. And in one fluid motion, I lift it up over her head. Heidi gasps as her arms raise, allowing me to strip her. As I go for the zipper of her skirt, she takes my dress shirt and rips it open.

Buttons fling across the room, clattering over the floor and vanishing into hidden corners, but I don't care. She can undress me with this kind of fire any day. I shove her skirt and panties down over her hips, and she kicks them aside, flinging her heels along with the bundle of clothes.

Then she reaches behind her to undo her bra as I unbuckle my belt and shove my pants around my ankles. I don't bother to untie my dress shoes or finish stepping out of my pants. Instead, I pull Heidi into my arms and kiss her deeply once again.

My hands roam freely over her curves, groping and kneading her flesh with fiery desperation. When I get to her thighs, I hoist her up, pressing her back against the wall as I wrap her legs around my hips.

Heidi clings to my shoulders, her fingers pressing into my back as she lightly bites my earlobe. Snarling, I find her entrance with the head of my cock and shove inside her.

The sound of her euphoric cry sends my need into overdrive. Keeping her back firmly pressed against the wall with my upper body, I hammer into her depths, seeking much-needed relief and at the same time, relishing the feel of her heart pounding in rhythm with mine.

Heidi's nails bite into my skin as she trembles in my arms, her breathing labored, her hard nipples pressed against my chest.

"Don't stop!" she pleads, her pussy tightening around my girth, and I love that she's on the verge of climax with such little buildup. She might fight me when it comes to rational choices and decision-making, but at least I still know how to make her body respond eagerly to my will.

If I were smart, I might use this ledge she's hovering on as leverage, to torture her into submission. But I can't. I don't have the self-control. I need to feel Heidi wrapped around me, falling apart in my arms more than I need my next breath.

Her perfect breasts start to bounce as I pound mercilessly inside her, and I know I've hit the spot when Heidi's nonsensical Southern euphemisms start spilling from her lips in quick succession.

I can feel she's close as her walls clamp down around me, and I shift my hips, wrapping an arm around her fine ass so I can better grind against her clit.

Her scream of ecstasy that follows slices straight to my core, and I groan as her pussy milks me forcefully, gripping my cock with almost painful strength. Again and again, she throbs around me, her slick arousal coating me as she comes hard and fast.

Holding her firmly against my chest, I turn and carry her to her desk. Swiping the papers and pencils off its surface, I lay her back on it so her hips are just at the edge, and when I stand straight, her pert, gorgeous breasts are on full display.

Hooking my arms beneath her knees, I grip her hips for better leverage, and then I resume my hard, fast thrusts. Heidi's arms reach above her head to grasp the edge of her desk, stabilizing herself as best she can.

But I'm fucking her so hard her body still rocks with each deep penetration.

"Play with your clit," I command, my blood scorching through my veins at the sight of her beautiful body on full display.

She's taking all my pent up emotions like she was built for the unrelenting onslaught. And God, is she sexy as she seems to revel in the heat of our passion. Reaching for the peak of her thighs, Heidi does as I say. Her fingers press and circle the sensitive bundle of nerves there.

I can feel the instantaneous release as her pussy tightens around my cock. Groaning, I continue my grueling pace, finding her G-spot with every deep thrust.

"Oh, H-E-double-L! *Maks!*" she groans, her voice strained with the intensity of her pleasure.

"Come for me, Heidi," I rasp, feeling my own release building in intensity as my balls tighten.

"I'm coming!" she whimpers, and her back arches up off the desk as she does.

This time, I'm right there with her, and I release her legs, leaning over the desk to capture her hard nipple between my teeth. As I release a powerful burst of cum deep inside her, I bite down ever so slightly.

Heidi cries out, her body twitching as her muscles strain with the force of her climax. Throbbing inside her, I come hard as she pulses around me, our simultaneous release just one more intensely satisfying sense of how perfectly we fit together.

Slowly, I still as the aftershocks of her orgasm fade away. Once we're both finished, I ease out of her. Gone is the fury that had reached a critical point of destruction. Gone is the overwhelming sense of lust that wiped away all common sense and consumed my soul with fire.

Now, as I dress, I can finally collect my thoughts to try again and have a more rational conversation with Heidi about how we might keep her safe. I pull up my pants and buckle them closed as she slides off the desk to collect her skirt from the floor. I watch her dress quickly as I tuck my now-buttonless shirt back into my slacks, overlapping the sides to try and mask the fact that it will no longer close.

"Please, Heidi. Let me take you somewhere safe," I say, keeping my voice intentionally low and calm this time in an effort to persuade rather than command. "It's only for a short time, I promise. I fully intend to kill Aleksandr Volkov, even if I have to do it in the middle of broad daylight. I intend to end this once and for all. But in the meantime, I won't let him hurt you. I can't."

My voice breaks on the last part, and I know I'm dangerously close to revealing my feelings for her. I was fooling myself, thinking I could keep a wall up when it comes to Heidi. She's unlike any woman I've ever met. Without even trying, she broke through all my carefully built defenses, slipped between the cracks like a soothing fountain of healing water that has cured all the raw wounds eating at my soul.

And now that I'm trying to bridge the distance between us, to convince her that I only have her best interests at heart, I find that I can't stand the thought of living without her.

Sighing as she slips back into her top, Heidi tucks it into her pencil skirt before facing me. "I can't, Maks. I have people counting on me, responsibilities I can't just shirk. You're the one with a target on your back, so from where I stand, my best chance of being safe is to stay away from you."

The words cut deep, and though I can see a hint of logic behind them, I find her calm, even delivery the most painful. Here I am, my heart on my sleeve—despite my determination not to fall for someone again—and Heidi's done exactly what she said she could and kept this a purely physical relationship.

She's not just *okay* with telling me goodbye. She would prefer it.

It hurts. I can't deny it.

But worse than that, she's backed me into a corner. We're at an impasse, and now I only see two options—let her have her way, or actually make her my prisoner. And as much as I might like the thought of keeping her locked away for my pleasure, I don't think I have it in me to destroy what trust we've built by doing that.

"Fine," I growl, struggling to control my rising temper before I change my mind and do something I regret. Frustrated by her complete unwillingness to budge, I turn and storm out, jerking the lapels of my suit jacket closed and buttoning them over my destroyed shirt.

I can't get her to see it my way, and I refuse to force her. But that doesn't mean I can't take matters into my own hands.

I'm vaguely grateful as I step into the reception area to find that Zoe and her daughter seem to have left. Hopefully, they were gone by the time things got physical between me and Heidi.

I push the thought aside as I pull my phone out of my pocket and dial Alexei's number. She might not agree to bodyguards, but I'm going to give her extra protection whether she wants it or not.

"Where did you head off to like a bat out of hell?" he asks by way of greeting.

"Heidi's office. Aleksandr knows about her. He sent me a text all but threatening to hurt her, but she's so fucking hard-headed, she's refusing to let me take her somewhere safe."

My men start to follow me to the car, but I stop them in their tracks. "You stay. I want eyes on Heidi at all times—from a distance—until Alexei can send a tail to put on her."

They give a single, synchronized nod and turn to take up posts where she won't see them watching.

"I'm sending a tail?"

"Yes. I want them to stay close enough to stop Aleksandr but far enough that Heidi won't know they're there." Opening my car door, I slip inside and slam it shut.

"You sure are bending over backward for this girl. You sure she's not more than a fuck toy?" Alexei teases.

"This is not the fucking time, man. Get it done!" I snap.

"Sheesh, Maks. It's done. They'll be there in ten."

I almost feel bad for snapping at my younger brother. I know he's just razzing me like he always does. But my nerves are beyond frayed, and I'm on the brink of losing it after everything that's transpired in the last twenty-four hours.

"I'm heading back to the office now. We are ending this war with Aleksandr once and for all. I don't care how many hours it takes. I don't care if I have to shoot him in the middle of the goddamn street. I want him dead, Alexei."

34

HEIDI

It was harder to watch Maks leave than I ever thought it could be. My heart sinks as his silhouette disappears from the frosted glass. A moment later, he exits my office building, swallowed by the shadows of uncertainty.

I've fallen for him, harder than I'd imagined I could.

I wasn't supposed to fall in love. We'd agreed it was just a contract, a business arrangement between us. And today, when I reminded him of that, he didn't argue.

I could see the concern in his eyes, a glimmer shining through the anger he carried like a shield. But that hint of worry is probably just the ghosts of his past haunting him, his post-traumatic stress stemming from the guilt he carries over his fiancée's death.

In the end, he seemed to accept my solution, which only confirms that his emotions have remained as unattached as he promised they would. I'm the idiot who read too far into things, who let my heart lead me astray.

As I stand alone in my suddenly silent office, I clench my fists, willing away the tears that threaten to spill. I might never see Maks again. And it hurts deeply to know that's how we left things.

Of course, I should be happy. After all, I'm the one who told him he should make this look like a breakup. What I didn't plan on was that he might put it into action without any intention of coming back once the danger is past.

Now, I'm not so sure.

Agonizing loss punches a hole through my chest, and I press a palm to my heart as I try to ease the pain. I knew better than to let my feelings run away with me. And now I'm paying for not following my instincts.

I can't live the way Maks does, going through life without attachment.

Even when I go in with a strong head and clear intentions, my heart leads the way. And as much as I like Maks—love him, even—I can't continue to call what we have casual sex.

So maybe this event came just in the nick of time, before I lost my heart completely to someone who can't protect it.

It's time to put my pain behind me, for my own sake and for Sarah's. My little girl is my world, and I need to protect her from the dangerous mess I've willingly waded into. Taking a deep, steadying breath, I solidify my resolve, ready to put my time with Maks behind me and find a way to go back to the simple, happy life I knew before him.

It's nearly the end of my usual workday, and after the intense emotions of the past twenty-four hours and a nearly sleepless night last night, I think it's time to call it quits. I do the bare minimum cleanup, scooping the papers and pencils up off the floor and depositing them in a messy pile on top of my desk. Then, I walk around the edge to collect my sport coat from the back of my chair.

Scanning the room to see if I've left anything behind, I pause as my eyes land on the wall Maks had me pinned against not long ago. My body heats at the memory, the way he knows how to lay claim to my body and still make me feel like he's worshiping it.

That angry sex is some of the best sex I've ever had. It was filled with so much passion, so much raw emotion that I could almost fool myself into thinking that it meant he cared. A knot forms in my throat, and I shove aside my thoughts of Maks, snatching up my purse and storming out the door a moment later.

I lock the front door and head out the back, making a beeline for my little white BMW and then home.

When I finally step inside the front door, I pause to listen for the happy sounds of Sarah and Zoe playing some game or whipping up a meal. It only takes me a moment to pinpoint my daughter's happy babble coming from the living room.

I find her there, playing with her toy horses, and her giggles prove a soothing balm to my wounded soul. She looks up at me with those big, innocent eyes and gives an excited, "Mommy!" before hopping up off the floor.

For a moment, I wonder how I can possibly let Maks go through life with no idea that he has a daughter. Not just any daughter, but the sweetest little girl on Earth.

But after being on the receiving end of his no-attachments philosophy, I can't stand the thought of Sarah knowing this kind of rejection and loss.

Pushing the thoughts away, I offer a tired smile. "Hi, sweetie," I say, bending down to hug her.

Zoe steps into the room from the kitchen, a mixing bowl tucked in the crook of her elbow and a whisk in her other hand. "Well?" she asks, her voice tinged with worry.

"What's for dinner?" I ask, diverting her question—a clear indication to her that we'll talk about it later.

Her dark-lined eyes flash with concern, but she forces her voice into a cheery tone. "I thought pancakes were in order for tonight."

"Breakfast for dinner?" I say in mock horror, giving Sarah a pointed look.

My little girl giggles. "Yeah! Breakfast for dinner!" She bounces up and down in her excitement.

I laugh, a smile stretching across my face despite the weight of my heart. Only Sarah could get so excited about breaking a simple convention like eating breakfast foods for dinner. She's going to be a handful when she gets older. I can already tell.

"I think you've been a bad influence on her," I say under my breath to Zoe as Sarah returns to her toys.

Zoe snickers wickedly. "I did warn you that I would be the favorite aunt because I intended to corrupt her."

"You're her only aunt," I point out.

Technically, even that is more of an honorary title, but I would never dream of taking it away from Zoe because I couldn't imagine my life without her in it, helping me raise my little girl, ensuring I'm not entirely alone in this world.

I've never felt so blessed to have a friend like Zoe than I do now.

As she gets the pancakes cooking, I set the table and make us each a drink. Orange juice for Sarah, and though I know it's late in the day, I make Zoe and myself a pot of coffee, a comfort I'm going to need to get through everything I need to tell her.

But first, I need to feed Sarah and put her to bed. The last thing I want is for her to hear about all the dangers slowly circling our happy little life.

We eat a quiet dinner together. Sarah's occasional laughter fills the room as Zoe makes faces at her, and their adorable play helps ease my anxiety. It's moments like these that remind me why I've kept my secrets and danced on the edge of this dangerous game.

It's my job to protect Sarah from the hardships of this world for as long as I can, and I intend to do that to the best of my abilities. Never again will I fall prey to my baser desires. My first priority is to be a good mother. The rest can wait.

After dinner, I put Sarah to bed, tucking her in with a goodnight kiss and promising to read her favorite bedtime story tomorrow. As I sit by her bedside, watching her sleep peacefully, I love the way she effortlessly fills the holes in my heart, patching me up and giving me more than enough reason to keep going, even when I'm sad.

After she's sound asleep, I slip from her room, turning off the light as I go.

I head to the kitchen, where I know Zoe will be waiting for me. She's been my confidante throughout this ordeal, the only one who knows the truth about Sarah's parentage and my tangled relationship with Maks. She might be the only person in this world who could possibly understand what I'm going through.

We sit at the kitchen table, sipping our coffees, a thick silence hanging between us. It's somehow both reassuring and troubling, filled with unspoken thoughts and emotions as my friend waits for me to begin.

Finally, I break the silence. "Zoe, I think I've made a terrible mistake."

As I meet her gaze, her eyes reflect the same worry that's been gnawing at me all evening.

"A mistake with Maks?" she asks gently.

I nod, my throat constricting with the weight of my confession.

"What happened?"

"I've fallen for him even though I told him I could keep things casual. But somewhere along the way, I started reading too much into things. And yesterday . . . last night . . ." I sigh, covering my face with my hands as I voice the ugly truth. "I should have ended things sooner. I let it get out of hand. Honestly, I never should have agreed to the arrangement in the first place."

"Oh, honey." Zoe's hand reaches across the table to hold mine. "You can't blame yourself for falling for him. That happens to the best of us."

"Yeah, well, it's over now." My voice cracks on the last word, and I swallow hard as I stare into my coffee mug.

"It's probably for the best," she says gently. "Did you . . . ever tell him about Sarah?"

I shake my head no. "I can't decide whether I should feel awful about it or that I did the right thing."

"You did what you thought was best to protect her," Zoe says fiercely, her support and loyalty bolstering my spirits just a hair.

"Thanks." Daring to meet her eyes once more, I give her a grateful smile.

She returns it, a hint of concern still lingering in her brown gaze. "Why did he come to the office today?"

Guilt twists my gut. "He came to tell me that I'm in danger. He wanted to take me somewhere safe because his enemies know who I am—know what I am to Maks—and they want to use me against him."

"But you said it yourself. He doesn't do attachment, so how do they think that's going to work?" Zoe frowns.

I shrug miserably. "It doesn't mean they won't hurt me in the hopes that it might hurt him."

"Maybe you should go to the police," she suggests.

"And say what? I don't know who these enemies are. I don't know what they might try to do to me, or when."

Zoe slumps. "Yeah, okay. I see your point."

"My biggest fear is that you and Sarah could get caught in the crosshairs. I'm so sorry, Zoe. I never should have taken the risk."

After a moment of silence, Zoe says, "Don't be sorry. I was the one who encouraged you to have some fun. Neither of us would have guessed it could get so . . . complicated." Zoe gives me a reassuring smile. "So, what kind of danger are we in, exactly?"

"I honestly don't know. Maks just told me he got a threatening message saying that his enemies know who I am and where to find me." My voice quavers, and I fall silent.

"And you didn't accept your Russian lover's protection? Why?"

I glance down the hall toward Sarah's room. "I couldn't be sure he would protect all of us," I murmur.

Zoe's lips twist in thought. "What did he say when you refused him?"

"He got mad."

"Mad?" Her head tilts, her expression shifting to concern once more.

I nod, glancing back down at my coffee. "He . . . can get kind of commanding. I think he's just used to people obeying him without question. And when I told him I wasn't going to go with him, he got frustrated. I might have yelled at him and called him an arrogant ass."

Zoe snorts, and I bite my lip to stifle my smile.

"And then?"

"Well, he kind of came at me, threatened to just take me if I wouldn't go willingly . . . so I slapped him."

My friend pales visibly at my confession. "Heidi," she breathes, her anxiety visible. "Did he . . . ?"

"Hurt me? No. No, nothing like that. We . . . actually ended up having sex."

Zoe covers her mouth with her hand, though her eyes tell me she's trying not to laugh. "Seriously? You're hopeless."

"Ugh. I know!" I let my head fall back against the head of the chair momentarily. "Afterward, he tried again to get me to leave with him. But I couldn't . . . I couldn't just leave without knowing whether you or Sarah would be safe. And when I told him I wouldn't go, he just . . . stormed out."

"Oh, Heidi." Zoe can read the sadness in my voice, and once again, she reaches across the table to take my hand.

"Maybe I should have risked telling him about Sarah. What if I've put us all in terrible danger by not taking the chance?"

Zoe furrows her brow, deep in thought. "I don't think so. I still think you did the right thing by not telling him about Sarah. After how angry he got when you didn't do as he said, I can't imagine he'd take it well if he found out you kept that kind of information from him for weeks—years. Besides, he's involved in something dangerous, something that goes far beyond us. You couldn't have known how deep this rabbit hole would go, but it's definitely not one you want Sarah going down."

Her words provide some comfort, and I take a deep breath, trying to steady myself. "What do we do now, Zoe?"

She leans forward, her eyes intense. "We'll figure it out, Heidi. If we don't feel safe here, we can leave town. Okay? We'll find our own way to protect Sarah, and I'm with you, always. You know that, right?"

A sense of relief washes over me. Zoe is my rock, the one who's been with me through thick and thin, and her unwavering support gives me hope. "Thank you," I breathe, giving her fingers a grateful squeeze.

35

HEIDI

Despite my invaluable conversation with Zoe last night, I barely got a wink of sleep. I couldn't stop thinking about the way things ended between me and Maks. And as many times as I told myself that it's for the best, I couldn't seem to get past the hollow ache his departure has left in my chest.

After hours of tossing and turning, I finally found a moment's peace from the heartache of knowing Maks and I are over.

That's when I started hearing bumps in the night.

I was plagued by the fear that the men who wanted to hurt Maks might follow through on their threat and come for me in the night. *And what if they found Sarah? Or Zoe?*

The anxiety kept me wide awake into the early-morning hours. I only managed to drift off after the first hints of sunlight graced the dark sky.

And now, as I drive Sarah to daycare, I'm afraid that my paranoia and lack of sleep might be making me see things. I grip the steering wheel, my knuckles turning white as I navigate the rolling hills of San Francisco's city roads.

Sarah chatters happily in the back seat, blissfully unaware of the unease settling in the pit of my stomach. We've taken this route a hundred times, and nothing has ever seemed amiss. Until today.

The morning sun seems to cast ominous shadows across the asphalt, and as I glance in the rearview mirror for the twentieth time in as many seconds, my heart skips a beat. I'm pretty sure we're being followed. A sleek black car has been trailing us for several blocks now, maybe longer.

My pulse quickens, and a cold shiver runs down my spine at the thought. Perhaps it's a coincidence, but after the fear in Maks's eyes yesterday, I don't really care to leave it at that. *What if these are the enemies Maks wanted to protect me from?* I pushed him away, and now I'm all on my own, trapped in a car, with my little girl in the back seat.

"Hey, sweetie," I say, trying to keep my voice steady as I look at Sarah in the rearview mirror. "How about we take a little detour on our way to school today? We'll go on a little adventure."

"Okay!" she says brightly, always enthusiastic about trying something new.

I force a smile as Sarah giggles, seemingly excited by the change in plans.

Taking a sharp right, I leave the path to her daycare. Then I take a second and a third, weaving my way into a neighborhood and off the busier city roads. The black car follows suit, staying nearly a full block behind without losing us as it somehow matches my every move. Panic starts to rise in my chest as my confidence grows to certainty.

This car is definitely following us.

My fingers fumble for my phone as I make a quick decision. I dial Zoe's number before holding the phone to my ear.

"Hey, Heidi? Everything alright?" A question she's asked me more times than I can count since we woke up this morning. But this time, I find I don't mind.

"Zoe," I whisper urgently, trying to keep my voice low enough to avoid alarming Sarah, "I think we're being followed. A black car has been tailing us for about ten minutes now. I don't know what to do."

Zoe's voice comes through the line, steady and reassuring. "Stay calm and go straight to the police station."

I nod and only recall afterward that she can't see me. "Okay, I'll let you know once we're there."

With trembling hands, I hang up and focus on the road ahead. My heart pounds in my chest as I make several sharp turns, trying to lose the menacing car as I weave in the general direction of the closest police station I know of. Sarah's eyes widen as her giggles fade. She seems to sense something is wrong now. I offer her a reassuring smile in the rearview, but it feels weak even to me.

As my eyes shift back to the road, I suddenly find myself in an unfamiliar neighborhood. In my effort to put some distance between me and the car following, I must have taken one too many turns, and now I'm lost. In a panic, I take another sharp turn, and to my astonishment, this time, I think I manage to ditch the black car.

Still, I don't dare wait around to find out.

I take several more random turns, praying none will bring me back to the same spot where my tail might be lying in wait. Finally, after my fifth clear street, I manage to breathe a sigh of relief. Now I just need to reorient myself so I can go to the police station. Pulling over to the side of the road, I open my Maps app and start to assess the larger area.

To my surprise, I've saved a pin just around the corner. And when I click on it, I discover I'm only a few blocks from my first client I'm supposed to meet today. I had intended to head over right after dropping Sarah off.

Biting my lip, I make a flash decision, changing my plan.

I shoot a quick text off to Zoe.

I've managed to ditch my stalker and am in the neighborhood of the client I'm supposed to meet. I'm going to ask if Sarah and I can hide there while I call the police. I'll have them send a car to escort us safely back home. Then you, Sarah, and I are leaving town. I'm not going to mess with whatever psychopaths Maks got himself wrapped up with.

Slipping my phone back into my pocket without waiting for a response, I take the quick detour around the corner and park in front of my client's vacant lot. "Sarah, would you like to go to work with Mommy today?" I suggest brightly.

"Okay," she agrees, her normally enthusiastic self seeming slightly unsettled by my erratic behavior and unusually reckless driving. At least she hasn't started crying.

Climbing out of the car, I scan the empty area to ensure the black car hasn't found me. Then I open the back seat to unbuckle Sarah from her car seat. My heart races as I scoop her up in my arms and race toward the restaurant's open glass front doors.

The restaurant is empty at this early hour, and Mr. Cherny stands behind the host stand, looking preoccupied as he scans something before him, a set of spectacles resting on the tip of his nose.

His eyes lift at our swift approach, and he raises an eyebrow at our unexpected arrival. "Ms. Turner," he says in his reedy, accented voice as he swipes the glasses off his face and sets them aside. "This is a pleasant surprise. What brings you here so early? Or have I lost track of the time? It can't be our appointment already."

He glances down at his watch as if to ensure he isn't mistaken.

I offer a strained smile, trying to hide the fear lurking beneath the surface. "Not at all. I'm really sorry, Mr. Cherny," I start, feeling the heat of embarrassment creeping up my neck. "I am absolutely here too early, and I don't usually bring my daughter to work, I assure you. I wouldn't be here if it weren't urgent, but I need your help."

"Your daughter?" he says, his eyes flitting to Sarah with apparent surprise and delight. "It's no problem at all. But what is so urgent, and how can I help?"

Taking a deep breath, I explain the situation as calmly as I can, recounting my tale about the mysterious black car and our sudden detour that brought us practically to his front door. "I hate to ask, but I'm concerned that if I keep driving around, I'll wind up in a more dangerous situation than before. I was hoping you would give us a safe place to wait for the police."

"Have you called them already?" he asks, his voice thick with concern as his hand goes for his own phone.

I shake my head. "I haven't had the chance."

Mr. Cherny's eyes soften, and he raises his cell phone to his ear. "You did the right thing coming here. Of course, I'll help. Leave it to me. I'll speak with the police. You just take care of your little girl, and we'll have this straightened out in no time."

Relief floods me as he moves quickly toward the front door, locking it behind us. He's being so thoughtful, I almost feel bad about having a negative reaction to his casual turn of phrase yesterday—even if it was insulting. He's clearly more than willing to help someone in need, and perhaps, in his world, the language he used with me is considered flattering.

Stroking Sarah's dark locks away from her face, I speak soothingly to her as I do my best to calm my own nerves at the same time.

But the relief is fleeting, and in an instant, it turns to icy terror as Mr. Cherny speaks into his phone. His voice shifts, and his new tone as he speaks in the now somewhat familiar sound of Russian comes out as nothing short of an arrogant drawl.

My arms tighten protectively around my little girl as I turn to face the man I just now realized I don't really know at all.

36

MAKSIM

The phone rings, and I jump, nearly knocking over the stack of paperwork cluttering my desk. The number flashing across the screen belongs to one of Alexei's men, and my heart clenches. They're supposed to be keeping an eye on Heidi, making sure she stays safe.

"*Da?*" I answer, trying to keep my voice steady, but my anxiety gnaws at me.

"*Pakhan*, it's Yuri," comes the hurried explanation in Russian. "We lost her."

"What do you mean you lost her?" I snap, continuing our conversation in our mother tongue. My fingers white-knuckle the phone. My mind races with images of Heidi in danger, and I can't help but curse under my breath.

"Boss, she drives like a damn madwoman," Yuri continues, frustration lacing his words. "And even though we kept a good distance, it seemed like she picked up on the fact that we were tailing her. She took a quite few wild turns into a random neighborhood, and we lost her. We've been combing the area ever since, but she's gone."

My heart feels like it's about to jump out of my chest with worry. *What could Heidi have possibly been thinking? Is she really so obstinately independent that she chose to refuse the small level of protection I could offer at a distance? How did she even know they were there?* I've seen my brother's men in action. They're not at all easy to spot.

Anxiety eating at my insides, I hang up and try calling her. The phone rings for what feels like an eternity before finally sending me to voicemail. Panic wells up inside me, and I dial her number again, then a third time. Each unanswered call feels like a dagger to my heart.

Is she intentionally ignoring me because of the way we left things yesterday? Or is she really in trouble this time? Once again, I'm plagued with doubts about her safety, and I hate it.

Try as I might to avoid this very situation, I've walked myself right into another relationship with a woman whom I don't know that I can live without. And now, Aleksandr Volkov might just have her by the throat.

The thought makes me want to vomit.

Unable to contain my anxiety any longer, I burst out of my office and head straight for Alexei's. As I push open the door, my youngest brother looks up from his paperwork, surprise etched on his features.

"What's wrong?" he asks, sitting up in his leather swivel chair. He looks exhausted after our long night of hunting down leads on how we might expose Aleksandr. But as soon as I step into his office, he's alert once more.

"Heidi's missing. Your guys lost her."

Alexei's brow furrows, and a moment later, Dimitri enters the room, his tall frame blocking the doorway. He looks just as ragged as I feel from the all-nighter I enforced, but there's no missing the concern in his eyes, telling me he heard something of our exchange.

"What's going on?" he asks, and I quickly fill him in.

"We need to find her," I say, my voice hoarse with anxiety. "She's not answering my calls, and something doesn't feel right."

"You don't think it has anything to do with the way you left things yesterday?" Alexei suggests. He knows better than Dimitri the heated exchange I shared with Heidi before storming out of her office—and how I put a tail on her against her wishes.

"No," I growl, frustrated because he might be closer to the truth than I want to admit.

My brothers exchange a look, that look that tells me they can see right through my short temper to the truth of the matter. As much as I want to deny it, I'm not only head over heels for this girl, but I'm going to go stark, raving mad if something happens to her.

Immediately, my brothers are on board with getting her back safely.

Stepping the rest of the way into the room, Dimitri places a firm hand on my shoulder. "We'll find her, Maks. We'll do everything we can."

Huddling in Alexei's office, we form a plan. His men are already out, searching the neighborhood, but we need a lead. Something to go by. The only thing is that the direction Heidi had been driving wasn't in any way headed toward her office. And I have no clue where else she might go.

She was probably headed to a client's property. But that could be any of the random houses. And how would we know?

Just as we commit to calling in more of our contacts, my phone rings. My heart leaps into my throat, and I grab it, praying it's Heidi getting back to me. The caller ID displays her name, and an intense, heady relief washes through me. I'm going to lose it over this girl.

"Heidi?" I answer, my voice gruff after such intense anxiety.

But the voice on the other end isn't Heidi's. It's cold, menacing, and oily as the man answers me in Russian. Dread consumes me as I recognize Aleksandr Volkov's reedy voice. "Maks, my boy, you seem worried," he says casually, making my blood run cold.

"Where's Heidi?" I snarl, my anger an effective mask for the fear coursing through me now. "What have you done with her?"

Aleksandr releases a low, sinister chuckle. "Don't worry. She's here with me. I have your girl, Maks. And if you ever want to see her alive again, you'll come alone, unarmed, to the Starlight Casino and Lounge within the next hour."

"Don't you fucking touch her," I snarl, my voice reaching an almost feral tone.

"Listen to you coming to your little slut's defense. I think I've finally found the one you're ready to die for. So, what do you say, Maks? Do we have an agreement?"

My stomach churns with a mix of rage and fear. I tried to have the best of both worlds, to keep Heidi and also protect her from my sick, twisted world, but she's fallen right into the middle of it. And now I see no way of saving her without laying down my life.

"Why should I believe you won't harm her if I come?" I hiss through gritted teeth, my fingers clutching the phone so tightly it feels like it might shatter.

"I guess you'll just have to take my word for it," Aleksandr replies. "But if you bring anyone else, if you try anything funny, I promise you'll never see her again."

He hangs up before I can say another word, and I'm left staring at my phone, my heart pounding in my chest. I can't believe I'm reliving my worst nightmare, but I won't let anything happen to Heidi. I refuse to watch her die in my arms like Symphony. No, Heidi doesn't get to die. She has too much life in her.

I glance up at my brothers as they watch me expectantly.

"He has her at the Starlight Lounge," I synopsize. "He wants me to come alone, unarmed, within the hour, or he'll kill her."

Volatile Russian insults stream from my brothers in sync as they rip Aleksandr apart with their insults.

"He can shove it where the sun doesn't shine if he thinks we'll let you go in there without backup. That's as good as handing you to him on a platter."

They both look at me with determination, ready to follow me into the fire. And I know I can't let them. I won't get us all killed trying to save the girl I love. If I die, I need them alive to bring Heidi home safely.

"Let's go, Maks," Dimitri says, his voice firm. "We're with you. We have a forty-five-minute drive to figure out how we're going to get your girl back safely."

Alexei nods, his expression grave. "We won't give that bastard an opportunity to hurt her."

I'm torn between the relief of having their support and the fear that they'll be drawn further into this mess. I know I can't do this alone. I can't leave Heidi in the hands of a monster like Aleksandr. But I also know my brothers can't come with me. Not this time.

"I'm going alone," I state firmly, stopping my brothers in their tracks. "And we're doing this exactly as he said. I refuse to risk Heidi's life by deviating from his demands."

"You can't be serious," Dimitri says flatly, his expression deadpan.

"I am."

"And you think we're just going to let you hand yourself over for some girl? Without even trying to fight back?" Alexei demands, his usually cheeky countenance replaced by a ferocity I've only ever seen him demonstrate once before—on the night he stepped in front of a bullet to save his wife.

"You will if I tell you that you will," I command, striding purposefully toward the door.

And to my surprise, Dimitri bars my path.

"Get out of my way," I command through clenched teeth.

"Not until we find a better way."

"Listen, we don't have time for this. I have an hour to save Heidi, and I will not stand by and let her die. You two have families, women you would die for. And they need you to stay alive. Well, I've finally found a woman I'm willing to die for. And right now, she needs me. Which means I need you two to be ready to get her out of there as soon as I have Aleksandr distracted."

My younger brothers share one of their silent looks, and I clench my fists as I see them debating whether my argument is worthy of the price I'm willing to pay.

"Fine," Dimitri says. "But if that's the plan, you don't get to just lie down and die."

"I assure you, I refuse to die without killing Aleksandr first."

37

HEIDI

It took only moments for me to realize just how terribly I'd screwed up. And worse, I walked my daughter Sarah right into danger as well. I can't believe I was so foolish, but I can't afford to dwell on it now. Not with the ominous figures dragging us out of the back of a van into the gloomy, dimly lit parking structure of what looks like a very dilapidated and fire-damaged version of one of San Francisco's local casinos.

My heart pounds against my ribcage, fear coiling like a serpent around my spine. I struggle violently against the men's iron grips as they wrench me from the van.

"Let us go!" I scream, lashing out wildly with my foot and connecting with something soft belonging to the man on my right.

He grunts, his hold slackening as he doubles over for a moment. And I take the opportunity to redouble my efforts to escape from my other captor. But as I turn to confront him, he's not willing to play games.

He backhands me with such force that the world seems to spin. The sharp crack of his skin on mine resonates through the still air, making my ears ring. I wince as pain radiates from my cheek, and I taste the metallic tang of fear as my world spins. Before I can determine which way is up, I hit the ground hard.

My palms scrape against the hard pavement, my knees bruising against the solid ground, and I glare up at them as I cup my throbbing cheek.

Sarah's cries pierce the dark, and I turn to see her thrashing in the arms of another of our captors. Her tiny face is red and contorted, her voice a terrified sob that tears at my heart as she tries to run to me.

"Please, don't hurt her," I beg, scrambling toward Sarah only to have my captors snatch my arms and haul me back to my feet.

Sarah wails, reaching for me, and I fight with all my might to take her, but I can't. One of the men holding me gives a low, cruel chuckle. It's as if they're using my little girl's fear and anguish as a weapon against me. They're reveling in the power of refusing to let me be with her, and I can see the utter panic on her face.

"Mommy!" she sobs, tears streaming down her cheeks as she continues to reach for me.

"Shh, sweetheart, it's going to be okay," I murmur, my voice trembling as I fight to calm her. I have to be strong for her. But I can't suppress the gnawing terror and guilt, knowing that I'm the one who got us into this living nightmare.

The men haul us into the abandoned building, and as we get lost in the labyrinth of hallways, they finally release their hold on me, perhaps believing I've been cowed into submission or maybe confident that I won't find my way back out.

But they don't know the fiery determination that courses through me, the mother's instinct to protect my child at all costs. For now, I'll bide my time, hide my anger and despair if that's what it takes to protect Sarah. They can't keep me forever.

After several long minutes of walking, we're ushered into a windowless room that reeks of smoke and melted plastic. Only then is Sarah released, and the men file from the room in quick succession. The heavy door clangs shut behind them, leaving us in eerie silence, punctuated only by Sarah's soft whimpers.

"Oh, sweet girl," I breathe, rushing to her.

I gather her into my arms, my trembling fingers brushing her tear-streaked cheeks. Her big, frightened eyes meet mine, and I tuck her head beneath my chin.

"It's going to be okay, baby. Mommy's here. I won't let anything happen to you," I whisper, my voice quavering. I only hope I can keep my promise, but I have no clue what they intend to do to us.

I hold Sarah close, the warmth of her little body providing me with some semblance of comfort as I rock her softly in my arms. She nestles against my chest, her sobs gradually subsiding into soft sniffles as she clings to me.

My mind races as I search for a way out of this nightmare, scanning the dim room with my eyes. I know I have to find an escape, to get Sarah to safety. *But how?* They might have underestimated me, thinking I'm just a pawn in this deadly game, but they have no idea what a desperate mother is capable of. And I will stop at nothing to protect my little girl.

The room looks like a private poker room, with two round tables occupying the medium-sized space. But it clearly endured a fire. The tables' felt has been scorched away, the plastic cup holders melted into warped plastic. Black smoke stains creep up the wall like an insidious paint job.

I've never really had the time to explore San Francisco's casinos, so I have no clue which one this is. But I vaguely believe it was up and running within the last few years. And judging by the smell, this fire must have been pretty recent. I wonder if the building is even safe to occupy. But it seems our captors have no concern with that.

I'm not sure the structural soundness is going to matter that much longer, either, and cold dread fills me at the thought. Redoubling my efforts to find a way out, I confirm that not only is the room windowless, but there is no second door. And the one we came through is thoroughly locked.

I feel horribly trapped and so helpless as I hold Sarah close, willing her, above all else, to be okay.

What feels like hours drag by in the dim, oppressive room. I can sense Sarah's exhaustion weighing her down, her eyelids drooping as she clings to me. But she doesn't want to drift into sleep. Every time she begins to, she starts back awake with a gasp. As heart-wrenching as that is, it might be for the best. We need to be vigilant, to seize any opportunity that might come our way.

As if on cue, the door creaks open, and the man who had introduced himself to me as Mr. Cherny enters the room, a wicked smile curling his lips. I know better than to think of him as a simple restaurant owner now. He made his true identity perfectly clear as soon as he took me prisoner in his restaurant.

Aleksandr Volkov, the very man Maks warned me about. I instinctively clutch Sarah tighter, my heart pounding in my chest. She stirs in my arms, sensing my worry, and tightens her grip around my neck. *What does this man want?* Maks told me he would hurt me, that he would use me to get to Maks. *But why? Why would he take us? And why here, of all places?*

"What do you want from me?" I demand, my voice shaking with a mixture of fear and anger.

Aleksandr's eyes glitter with malevolence as he steps closer, his gaze locked on Sarah. "I want to put an end to the Federov Bratva. And you, my dear, are the bait to bring Maks in so I can kill him once and for all. The Federov brothers have been a plague on my city, taking all the best businesses and running this town for years. So tonight, I intend to butcher their leader. Then I'll deal with the rest of his family."

The words send a shiver down my spine. Maks, the man who offered to protect us, the one I foolishly rejected believing I could protect not only myself but my little girl, he's the one Aleksandr wants. And Aleksandr's intentions are far from noble. He's out for blood, and it's Maks's blood he craves. But I sense that my life, and Sarah's, would mean little to him if our deaths would help him capture his prey.

Sarah's small voice pierces the tension. "Mommy, I'm scared."

I hold her close, stroking her back with my palm. I keep my voice soft but firm as I respond to Aleksandr. "Maks won't come for us. He doesn't care about me. I'm nothing to him, just his . . ." —I hesitate, the word sticking in my throat— "whore."

It pains me to say it, now that I know how deep my emotions run for him. It might be the truth, that I'm little more than a prostitute in Maks's eyes, but the truth still hurts.

Aleksandr tsks, his expression unimpressed. "Now, Heidi, I thought you and I were building a bit of trust between us. The least you could do is be honest with me. To be a whore, one must accept money, my dear. And you don't do that, do you? Besides, I've been watching you two together. You can't fool me. I might not have a heart, but I'm not blind or dumb. Maks is obviously in love with you. Or hasn't he told you that?"

I scoff at the obvious attempt to upset me. Perhaps *Aleksandr* is the one who's underestimating *me*.

"What? You don't believe me?" he asks, his voice riddled with mock indignation. "You would if you'd heard him on the phone when I told him I plan on killing you. He nearly lost his mind. He didn't even try to argue when I told him he had to come alone and unarmed if he wanted a prayer of saving you. Not that I intend to let either of you live once I have him. No, I intend to let him watch your slow, excruciating death."

It terrifies me to hear Aleksandr's plans for me spoken so casually, as though he might as well have been saying he intended to take me for some ice cream. And yet, somehow, the suggestion that Maks has feelings for me dulls that fear. Even in our dire situation, the possibility that he might love me still manages to exhilarate me.

But I can't help the dread that coils in the pit of my stomach at the same time. My heart aches as I think about the danger I've put Maks in. Regardless of whether he cares for me or not, I know he feels a sense of responsibility to protect me. And I can't imagine he would handle my death well at all after what happened to his fiancée.

And if he *does* come for me, he'll be walking right into a trap. I don't want him to die for me. Which is exactly what it sounds like would happen if he chooses to do as Aleksandr commanded.

I can't let that happen. My mind races as I hold my daughter close, formulating a plan, desperate to ensure Sarah's safety and to make amends for the terrible mistake I made.

38

MAKSIM

Speeding to the casino in my red Corvette, I try to calm my heart's furious pace. The road blurs past my speeding car, each moment feeling like an eternity as I race against the clock, my life spiraling toward a precipice of impossible choices.

The image of Symphony's lifeless eyes staring up at me haunts my thoughts, and the guilt that claws at my soul threatens to consume me. How horribly I failed her, how I let her down in the most profound way. I'll never forgive myself for it.

But somehow, this fear that grips me as I hurtle toward Aleksandr's casino is a thousand times worse. Because I now know that I care more deeply for Heidi than I ever did for Symphony—even though I got engaged to Symphony and was with her for years, even though I've only spent a grand total of a few weeks in Heidi's presence.

Heidi is the sun that warms my days, the gravity that keeps me grounded. The brief time we've spent together has been the happiest of my life. And the last few nights have proven to me just how much I was missing out on by trying to keep her at a distance.

I've never felt so deeply connected to another human, so perfectly safe to be myself. Heidi doesn't just accept me as I am. She appreciates me for it. And I feel the same way about her—stubborn streak and all. I love her realness, her honesty, her unbreakable optimism even after she's suffered great loss.

And the more I know of her, the more I want.

I tried to end things with her. I was ready to walk away if that's what it took to keep her safe. But quitting Heidi was harder than quitting nicotine. And her plan failed miserably, anyway. I never should have agreed to it. I never should have left her exposed.

And now I'm paying for my mistake.

If we both make it through this situation alive, I intend to never let her out of my sight again. Because it's too late for me to quit her now. I'm crazy about Heidi. I don't want to keep things casual with her. I never want to live without her again. I don't know that I even can.

And that realization has my gas pedal plastered to the metal as I fly to her rescue.

I will do whatever it takes to save her.

Even if it takes laying down my own life.

I'd just better not be too late.

The plan is simple—as simple as it can be in our twisted, messed-up world. I intend to turn myself over. I'll gladly die if that's what it takes to ensure Heidi lives. And I'm confident that's exactly what Aleksandr wants. His message was clear—come alone, come unarmed, and come within the hour, which left me little time to formulate a strategy beyond compliance.

But I'm not naïve. I have no doubt that Aleksandr likely intends to kill Heidi as soon as he has what he wants. Hell, if I know anything about Aleksandr Volkov, he probably means to kill her slowly, painfully, and make me watch the entire time.

Because he's a sadistic bastard who doesn't just want to kill me. He'll want to break me first.

I won't let that happen.

Not at Heidi's expense.

That's why I've rallied Alexei and Dimitri to head the charge with all our men. Armed to the teeth, they're shortly behind me, ready to storm in as soon as Aleksandr's men believe I'm alone.

It's come down to a violent showdown, one I've spent years desperately hoping to avoid. I know we will lose good men over it and we could far more easily end up in jail for our crimes if this becomes a bloodbath. But I'll accept whatever fate awaits me as long as Heidi makes it out alive.

The tires of my car screech in protest as I pull into the casino's parking lot. My hands shake with unbridled fury as I yank the keys from the ignition and jump out of the vehicle. There's no time to waste, no room for hesitation. Every second counts.

As soon as I close my car door, I'm surrounded by a group of armed men, Aleksandr's men. Their faces are masked with a brutal stoicism, their presence a tangible reminder of the gravity of the situation.

Silently, one man steps forward to warily pat me down, checking to ensure I came unarmed before they escort me through the ruined casino's front doors at gunpoint. The tension in the air is suffocating, an invisible vise that constricts my chest and squeezes my heart.

Still, I feel a sense of pride at seeing the level of destruction we wrought on Aleksandr's favorite cash cow. The Starlight Lounge is little more than a ruin now, a scorched shell containing graveyards of melted slot machines and broken card tables. It's amazing what a little accelerant and a flame thrower can do.

By the time the police arrived, and the fire engine, there was little they could do.

Aleksandr's men lead me down winding corridors, past the ash-covered slot machines and the scorched roulette tables, toward the epicenter of the casino. My pulse quickens with every step, knowing that Heidi's life hangs in the balance, her fate determined by the relentless march of time.

As we approach the room where Aleksandr is holding her, I can hear his voice dripping with sadistic delight. My blood runs cold as he taunts her, seeming to savor her fear.

"Well, my dear, it seems you might be right after all. Maksim must not love you because it's been an hour and he's not here. Which means you're out of time."

"Wait, wait!" she cries. "If I mean so little to him, why do you need to kill me? Couldn't you just let me go?"

Aleksandr laughs cruelly. "And miss the opportunity to hang your mangled corpse in the lobby of his new hotel? I don't think so. Even if he doesn't care enough to try and save you, I'm sure he won't like your dead body frightening off his guests."

"Please don't," Heidi sobs, her voice growing frantic.

My stomach drops, and I move more urgently toward the door at the sound of Heidi's terrified plea.

But Aleksandr sounds completely unaffected as he delivers a horrifying ultimatum. "Would you rather I shoot you or your daughter first?"

I barely have time to process his question before Heidi's horrible choking sob drives me into desperation.

"No, *please*," she begs, the panic in her voice piercing through me.

The urgency of the situation grows unbearable, and true fear surges through me. *What if I'm just seconds too late?* I can't stand the thought. I can't fail Heidi, not now, not ever.

Panicking, I shove my way past the guards surrounding me and burst into the room. "I'm here," I growl, drawing all eyes to me in an instant. "You can aim the gun at me, Aleksandr, where that bullet belongs."

A malevolent smile plays across Aleksandr's lips as he turns to face me, his finger still poised on the trigger.

And because I can't help myself, I spare a glance toward Heidi. The scene that greets me is one of pure horror. Her face is streaked with tears, and I can see the start of a purple bruise coloring one cheekbone. She stands trembling with little Sarah, the innocent child I met at Heidi's office yesterday, clinging to her, eyes wide with terror.

Why would Sarah be with Heidi?

Somewhere in the back of my mind, I register the fact that Aleksandr called the little girl Heidi's daughter. A horrible, sinking feeling settles in my gut. But I don't have time to process that now.

"Ah, Maksim," Aleksandr purrs, his gaze icy as my eyes shift to look at him once more. "You finally decided to show up. I thought you might not come after all."

The room feels like it's closing in on me, like the walls are moving in, slowly squeezing the life out of us all. Every instinct in my body screams for me to act, to protect Heidi and her daughter at any cost. But I keep my hands visible, my palms open in a sign of surrender, even as my heart races.

What I need is to stall until I find an opening.

"Well, I did come," I reply, my voice steady, though the turmoil inside me threatens to explode. "Let them go, Aleksandr. You have me. You've won."

Heidi's round hazel eyes lock onto mine, gratitude and fear mingling in their depths. The room is charged with tension, the silence as heavy as death. I've put my life on the line, offered myself up as the ultimate pawn in this twisted game, all for her sake. And I can only pray that my plan works.

Then Aleksandr's smile widens, revealing the predator within. He's a man who revels in his power. He flaunts it and soaks up the fear that his reign of terror creates. There won't be a way out of this one.

Not for all of us, anyway.

39

HEIDI

Aleksandr's smile sends icy horror through my chest. Maks came. He actually came, unarmed and alone, as requested. And it rips me apart to know he's sacrificing himself for me.

In an instant, two realizations hit me hard enough to nearly knock me off my feet. One, I can't stand the thought of watching the man I love die—and I do love Maks, with my whole heart, regardless of how he feels about commitment or love or even me.

The second realization is that Aleksandr might actually be right. Maks does care for me. At least he cares enough that he's willing to die for me. And the moving realization steals my breath away, leaving me filled with overwhelming joy for one fractal moment.

Then reality comes crashing back down around me as I face the fact that he probably is going to die for me. Right here. Right now. In front of our daughter whom I never told him is his.

I've made such a mess of everything.

As if he heard my thoughts and finds them particularly humorous, Aleksandr sneers, his eyes as dark as the devil's as he looks me up and down with scorn.

"I have to give it to you, Maks. She is beautiful. But you Federov brothers are just too easy to manipulate because you're all the same." Aleksandr pauses, letting his gloating jab really sink in before he continues. "I've never met a family with such a hard reputation, and yet you're all a bunch of soft-hearted romantics willing to give up your lives for the women you love."

Maks stands stock still, his silver eyes brimming with hatred as he follows Aleksandr's slow stroll around the room. "At least we're not heartless monsters willing to poison a frail old woman living her life in peace on her country estate."

Confused, I frown as my gaze shifts to Aleksandr, but Maks's comment seems to have the desired effect as my captor takes an unexpected pause.

"Dimitri did get my chef to break, then, did he? I must admit, I'm a bit surprised." Aleksandr resumes his walk, seeming to make peace with the new knowledge.

"Actually, no. Believe it or not, I worked that one out for myself, thanks. You've gone after both of my brothers' wives, killed my fiancée. It's not a far leap to assume you're responsible for poisoning my mother."

Aleksandr scoffs. "Pity it didn't work."

My jaw drops at the new revelation, and I cling more tightly to Sarah as the reasons behind Maks's wrath toward Aleksandr grow more apparent by the second. No wonder he was so worked up about the living agreement he wanted me to enter into. I'm actually shocked he was willing to compromise at all.

"Pity I didn't see you for the snake in the grass Dimitri always knew you were. I could have removed your head before you turned into such a bothersome nuisance," Maks spits.

From the shift in Aleksandr's expression, I can tell he doesn't like being belittled at all. And from what I understand of him, I imagine that's because he wants to be feared and respected, not thought of as a minor inconvenience that Maks didn't even bat an eye at.

"You and your brothers are not worthy of the brotherhood you claim," Aleksandr snarls, losing his cool for the first time. "You're not strong enough to hold the territory your father won for you. You're all weak, and that's why you're all going to die. I look forward to killing each and every one of you. Starting with you."

By the end of his tirade, Aleksandr has regained some of his cool. But I can still see the mad dog lying beneath the surface, ready to attack at the smallest provocation. Maks might be a dangerous person, but Aleksandr Volkov seems positively unhinged.

"I hate to disagree with you," Maks says calmly, seeming to know just what buttons to push to keep Aleksandr talking rather than killing us, "but I'm going to anyway. A weak man is a man who stands alone. There's strength in loyalty, strength in family, and strength in numbers. All of which we do have."

Aleksandr's eyebrows buckle, forming a dark scowl as he stops to search for the insult in Maks's words.

I'm nearly as stunned by the statement myself as I study Maks's face with new regard. Not only is he clearly in his element and a master at negotiation and stall tactics, but I hear a ringing truth in his argument that flies in the face of all his no-emotional-ties business. After all, you can't have loyalty, and you certainly can't have family, without love.

The room is silent for a moment, even Aleksandr's men pausing in their diligent efforts to keep their guns trained on Maks.

That's when the distant sound of gunfire begins.

Faster than my eyes can track, Maks is in motion. He closes the distance between him and the nearest of Aleksandr's guards before the man has time to aim. He grabs the man's gun wrist and with a violent jerk, Maks both disarms him and wraps his arm around the man's throat.

The guard chokes, his hands flying to Maks's arm to relieve the crushing pressure. But Maks hardly seems to notice as he points the guard's gun at one armed assailant after the next and kills them before they can stop him.

Amazed by Maksim's dexterity and unwavering bravery, I watch in stunned silence for a moment before realizing I'm standing out in the open, leaving me and Sarah completely exposed. Tucking my little girl's face into my shoulder, I cover her head as best I can, then duck behind a table, enveloping Sarah with my body as best I can.

It's not the ideal kind of cover. I can still see everything happening in the room, but at least I've minimized our exposed surface area as I try to hide my daughter from the bullets pinging around the room.

And as I crouch over Sarah, I watch Maks take down one man after the next, using the guard he disarmed as a shield. His aim is astonishing, and though my heart falters at the sight of bullets whizzing past him and riddling the man before him, he doesn't fall.

He slaughters men with a cool, emotionless confidence that I might have found terrifying if not for the fact that he's doing it to save my life. And now, as I watch him singlehandedly clear the room of my captors, all I can feel is intense, overwhelming gratitude and growing relief.

Finally, only Aleksandr remains standing, and he unloads five bullets with a furious shout, his face twisted into a mask of fury as he tries and fails to hit Maks around his human shield.

Aleksandr's gun clicks once, twice, three times, informing us that he's out of ammo. His face pales as the gunfire grows louder down the hallway. Maks's backup is getting close.

Releasing the now-lifeless corpse with a harsh thud, Maks unleashes a murderous grin, his eyes glinting as he watches Aleksandr like a lion who's cornered its prey.

As if only just realizing the imminent danger, Aleksandr drops his gun, sprinting for the door at a pace I hadn't imagined a man of his physique could muster.

Maks tracks him calmly, almost lazily with his gun, and as the fleeing villain comes within feet of the door, Maks gives his trigger one final squeeze.

The report echoes down the hallway, the sound three times louder than I had anticipated and oddly delayed.

A moment later, Aleksandr spins, his body twisting almost involuntarily until he's facing into the room once more. Only then do I see the bullet in his chest. My eyes shift upward to find a third bullet hole squarely in the center of his forehead. A vacant expression falls like a curtain over his face.

Then Aleksandr Volkov crumples to the floor. Dead.

40

MAKSIM

My bullet hits Aleksandr square between the shoulder blades. And to my surprise, his body whips around as two more bullets find their home in his chest and head. Dimitri and Alexei appear in the doorway a moment later, their presence all the explanation I need.

Those seem to be the final bullets in our old-school shootout, and as the din dies down, the room grows deathly still in the wake of our victory.

This is going to require a massive clean-up job. But at least the casino is out of commission after our last attack on it, and it's far enough outside the city that we'll have more time to clean up the evidence before cops arrive.

Soft sniffling redirects my attention from my brothers' broad smiles to the girls huddled beneath the poker table, and I turn to see Heidi cradling Sarah protectively in her arms. The sight of the incredibly maternal way Heidi holds her brings Aleksandr's questions back to mind in an instant. And though I might have questioned it then, there's no doubt in my mind now. Heidi has a daughter.

I don't quite know how to feel about that—not because I have anything against children, and this one in particular, I truly enjoy. *But why did Heidi never tell me?* We've spent weeks in each other's company, and while we tended to keep our conversations more impersonal, I told her about my family, and she told me all about Zoe and her mom.

None of that matters now, of course. My first concern is that they're both alright, and I stride purposefully across the room to check on them. As I reach her side, Heidi looks too shaky to stand on her own, so I stoop to wrap an arm around her waist and help her out from under the table.

"Thank you," she whispers tearfully, one hand clinging to my arm for support until she's back on her feet.

Then her hand returns to Sarah's head as she cradles the little girl close to her chest.

"Are you both alright?" I ask, keeping my voice low so as not to startle the little girl.

"I–I think so," Heidi says, gingerly wiping the tears from her cheeks.

Little Sarah peeks shyly out from under her thick curtain of dark hair after a moment's hesitation to look up at me. And as soon as I meet her eyes, I wonder how I could have thought she was anyone but Heidi's daughter. They have the same striking hazel eyes, round with innocent wonder.

"You're safe now," I assure the little girl, offering her a soft smile.

And to my relief, she straightens a little in her mom's arms, turning to return the smile more shakily.

"Did they hurt you?" I ask, carefully inspecting Sarah before turning my attention to Heidi.

"Not bad. A few bumps and bruises," she admits, showing me one of her skinned palms.

Tenderly, I brush the back of a knuckle across the bruise that's swiftly darkening on her cheek. Heidi flinches, air hissing between her teeth, though she tries to mask the pain.

"Mommy?" Sarah says, her voice warbling with the threat of fresh tears.

"I'm okay, baby," Heidi promises, pressing her lips to her little girl's temple. "Everything is okay."

The sweet exchange is a lance through my heart as it confirms any lingering thoughts I might have, and despite my deep concern for their well-being and my need to ensure their safety, a hint of anger starts to rise within me.

It hurts to know that Heidi lied to me. It's a deep betrayal after I've felt I could trust her all this time. I want to confront her about it, but I don't want to scare her little girl.

"You never told me you have a daughter," I state as quietly as I can manage, my voice rigid with the effort to keep my anger from my tone. "Do you have a husband I should know about too?"

"No. No!" she says, startled, her eyes flying wide in a look of shocked innocence that I no longer know whether I can believe.

"Then, what? An ex, a boyfriend, or are you going to tell me she was born from immaculate conception?" The hurt in my voice comes out bitter, and I bite back my words before I say something I might regret. Taking a deep breath, I try to collect myself before asking a more civil question. "What's the story on her father?"

Fresh tears spring to Heidi's eyes, revealing a deep sadness I hadn't anticipated. A tinge of regret tightens my stomach. Maybe I was too quick to anger.

"I'm so sorry, Maks. I should have told you. I wanted to tell you so many times, but I couldn't because . . . well, she's your daughter. I got pregnant from our first time together—four years ago. I didn't tell you because you said you didn't want love or a family. And I thought it best to keep Sarah out of this"—she gestures between me and her, indicating our arrangement—"because I didn't want to put her through the confusion and loss after we ended things."

I'm stunned to hear I have a daughter, and an intense warmth radiates through my heart at the possibility that Sarah is mine. That overwhelming joy is quickly followed by guilt, however, and deep remorse that I did something to convince Heidi that I shouldn't be in my daughter's life.

And just as quickly, my emotions shift again to an ugly suspicion that I want to crush before it takes control. But after Heidi's kept such a big secret all this time, I find I'm not entirely ready to trust her.

"How can you possibly be sure I'm the father? I mean, it was one night, and we used protection. Couldn't it have been a boyfriend around that time, or . . .?" My voice trails off as I recall that night we shared, how inexperienced she seemed, how nearly virginal. And before she says anything, I know she's telling the truth.

"I haven't been with anyone except you since that night, Maks," she confesses, her cheeks turning a deep shade of rose. She doesn't sound defensive. Instead, she seems determined to lay it all out there now that I know, her explanation gushing from her without prompting. "I wasn't with anyone before you either, not for a long time."

Sniffling, Heidi wipes her face once more, pulling herself together. "I was ready to keep it a one-time thing, and like I told you before, your generosity made it so I could quit Lady Venus and get my life back on track. Then, about a month into school, I found out I was pregnant."

Her hand strokes Sarah's hair as if to comfort herself as much as to soothe the little girl, and despite myself, it makes my heart swell to see Heidi be such a good mother. Snuggled in her mother's arms, Sarah looks like she's on the verge of falling asleep at this point. She's probably exhausted from all the fear and trauma she just survived.

"I knew I wanted to keep the baby and that I should tell you," she says. "But I had no clue how to find you or where I would even start. By then, I couldn't even recall your last name. I didn't know where you lived, where you worked . . . So I made peace with becoming a single mom."

I remain still, listening to her tale though I think at this point, she needs to tell me more than I need to hear it. Because the truth is that whatever she's hoping I'll forgive her for, I've already forgiven. In my mind, there's nothing to forgive. She's taken care of our daughter without my help for the first three years of Sarah's life. She's done it with a devotion that astounds me, and all I can feel is gratitude for her strength and dedication to our little girl.

"I swear, Maks, I didn't even have time to think about dating, what with Mom being so sick and then passing away ... then trying to start my own business and raise a child ..."

Softening further as I hear the anxiety behind her words and see the tearful apology in her eyes, I can't let her go on any longer. Stepping close to Heidi, I cup her face tenderly in my palms. "Shh," I soothe. "I'm sorry I doubted you for even a second," I murmur. "You did more than anyone could ever have expected of a young single mother, and I only wish I had been there. I want to help, to do my part as a father. I want to make it up to you both."

"Oh, Maks," Heidi breathes, her tears coming hard and fast once more. As they trickle down her cheeks, I gently brush them away with my thumbs. "Don't you know you've already done more than I would ever ask? Even in my hardest moments, when I felt most alone, I never had to worry about how I would feed Sarah or put a roof over her head. And that's because you gave so generously to me without a second thought. I don't want you to feel guilty, and I definitely don't want you to feel obligated to be a part of our lives if that's not what you want."

"But it is," I insist, her words triggering a deep ache in my heart. I fear she might not believe my words now after everything I've said and done to prove otherwise. "I *do* want to be a part of your lives. I'm overjoyed to know I'm the father of such a beautiful, smart, good girl —just like her mom."

Heidi's eyes shine with love and devotion, and she places one hand over the back of mine, nuzzling her cheek into my palm.

"I want to be a part of Sarah's life—and yours—for as long as you'll let me. I'm sorry it's taken me time to realize it, to work through all my junk. But I'm crazy about you, Heidi. I want to be with you and raise our daughter together. I would do anything to protect you—both of you."

"I know," Heidi breathes, her eyes casting around the room to acknowledge the lengths I went to in order to keep her safe today. Then her eyes return to me, a grateful smile curving her lips.

I mirror her warmth, my own smile drawing from within me all the joy and love and devotion I've spent so long trying to suppress.

"Against my wishes, and my very best efforts, I've fallen for you, Heidi, and after almost losing you, I know that the love I was trying to avoid found me anyway. I don't want to run from attachment anymore. I want to tie myself to you in every earthly way possible and spend the rest of my life making up for all the years I've wasted."

Heidi giggles, her happiness radiating from her with an almost angelic glow. "I want that too," she murmurs, her eyes glistening.

41

HEIDI

It fills me with overwhelming elation to hear Maks say that he not only loves me but that he wants to raise our daughter together. Telling him the truth about Sarah was one of the scariest things I've ever had to do—almost as scary as facing my death at the hands of Aleksandr Volkov.

I had expected Maks to be angry that I kept my secret from him, possibly indifferent about having a daughter. I thought he might even want nothing to do with me or Sarah, but he took me completely by surprise.

As a giddy burst of joy bubbles from my lips, Maks leans in to kiss me, right in the middle of the casino. Heat races through my veins and pools inside my belly at his touch, and as I hold Sarah's sleepy body close with one arm, I melt into Maks, soaking up the reassuring strength of his powerful arms.

Catcalls from the doorway of the dim room call me back to the present, and Maks breaks the kiss with a roll of his eyes.

"You two are the worst," he growls toward the two men who paused their inspection of Aleksandr's lifeless body to interrupt our moment.

They both flash devilish grins that instantly confirm they must be

Maks's brothers. All three have the same gray eyes and dark hair flecked with just the right amount of silver. Their features are similar, too, with square jaws and straight noses. From a distance, I might have a hard time distinguishing one from the other.

"Sorry," Maks grumbles, turning his attention back to me. "I would say they're not normally this bad, but then I'd be lying."

A startled laugh bursts from my lips, and Sarah perks up once again, looking around to see what I thought was so funny.

Anxiety tightens my stomach as I think about all the dead bodies littering the floor, and I try to shield her from the worst of it. "Maybe we could take this outside? I'd like to talk to Sarah about... well, you. But I want to do it somewhere she'll feel safer."

"Of course." Without a moment's hesitation, Maks shrugs out of his suit jacket and drapes it over Sarah, giving her a warm blanket that I can tuck close to help hide the graphic sight around us. Then his arm shifts around my waist to support me as he helps guide me through the maze of bodies.

"Dimitri...?" he starts as we near the doorway, and the older-looking of his two brothers rises with a momentarily serious expression.

"I'll handle it. You do what you need to do." His chin juts in my direction, and for a moment, sharp, intelligent eyes scrutinize me with open curiosity. Then Dimitri gives a subtle bow. "Heidi, it's a pleasure to finally meet you," he says. "Though the circumstances are rather unfortunate." His eyes take in the gory scene around us.

Then Maks's other brother rises from his crouch to elbow Dimitri in the ribs. "What he's trying to say is we've heard a lot about you, and we look forward to getting to know you better. Not just any girl could work your kind of magic on the old grizzly bear here."

He pats Maks on the shoulder and receives a shockingly bear-like growl from his older brother in response.

"I'm Alexei, by the way. The handsome Federov brother." He gives me a playful wink.

"It's nice to meet you both," I say, smiling despite the grim atmosphere.

"Come on. Let's get you two outside," Maks says, his arm wrapping protectively around my shoulders as he moves me along.

It fills me with relief when he doesn't take me through the same flickering maze of hallways into the parking garage. Instead, Maks walks me right through the boarded up front doors of the casino and back out into the startlingly bright day.

From the angle of the sun, I'd guess it's late afternoon or early evening, and I'm almost shocked to realize we must still be on the same day as our abduction. It feels like a lifetime ago that I shook off that black SUV tailing me.

A thought hits me all of a sudden, and I look up at Maks. "Did you ... send a car to follow me?"

Maks gives me a somewhat sheepish grin. "Yeah. Although apparently, you're a crazier driver than a couple of Russian Bratva members."

I chuckle at that and shake my head. "After your warning yesterday, I thought they might be the men you were talking about. They scared the daylights out of me."

"I should have just told you about them. But I thought you might try to sneak away from them if I did."

My lips press into a warm smile. "You're probably right. But how about, from now on, we agree to no more secrets?"

"I can live with that," he agrees, and he pulls me close to press a kiss to my forehead.

Outside, in the front drive of what proves to be the Starlight Casino and Lounge, I'm relieved to find that the world around us could almost be considered normal. This will do just fine to talk to Sarah about Maks.

Stooping, I set her down on the sidewalk, and Sarah leans close, not wanting to be left alone after everything she's been through.

"I have something to tell you," I say gently, smoothing my fingers over her delicate cheeks and chin before taking my daughter's tiny hands. "Sarah, this is Maks. Do you remember him?"

"Yeah. We met yesterday," she says, looking shyly up at him over my shoulder.

Even though he's brought himself down to Sarah's level behind me, he's still tall enough that she has to raise her eyes, and she swings her body from side to side in a bashful dance.

"That's right," he agrees. "And you told me about your birthday plans to go to the zoo."

I peek over my shoulder at Maks to find a soft, tender smile breaking across his face.

Sarah's nodding when I turn back to her, and after a moment's hesitation, she asks, "Do you want to come?"

My heart positively melts. It seems our daughter has already taken a shine to Maks, and I'm speechless for a moment as happy tears sting my eyes.

"I would love to come to your birthday," Maks says, his low voice rich with emotion.

"Sarah, honey, you know how you asked me about the dads your friends at school have?" I say, trying to break into the topic gently.

"Yeah?"

"Well, Maks is *your* dad. And if it's alright with you, he would like to start spending time with us. What do you say?"

Sarah's eyes grow round before her brows crumple in confusion, and she looks at Maks once more. "Dad?" she says, trying out the word.

The utter vulnerability that transforms Maks's face is devastatingly beautiful. I can see the deep emotion in his eyes, and I know that even though he couldn't be there in the hospital on the day Sarah was born, he's experiencing that same earth-shattering experience now. That feeling like the entire gravity of the planet has suddenly shifted to revolve around one single, tiny human being.

"Yeah, that's me," he agrees, his voice rasping adorably, and he clears his throat, sniffing to pull himself together.

Tentatively, as if unsure whether it's allowed, Sarah releases my hands to step closer to her father. Then she commits, taking two toddling steps before she wraps her arms around his neck in a fierce hug.

Maks freezes, his body tensing with the shock of her affectionate display. Then all at once, he relaxes, his big arms wrapping around her tiny frame with a delicate tenderness that puts a lump in my throat. Holding Sarah close, his palm nearly covering the expanse of her tiny back, Maks meets my eye, and I can see the unconditional love there, the devotion that goes beyond words.

How I ever could have doubted that he could love our daughter, I don't know. But it's clear to me now that Sarah's life is about to get so much richer for having her father in her life.

When she finally releases him, Sarah steps back into my arms with a shy smile.

"Shall we go home?" I offer, giving her a tight squeeze from behind.

She just nods and turns to let me lift her back into my arms.

Maks and I agree that the best place for Sarah tonight is going to be in her own home, where she'll feel safest, surrounded by the people who love her most.

Zoe's there when we arrive, in a full-on panic as she bellows into the phone at the police about the ludicrousness of waiting twenty-four hours to file a missing persons report. As soon as she sees us, she hangs up without another word before sprinting across the room to give us both a fierce hug.

After telling her the full story of what happened once I got off the phone with her this morning, Zoe astonishes me by not just hugging me and Sarah again but also by throwing her arms around Maks in a fierce embrace.

"Thank you for bringing them home safely," she says tearfully.

Maks gives her a gentle pat on the back, his expression baffled by her emotional display as he looks at me. I grin, shrugging to indicate he should just accept the fact that he's proven himself a knight in shining armor today.

"Of course," he says.

We all sit down for an early dinner together, and afterward, Maks joins me and Sarah for her favorite bedtime story. The poor thing is so tired that we don't even make it through the children's picture book before she's sleeping soundly, tucked between us.

Sneaking quietly from her room without waking her, Maks and I head back to my room down the hall. As I close the door behind us, we're finally alone, free to talk uninhibited about everything that's happened.

Maks doesn't waste a moment, pressing me gently back against the closed door to capture my lips in a fiery kiss. And it feels so good to have him near. I thought I'd lost him. First yesterday, when he walked out the door. Then again today, when he came barging in to rescue me. I've never been so scared to lose someone in my life.

It's heavenly to have my hand resting over his heart as I feel the powerful beats against my palm. "You're really ready to give love another try?" I breathe when he finally pauses to come up for air.

Maks releases a low, dark chuckle. "I don't see that I have much of a choice because I'm already in love."

My heart throbs at the sound of those words, and a slow smile stretches across my face.

"But this time, I promise I will do whatever it takes to keep you and our daughter safe."

"Aw." Emotion threatens to choke me once again at his deeply meaningful words.

"What?" he asks, leaning back to meet my eyes.

"You said 'our daughter'." I sniffle, then I giggle as Maks gives a soft laugh.

"I like the sound of that," he agrees as he leans in to kiss me once again.

The electric connection between us starts to build as his tongue traces my lower lip before stroking inside my mouth. His hands explore me gently, careful not to hurt me in any way.

Something about this newfound tenderness makes my heart flutter. I love the rough, passionate way he fucks me, and I adore the slow, intimate sex we had during the night we spent at the spa. But this, without a doubt, is how Maks intends to make love to me for the first time, and it warms my soul, filling me up with the sweetest kind of happiness I've ever known.

Slowly, carefully, he undresses me before he scoops me into his arms to carry me to my bed. I watch as he strips his own clothes, his eyes never leaving my face as if he fears I might vanish if he looks away.

Then he climbs into bed with me, his body aligning with mine with effortless perfection. "I know I'm doing this all out of order," he murmurs as he trails soft kisses down my throat to my breasts. "And I don't have a ring—yet. But, Heidi Turner, I love you. I love you more than I've ever loved anything. And I want to show you that every day for the rest of our lives. Will you marry me?"

His lips draw kisses back up to my mouth, and he presses a single chaste kiss there before pausing, his arms resting against the mattress on either side of my shoulders, as he waits for my answer.

"Yes," I breathe, tears of joy stinging my eyes as I nod emphatically. "Yes, I'll marry y—"

Maks's lips find mine, cutting short my response as he kisses me with renewed passion, and I groan with pleasure as he eases inside me a moment later. I can hardly breathe, I'm so overcome by the euphoria of being in his arms, of feeling the love radiating from his body in tangible waves.

All that potential I could see hidden behind his thick walls floods forth now, wrapping me in deep emotion that leaves me speechless. Maks said he loves me. He said it without fear or hesitation. And I know I'm in love with him too.

I can't believe I'm so fortunate that he is the father of our child because he's the only man for me. I think somewhere, deep down in my soul, I've known it all along.

We've both suffered so much pain and loss in our lives, and I know those people will never truly leave us. But now, I can't wait to discover all the new, wonderful possibilities of a life with Maks.

This is my happily ever after. With the man of my dreams, the most wonderful daughter in the world, and the best family a girl could ask for.

EPILOGUE
HEIDI

I stand in the soft glow of the late-afternoon sun, my heart fluttering with anticipation. We decided to keep our wedding day simple after a short engagement. Maks didn't want to wait, and honestly, I couldn't agree more. But as I stand waiting for the guests to arrive, the day almost feels surreal. It happened in the blink of an eye.

But I'm just excited that tonight, I'll go to bed the wife of Maksim Federov.

Excitement bubbles up inside me, threatening to overflow as I watch the final preparations for our special day unfold at Le Fleur. By happy coincidence, I learned that the favorite French restaurant Zoe, Sarah, and I have been going to for years happens to be owned and run by none other than Maks's sister-in-law Camille.

Camille—Dimitri's wife—has proven to be nothing short of a delight in helping with wedding preparations, and I'm so grateful that she's closed the entire restaurant for the evening to accommodate the celebration of our nuptials. It's mostly family in attendance, and our closest friends, which for me is one and the same. And that's just how I like it.

The scent of fresh flowers fills the air as a gentle breeze rustles through the open front doors. I take a deep breath and savor the moment. The guests who made our very short guest list are arriving, and everything feels perfect.

I look over at Sarah, our adorable flower girl, her giggle of excitement contagious as she twirls in her tiny white dress. I can't help but smile as I watch her. Having her here today, playing a part in the wedding, is a dream come true, and I love that she's as excited for us to become a family as I am.

Zoe claps enthusiastically at her performance, and once again, I'm grateful for my lifelong friend who was more than willing to accept the responsibility of watching Sarah today and taking her home for a sleepover tonight so Maks and I can have time alone on our wedding night.

Maks's brother, Alexei, approaches me, his tuxedo impeccably tailored and a warm smile on his face. He leans in to kiss my cheek, and I can't help but feel a surge of gratitude for the strong bond that has formed between us since he and Dimitri helped Maks come to my rescue.

Already, I feel like part of the family, and the ceremony hasn't even happened yet.

"Congratulations, Heidi," he says, his Russian accent adding a touch of charm to his words. "You look stunning."

"Thank you, Alexei," I reply, a blush rising in my cheeks.

He nods, his eyes scanning the well-decorated space. The space didn't need much more than a few bouquets of fresh wedding-white flowers to add a bit of formality to the already charming ambiance. They made the perfect touch to the restaurant adorned with extravagant, curling chandeliers that drip glittering crystals. The vaulted exposed-beam room is cast with a soft, romantic light.

The rustic wood chairs and tables give it a countryside cottage feel, and the green vines that wind around the solid wood beams give the space a hint of an enchanted-forest atmosphere. It's the vision of a true artist, and I've always admired whoever chose Camille's decor.

"It's a beautiful day for a wedding," Alexei observes. "I'm glad my brother didn't want to wait any longer."

I smile in silent agreement. Maksim's impatience to start our lives together is one of the things I love most about him. Since the day he told me he loved me, Maks has proven more devoted, more caring, more attentive as a father and as a partner than I ever could have imagined. And his eagerness to marry me is just one more endearing piece to the man I fall more in love with every day.

"Me too."

Alexei gives me a signature wink and walks away to greet other guests.

I watch the children playing together, their laughter filling the air, and it warms my heart to see Sarah having such a great time with her new friends, cousins she's quickly grown close to and looks forward to seeing. It's moments like these that make me believe in the magic of love and family.

I feel so blessed to be joining Maks's.

We keep the ceremony simple—no more than fifteen minutes—but filled with heartfelt vows and promises. Maks asked his brother Dimitri to officiate, and he knocks it out of the park with a few choice words about love, devotion, and the significance of finding someone you want to hold onto forever.

Then Maks and I exchange rings, sealing our commitment with a kiss that sets my soul on fire. I can't wait to start this new chapter of our lives as husband and wife.

After the ceremony, we move upstairs to the beautifully decorated loft we intend to use as the reception area. A long table is set for dinner, and the aroma of delicious food wafts through the air, making my stomach rumble with hunger. The delicate clinking of glasses and the murmurs of our guests create a comforting background melody.

We settle at the middle of the table and share a few quiet moments together as the food starts to leave the kitchen, the staff placing it before our guests with practiced finesse.

"Well, wife, is today everything you dreamed?" Maks asks, lifting our intertwined hands to place a kiss on the back of my palm.

"More than," I breathe, and I mean it.

His smile is radiant, and it fills me with a warmth that words can't capture. I lean close, and we share a tender kiss as the sun dips lower in the San Francisco sky, casting a golden hue over our celebration.

At the end of the evening, after a full night of celebration and fun, our family and friends give us a big send off. Then Maks and I climb into his red Corvette to head to his penthouse for a little alone time.

As we drive, I can hardly contain my excitement. I've been holding onto a secret all day, and now I can finally reveal it.

"At last, I have you all to myself," Maks growls, pulling me into his arms as we step off the elevator into his spacious home.

I giggle, rocking with him as we sway in the entryway. When he leans in to kiss me, I hum appreciatively, relishing in the feel of his soft lips commanding mine.

"I have a surprise for you," I whisper, pulling back just enough to meet his molten silver gaze.

His eyes search mine, filled with a mix of curiosity and desire. "And what surprise is that, my love?"

I can barely contain my smile as I gently disentangle myself from his arms and lead him to the kitchen where a small, neatly wrapped box sits on the kitchen island. I hand it to him, watching as his eyes widen with anticipation.

"Open it," I say.

He does, setting the box aside as he lifts a tiny pale yellow onesie decorated with giraffes from the tissue paper. His gaze moves from the little outfit to me, a puzzled expression on his face. Then, it clicks as his eyes fill with wonder and his lips part in awe.

"You're pregnant?" he breathes, his voice tinged with emotion.

I nod, tears of joy filling my eyes. "I've been bursting to tell you all day, but I wanted to wait for a moment when we could celebrate together."

Maksim pulls me into his arms, holding me tightly. "Heidi, this is the best surprise I could ever imagine. We're having a baby?"

I nod more emphatically this time, giddy with excitement.

His joy is contagious, and we both laugh as the tears start to stream from my eyes.

"But why are you crying?" he asks, his thumbs brushing across my cheeks as he peers into my eyes.

I laugh again, waving the tears away. "This is just the hormones kicking in. I hope you're prepared because they don't get easier from here."

Maks chuckles in response, pulling me close to his chest once more. "I think I can handle that."

His steadfast support fills this special day with an even deeper sense of happiness and love. I can't believe my family is growing, this time with the man I adore, the man who completes me.

Maksim kisses my forehead, then my lips, a tender promise of all the love and support he'll give me as we embark on this new journey together.

"How long have you known?" Maksim asks, his eyes locking onto mine.

"I took the test this morning." My heart swells with love for him. "I wanted to tell you right away, but I also wanted to just enjoy our special day."

Maks smiles, then leans down and kisses my belly, his lips tender against my skin. "I can't wait to meet our little one."

Combing my fingers into his hair, I smile down at him. "Me too. Now, take me to bed, husband."

With an appreciative growl, Maks rises from his crouch. In a flash, he scoops me up into his arms. I squeal at the sudden shift in balance, then I wrap my arms around his neck as he carries me across the threshold into the bedroom.

I can't help but smile as I think about the adventures that lie ahead. With Maks by my side, I know we can face anything. Our love is a beacon that will light our path as we journey together into this new chapter of our lives. Life is good, and it's only going to get better as we welcome a new member into our family.

We are surrounded by the love and warmth of our friends and family. This is a moment frozen in time, one that we will carry with us as we step into the future hand in hand, ready to embrace the blessings and challenges of parenthood together.

EXTENDED EPILOGUE
MAKSIM

One Year Later

Now that Aleksandr Volkov is gone, the war is over, and I'm not ashamed to admit that the Federov brothers are back on top. I can feel it as I step out of my car onto Mom's estate and am greeted by my two younger brothers, Dimitri and Alexei.

"Took you long enough," Alexei ribs. "What, did you get stuck in traffic?"

"What traffic?" Dimitri piles on. "It's two o'clock on a Saturday."

"Maybe rather than giving me a hard time, one of you lazy slouches might offer my wife a hand," I suggest, adopting my best gruff tone. But in truth, nothing can put me in a bad mood these days.

"Heidi," Alexei greets her, taking little Efrem from her before wrapping her in a one-armed hug. Then he holds my son above his head, exacting a giggle from the little boy as he jiggles him playfully.

"Ready, Sarah?" I ask, opening the back seat to find she's already unbuckled herself and is doing her best to crawl down from the car on her own.

Just like her mother—independent as hell and unwilling to ask for help, even when it's perfectly within reason.

"Daddy, can I go find Cousin Liam?" she asks as she drags the little rainbow-colored backpack of art supplies from the car floor and slings it, upside down, across her back.

"I bet your Uncle Dimitri will know just where you ought to look," I suggest.

"Come on, kiddo," Dimitri says, offering Sarah his hand.

She takes it, and the two vanish into the house as I stoop to reach into the back seat of the car to help Heidi unload supplies.

"I thought I heard that car of yours," Camille says brightly, stepping onto Mom's pillared front patio.

The voluptuous and talented young chef married to my brother Dimitri shields her eyes as she smiles down on us. Next to her, my brother Alexei's wife, Nadia, has a newborn baby girl cradled in her arms.

That makes three kiddos for my youngest brother, a miracle, really, considering Nadia thought she would never be able to have kids of her own until Alexei came along. Her petite dancer's frame is a stark contrast to Camille's, and yet they're both strikingly beautiful women in their own ways.

"We brought the fruit salad, as requested," Heidi says, displaying our contribution to the barbecue as we ascend the porch steps.

My wife shares a warm hug with both of my sisters-in-law before they give me a hug. I love how well all three of our wives get along. It makes being so close to my brothers—both in business and as family—far easier, and in my book, more meaningful.

"Maks, when did you get here?" Mom, her steps growing frailer by the day, hobbles out to greet us, using her cane for balance and support.

"Hi, Ma," I murmur, grasping her forearm to gently steady her before I press a kiss to her temple. "We just arrived. My brothers have kidnapped both of our children, however, so you'll have to chase them down if you want to see your grandchildren."

"Are you all hungry?" Camille asks. "The grill's nice and hot. If we want to head out back, I can get started on the brats."

"I'm famished," Heidi confesses. "I only just finished with my client this morning and haven't had a chance to eat yet today."

"You are going to work yourself to the bone if you keep up like that. Hasn't Maks told you it's okay to take a break every now and again?" Nadia teases, linking arms with my wife as we all head toward the back porch.

My brothers' herd of children are already playing on the lawn past the cement patio, chasing each other across the lawn with excited squeals. It would seem that Sarah's found them as well, and she and Liam giggle as they run circles around the younger ones.

"I brought you the fixings, love," Dimitri says, exiting the house from the kitchen with a platter of garnish and a pair of tongs. He presses a kiss to Camille's cheek as he sets the food down next to the grill she's busy manning.

It doesn't take long before the burgers are ready, and after a bit of a challenge wrangling the kiddos into chairs at the kids' table, we all sit down to eat beneath the warm summer sun. The chatter is light, my brothers offering up an endless stream of banter as we all laugh.

I can't think of a time in my life when we have all been so happy, and I sit back in my seat to soak up the joy that surrounds me now.

"Your father would have loved to see this," Mom says, leaning toward me conspiratorially as she gives my hand a soft pat. "He might have been hard on you boys growing up, but all he ever wanted was for you to live good, happy lives. And I think you've each managed that beautifully."

I give my mom's hand a gentle squeeze, and a moment later, I catch Heidi's soft grin as she watches our exchange.

"You know, I don't think I've ever heard the story of how you met your husband, Mrs. Federov," Heidi says.

I love that no matter how many times my mother has told my wife to call her by her first name, Heidi's Southern upbringing won't permit it. And as my mom gives Heidi a scolding look now, I can't help but chuckle.

"You haven't?" Alexei asks, surprise dawning on his face.

"Come to think of it, I don't know that I've heard the stories behind how any of you met," she adds, glancing at Nadia and Alexei and then Camille and Dimitri.

Camille snorts a laugh, drawing everyone's attention, and a hint of color stains her cheeks. "You don't want to know how Dimitri and I met," she says, quirking an eyebrow at her husband, daring him to defend himself.

"Okay, now I have to know," Heidi insists, sitting forward in her chair.

"He walked into my restaurant one night, bold as brass, and told me that I owed him half a million dollars or my restaurant."

"What?" Heidi nearly shrieks, her eyes bugging out of her head. "And you said?"

"Perhaps we can discuss this over a meal," Dimitri offers, a twinkle in his eye.

"That is *not* what I said," Camille counters. "I'm pretty sure it was closer to 'you can just go straight to hell.'"

"No, that was after I suggested you could pay me back in sexual favors," Dimitri states, his eyebrows doing a suggestive dance.

"Wow, and still you married him?" Heidi jokes.

"Let's not pretend like that's the worst meet cute we have at this table," Nadia says, laughter in her voice as she casts Alexei a fiery look.

"What?" he asks around a mouthful of burger. "Oh, come on. Don't tell me you mean us. I was nothing but charming when we met."

"Aside from the fact that you came barging into my dressing room to demand I go on a date with you?" she says, one eyebrow creeping up her forehead.

"That's not how I recall it going at all," he says.

"Well, it was," Nadia explains, her Russian accent thickening as she leans closer to Heidi. "Which is why I turned him down flat."

"What's with the Federov men and their commands, am I right?" Camille jokes.

Heidi shares a smile with me, and we don't need to speak for me to know that she's thinking of all the times she's asked me the same question when she thinks I've bossed her around enough for one day.

"So . . . then what happened?" Heidi asks, turning her attention back to Nadia.

"He bought the ballet company I dance for."

Heidi gapes openly at my youngest brother, seemingly at a loss for words.

"Alexei," Mom scolds. "You told me you bought it because you thought it would be a valuable investment."

"Was I wrong? In my eyes, I would consider that the best investment of my life." He flashes Nadia a devilish smile, and despite herself, she melts visibly beneath his powerful charm.

"Well," Mom says, cutting in with a mischievous grin, "I assure you they didn't learn any of that from me."

The chorus of snorts that issue from me and my two brothers sends our wives into a fit of giggles.

"Okay, why do I get the sense there's a story behind that?" Heidi says, propping her elbows on the table and planting her chin in her palm as she waits for my mom's story.

"Because our father was far worse than any of our antics," Alexei explains.

The table goes quiet as the girls wait for further explanation, but none is forthcoming.

"Oh, come on. You have to tell us now," Camille pleads, mirroring Heidi's posture as she looks at my mom as well.

Mom simply laughs. "Alright, if you must know, their father saw me working in the garden one day, and he walked right up to me and asked for a kiss. Of course, I told him no, so he went on his way. The next day, he came with a bloody lip and explained that he'd gotten into a fight—could I kiss him and make it all better. Again, I told him no. But on the third day, he hired a man to chase him down, and as he ran past my house, he begged me to kiss him so the man would just keep walking. He said it was a matter of life or death, so I finally agreed. And the rest is history."

"What a scoundrel!" Heidi objects.

Mom gives a soft chuckle. "Yes, I'm sorry, Ladies. I did my best, but my boys do take after their father in some ways. And it would seem that setting their sights on a woman and never relenting is one of them."

Again, Heidi and I share a look. Only this time, her smile is filled with a deep love and appreciation.

She reaches across the table to give my hand a squeeze. "I, for one, am very grateful," she murmurs.

I brush the pad of my thumb across her knuckles, returning the smile she gives me.

"Wait, Heidi, what did Maks do to coerce you into dating him?" Nadia asks, confused.

"Date? No. He offered me a hundred thousand dollars to sleep with him."

"Maksim!" Mom scolds me this time.

"I know, I know. Don't worry, Ma . . . I ended up paying her two hundred thousand."

Loud guffaws erupt around the table at that, and Heidi's cheeks blush adorably at the mention of our first meeting.

"Well, it seems fate must have had a hand in all of it," Nadia observes. "Otherwise, how could we all have had such . . . rocky starts and still have found the ones we love?"

"I think that just means my sons are good at picking patient and forgiving women," Mom jokes lightly.

And once again, the table erupts in laughter. She's not wrong. Each of my brothers and I are truly blessed with the women we found. At a point in time not too long ago, I was convinced neither of my brothers would settle down. And I had committed to a woman, not because she was the right fit for me but because I didn't want to be alone.

Now, we're with partners who couldn't be more perfectly suited to each of us in our own unique way. It fills me with pride and joy to see our family not just thriving but so full of contentment. My mom was right. My father would have been very happy to see the life we've built together.

And I couldn't have done any of it without my soulmate by my side.

Loved this story?
Ready for ALL books in the series?

Season of Malice (Dimitri and Camille)

Season of Desire (Alexei and Nadia)

Season of Wrath (Maksim and Angel)

SEASON OF MALICE (PREVIEW)

DESCRIPTION

He's old enough to be my father.
He might be the one who killed my boyfriend.
And I can't resist him any longer.

Not only is my boyfriend dead, he left me with a sizable loan in my name to a mafia boss.
When Dimitri Federov, a handsome, loaded Russian playboy, appears on my doorstep, I panic.

He wants money to repay the debt. Money I don't have.

The prick offers me a solution - pay with my body. I turn him down flat, but the indecent proposal remains in my thoughts, forever reminding me of what could have been...

But when Dimitri turns on his charms, it gets even harder to resist him, and much easier to forget he's a ruthless kingpin... a *killer*.

And once I let him have what he so desperately wants, give into our desires and follow this basic instinct to its heady climax... There will be no stopping Dimitri's dark desires.

One night leaves me with the biggest secret of my life... and I have to make sure Dimitri never finds out he got me *pregnant*.

1

Camille

"No, no that's way too hot!" I shout, snatching the saucepan from the stove as I watch the creamy beurre blanc break before my eyes. Then I burst into tears.

Poor Louis looks like I might as well have slapped him across the face as his eyes widen with fear. "I'm sorry, Chef. I just turned away for a moment…"

He looks utterly crestfallen as my tears come hard and fast, spilling down my cheeks in a torrent. I can't help myself. Normally, I wouldn't cry over something so minor as broken sauce—even in the middle of the dinner rush—not when it's a simple fix of adding water while whisking to re-emulsify the butter. But the last two weeks have been some of the worst of my life. And that's saying something.

"It's f-fine," I stutter, wiping brusquely at my cheeks. "You know how to fix it?"

Louis nods his head vigorously.

Hannah, my best friend and front-of-house manager, steps into the kitchen at the commotion, and when her eyes find mine, her shoulders drop.

"Cami, go home," she insists for what must be the hundredth time.

But I can't. I'm the head chef—the only head chef at my restaurant, Le Fleur—and I have an obligation to see us through the Friday night rush, no matter what state I'm in.

Sniffling, I shake my head and step back up to the grill. "I'm fine," I insist, avoiding Hannah's stern hazel gaze.

She plants her hands on her hips and steps close to speak in a low voice. "You've suffered a major personal loss, honey. Nobody would hold it against you if you closed the restaurant for a few days—hell, even a week—if you need to. And I'm sure we would survive—broken sauces and all—even if you left us to run the restaurant without a head chef."

"I didn't *suffer a loss*, Hannah. Roy was murdered. Why else would the police ask if he had any enemies?" Fresh tears threaten to spill at the memory of that call notifying me that my boyfriend of two years had been found dead in a house fire.

The term 'suspicious circumstances' had been thrown around more than once while I'd bawled my eyes out, but no one had been willing to tell me what those suspicious circumstances were because of the pending investigation. Therefore, I'd been left to speculate and grieve all in one fell swoop.

"I know what you think, Cami. And I totally get it. I just think you're putting yourself under a lot of pressure trying to cook and run a business seven days a week when you haven't even had the time to process."

Sliding the pan-fried sol from the stove and plating it, I keep my hands busy. "I don't need time to process. Cooking helps clear my mind, and right now, the less thinking I do, the better. Besides, Daddy never took a day off, and I don't need to either."

"You're not helping your case with that last statement, hon," Hannah says dryly.

When I shoot her a withering glare, she puts her hands up in surrender. But I suppose she's right. My dad died of a massive heart attack before his forty-fifth birthday—probably due in part to the amount of stress he endured from working so many hours to raise me on his own and put me through college.

But opening this restaurant was Daddy's and my dream, and I won't let it fall apart just because my personal life has.

"I'm fine," I state definitively. "I'll be fine. You just go back out there and win over our customers. I'll get my act together in here."

Hannah releases a heavy sigh, then gives my shoulder a squeeze before heading back through the swinging door to the front of the house, her honey-blond ponytail swishing.

"The beurre blanc is ready, Chef," Louis says apologetically, stepping up beside me.

"Good, good. Thank you, Louis." I take the saucepan from him with a forced smile and finish plating the sol.

It's a long night of grueling work as the rush never seems to end, and after my meltdown, my eyes feel tired, my body heavy with grief. But we make it. At ten o'clock, I glance around the kitchen at my staff. They're cleaning up for the night, hauling dirty dishes toward Marie, our dishwasher, and sanitizing the stainless steel surfaces.

Wiping the sweat from my brow, I turn back to my own station to ensure it's spotless.

"Um, Cami?" Hannah says tentatively from the kitchen doorway.

"Hmm?" I glance up and immediately stop my cleaning from the look of apprehension that scrunches my best friend's face.

"There's a man out front who asked to speak with the owner."

"At this time of night?" I'm baffled. Usually, food critics would alert me to their presence before the kitchen closes, and I can't think of anyone I had an appointment with. "I'll be right out," I add, wiping my hands on my apron.

I scan my station to ensure I've turned everything off—a habit my father drilled into me as a child—then follow Hannah into the dining area.

It's empty and still, the soft jazz music trickling through the speakers sounding almost too loud without the din of customers eating and talking and laughing.

Brushing the stray wisps of auburn hair back from my face, I approach the host stand, and my heart skips a beat. The gentleman waiting there—a businessman from the looks of him in his fine-tailored suit and dark, wavy hair styled to perfection—is gorgeous. He must be over six feet tall with a trim, muscular physique. A healthy amount of facial hair shadows his strong jaw, calling attention to his lips.

Gray eyes meet mine as I approach, and a predatory smile lifts the corners of his mouth as he looks me up and down in a way that leaves me feeling exposed, almost naked. And though he looks nearly old enough to be my father, the appreciative gaze that comes to rest on my face once more makes my stomach quiver.

"Hi, I'm Camille Anderson," I state, my voice sounding more confident than I feel in this stranger's presence. Extending my hand as I close the distance between us, I strive for professionalism, even though he's asking for me at such a late hour.

"Dimitri Federov," he introduces himself, the hint of a Russian accent rolling off his tongue.

He accepts my hand, and rather than shaking it, draws my knuckles to his lips. His gray eyes never leave mine as he brushes a soft kiss over the back of my hand.

Gasping in shock, I pull my hand back quickly, balling my fist in an attempt to subdue the tingles that race up my arm. "How can I help you, Mr. Federov?" This time, my voice wavers slightly.

"Please, call me Dimitri," he insists, his low voice making my stomach quiver. Then the businessman's smile creeps higher as his eyes flash dangerously. "And I've come because your loan payment is overdue. I'm here to collect."

His soft, inviting tone is an utter contradiction to the words that leave his mouth, and for a moment, I stand frozen, not quite sure I heard him right.

"I'm-I'm sorry? You must have the wrong person. I don't have a loan," I state when I finally find my voice.

His dark eyebrows raise as if in mild surprise, but that smile never falters. "No? Then why does my paperwork put your business as collateral for a significant personal loan that is now overdue?"

Is that amusement in his voice? He must be joking. Irritation flares inside me. Whatever stunt he thinks he's pulling, I don't have the time for it. Or the energy. All I want to do is put on my comfiest pair of pajamas, curl up on my couch with my favorite chick flick, and mourn my dead boyfriend. But this jerk thinks tonight's the night to pull one over on me? I don't think so.

"I already told you I haven't put a lien on my business, nor would I ever. So, you need to leave." I force as much authority into my voice as I can muster, though my still-trembling stomach does nothing to help me.

"I have paperwork that would disagree with you, Miss Anderson," the handsome stranger states.

Scoffing, I plant my hands on my hips. "Alright then. Why don't you show me this supposed paperwork?"

"Gladly," Dimitri says. Then he gestures to a nearby booth. "May I?"

"Be my guest." I wave him toward it, though my tone would say he's anything but welcome in my restaurant.

The tall businessman sets his briefcase on the table and pops the clasps before withdrawing a document from inside. I take the opportunity to study his chiseled face, the hint of silver at his temples, looking for any underlying motive he might have. I can find nothing in his expression.

He skims the document as if to ensure it's the right one before flipping it to face me and handing it over. I snatch it from him with unnecessary sass and slowly lower my eyes from his to read the paper's contents.

The document looks official enough. And it outlines a loan for half a million dollars, putting *my* restaurant up as collateral. My blood turns to ice in my veins as I reach the bottom of the page and find a rather adept forgery of my signature. And next to it. Roy's. My boyfriend of two years betrayed me. Used me.

It appears he granted a lien on my business six months ago without telling me. Though what he needed half a million dollars for, I haven't the slightest clue. He never mentioned anything about needing a loan.

"This is my boyfriend, Roy. Not me. And he did this without my knowledge," I state flatly, shoving the condemning paperwork back toward Dimitri Federov.

"Yes, well, your boyfriend stopped making payments a few months ago, and my men have informed me that he was spending a lot of time at the casinos before that, so he probably gambled it away," he explains casually. "The contract states that failure to make payment entitles me to claim this restaurant as collateral. So, seeing as your boyfriend has stopped returning my calls, I've come to collect. You have two options, Miss Anderson."

He steps close to me, invading my personal space and forcing me to look up at him. My heart hammers in my chest. The masculine scent of leather and pine fills my nose as I inhale sharply, and I swallow hard.

A mere foot from me now, the man feels far more intimidating than I had realized upon first meeting him, and a shiver races down my spine. But I refuse to back up.

"Either you can pay me back in full, or I'll take your business," he states softly, his voice almost a caress, even as he threatens to take away my entire life.

"You can't do that," I say firmly, standing my ground. I lick my suddenly dry lips and glare up into Dimitri Federov's penetrating gaze. "I didn't even know about the lien, and besides, my boyfriend is... dead." My voice cracks on the last word.

Dimitri's face maintains the same calm, watchful expression, and I slowly realize with growing horror that he already knows. Cold terror seeps into my bones as a new thought comes to mind. If he already knows Roy is dead, does that mean this is the man who killed him?

As soon as the thought occurs, it solidifies as an undeniable fact inside me. Roy lost the money. He couldn't pay back what he owed, so Dimitri killed him. And now he's here to collect. If I'm not careful, he might just do the same to me.

2

Dimitri

The fear in Camille Anderson's striking features tells me she doesn't have the money. Who would? I'm not surprised that Roy Lochte went behind his girlfriend's back and took out a loan he couldn't afford. He seemed like a slimy git from the start.

But now that we're in this situation, I can't simply rip up the contract and walk away. My brothers and I don't make the kind of money we do by forgiving unpaid debts. We always collect, and that's why they send me.

Still, I have a few alternatives I could suggest for this alluring, voluptuous beauty if she doesn't think she can pay. Though I know my brothers would be pissed, I feel inclined to cut this enticing and fiery young chef a break.

"If you don't think you can pay the debt in full, I might be willing to let you pay it off in installments..." I suggest.

Immediately, the worry lines around her blue eyes soften, telling me her greatest fear is losing her business.

"You could compensate me with sexual favors," I suggest playfully, reaching out to touch a stray lock of auburn hair that falls from her messy bun. I mean it more as a joke. The stunning young woman looks nearly half my age. But still, the idea *does* appeal to me. If she were interested.

"How dare you," she demands, her cheeks turning a delicious shade of red as she takes a step back from me and bumps into the wall behind her. "I would never sell my body to you."

That last statement burrows under my skin in a way comments don't usually, posing a challenge that makes me eager to change her mind. "Not to me?" I press, moving closer once again.

"To anyone," she clarifies forcefully, her eyes snapping with cold fire. "And my business is perfectly capable of paying off the lien if you'll just give me more time."

"Hmm," I hum, considering the offer.

Camille takes a step to the side, moving away from the wall before retreating farther. "I can prove it to you," she offers, her voice growing urgent. "Just... just let me prepare something for you, and you can judge for yourself if my business is worthy of a long-term loan."

Amused by the suggestion, I shrug. "Alright. Impress me."

Camille releases a breath of relief, calling attention to her generous breasts, and I trace my eyes down her body once more. She's on the shorter side, with curves in all the right places, and when she turns to retreat into the kitchen, I can't help but follow the sway of her hips.

Unwilling to let her out of my sight, I join her in the kitchen, stepping through the swinging door a beat after she does. The staff members, dressed in chef's robes, cast curious glances in my direction, but none say anything as they go about cleaning the pristine space.

"How long have you been in business?" I ask, coming to rest beside the stove as Camille turns it on.

A startled squeak bursts from her as she jumps away from me and presses a palm to her ample breasts. "You scared me. What are you doing in here?"

"I want to see you work, watch the magic, know that my investment would be worth my while." My lips tug up into a wicked grin as she throws a thunderous scowl in my direction.

"Fine. Just don't touch anything... please." She seems to second guess her harsh tone and tack on the please at the last minute.

Lifting my hands to show I'll keep them to myself, I lean back against the counter so I can watch her cook. "You didn't answer my question," I state after several moments of silence.

Camille bustles around the kitchen, collecting supplies with a confidence she didn't have when we first met. And the sight of her in her element makes her that much more attractive.

"What question?" she asks, casting me a sidelong glance.

"How long have you been in business?"

"Oh, um, a little over a year."

Impressive. I'm aware of how well her restaurant has been doing in the culinary mecca of San Francisco. I did a bit of digging to learn its value when Roy first took out his loan—to ensure it would make appropriate collateral. But to rise so quickly after just a year in business? That takes talent.

Falling silent once more, I watch with interest as she pounds a piece of meat, her intent expression making me wonder if she's picturing my face beneath her tenderizer. After it's been thoroughly pounded, she seasons the meat before putting it on the grill. Then she moves on to the stove to start a sauce.

As soon as Camille appears to accept my presence, the rest of the staff do as well. I respect that. They seem to trust her as their employer and demonstrate that her opinion is both valued and taken without question. The kitchen staff swiftly finish their work and trickle out the back door, wishing the restaurant owner and chef a tentative good night as they go.

She goes the whole nine yards, cooking me a lamb cutlet drizzled with what looks like a cranberry sauce, adding caramelized carrots and fingerling potatoes as my side. She plates the whole thing like an artist, adding rosemary for garnish.

Then she gestures toward the swinging door, indicating I should lead the way.

I pick a table in the center of the room, one that still has silverware set, waiting for its next customer. Rather than following me directly, Camille stops at the bar, speaking in hushed tones to the bartender, who had been busy restocking a moment before.

He pauses to uncork a bottle of red wine and pours a glass.

With familiar ease, Camille approaches the table with my meal, and the sight of her makes my mouth water. Not just from the fact that my long day at the office delayed my dinner but also the way her blue eyes trap me in a daring gaze.

"Your dinner, Mr. Federov," she says smartly, emphasizing my last name as she sets my plate and glass of wine before me. "Lamb cutlet with a cranberry balsamic drizzle, glazed carrots, fresh from our garden, and roasted fingerling potatoes; paired with a 2016 cabernet sauvignon, for your pleasure."

She takes a step back and clasps her hands behind her, as if waiting for my verdict. And suddenly, I know she's dangerous. Because I find her entirely too appealing. And I'm supposed to be here on business, acquiring another restaurant for my family's considerable empire.

"Come sit," I say, pulling out the chair to my right and refusing to touch my food until she obeys.

After several seconds of hesitation, Camille slides into the seat beside me. Only then do I cut into the impressively tender meat and place a bite in my mouth. The explosion of flavor stuns me momentarily, and my chewing slows as I savor the best bite I think I've ever tasted.

Flicking my eyes toward the heart-shaped face beside me, I find a smile tugging at her bee-stung lips. She knows just how good she is. And that proud smirk might be the sexiest thing I've ever seen.

Following my bite with a sip of wine, I take my time relishing the culinary masterpiece she's put before me. I don't know how she can be so young and so talented all at once, but I would eat here every single day of the week.

"Well?" she asks nervously as I continue to sample my plate without a word.

"How old are you, Miss Anderson?" I ask, and though it's a forward question, I'm dying to know.

Color stains her porcelain cheeks. "Don't you know it's rude to ask women that?" she demands, her eyes flashing.

I chuckle, low and soft, enjoying her consternation. "I only ask because this is some of the best lamb I have ever tasted, and I've never met a chef with this level of skill at such a young age."

Her blush intensifies, and Camille drops her eyes to the table. "Well, thank you."

"You are... I'm going to guess twenty-five." She looks younger, but a man can hope.

Blue eyes snap up to meet mine, and then she narrows them. "I'll be twenty-five in June," she says slowly, her voice laced with suspicion. "How did you know?"

I shrug. "Lucky guess."

Camille purses her lips but doesn't argue. Instead, she watches as I eat another bite.

I swallow deliberately and turn to face her. "And you opened this restaurant by yourself?"

She shrugs one shoulder. "My friend Hannah helps me run it. She hires and manages the restaurant staff while I manage the kitchen. But yes, Le Fleur is *my* restaurant." She says the last almost possessively, reminding me of why I'm here.

Now that I've indulged in what's proven to be one of the best meals of my life, I need to get back to business. But before I do, I have to try something.

Turning to face the young chef, I take her hand and pull her close, moving Camille from her chair to my lap in one swift move. She has time to release a startled yelp before I capture her lips with mine.

Electric attraction sizzles like a live wire between us. She tastes faintly of balsamic glaze, tangy and crisp. And her soft lips yield to mine, molding to my kiss as if made for me. Her rigid body demonstrates her shock, and yet, as I tease her lower lip with the tip of my tongue, she does not pull away.

Instead, she seems to relax, her muscles releasing as I hold her close. Her lips part on a sigh, and I take the opportunity to deepen the kiss, so tempted by her sultry figure and delicious flavor that I have to try more.

We kiss for a long moment, and when Camille finally pulls back, she looks flustered in the best way. Her cheeks are flush with excitement, her lips red and swollen from my exploring touch.

She scrambles back into her seat, her blue eyes wide with confusion and shock. "What was that for?" she gasps, her breaths coming hard, her breasts rising and falling dramatically.

"I've decided to make you a new offer," I say calmly, ignoring her question. My brothers won't like the bold move, but I can't let Camille slip through my fingers. "Rather than taking your restaurant from you or making you pay back the loan in full, I'll buy your restaurant outright. I believe it is worth enough that I can pay you $1.5 million. Cash. We can take the amount of the loan from that. And then you and I will be business partners."

Her look of utter horror tells me her answer long before she manages to regain her voice. Her lips move silently for several seconds, opening and closing as if trying to formulate a sentence.

Finally, she gasps, "How is that in any way a business partnership? That sounds like you're just taking my business from me!"

"Only you would be a million dollars richer," I counter logically. "And you would stay on as head chef, managing your restaurant exactly as you have been for the last year. I would be a silent investor of sorts."

Camille's expression brews with a storm of fury, her eyes flashing like lightning, and her beauty in that moment is breathtaking.

End of preview. *Continue reading this sizzling hot, Bratva romance here.*

Ready for ALL books in the series?

Season of Malice (Dimitri and Camille)

Season of Desire (Alexei and Nadia)

Season of Wrath (Maksim and Angel)

Printed in Great Britain
by Amazon